SPECIAL EDITION

NICKY THE DRIVER

UNDERBOSS INSURRECTION #2

CATE C. WELLS

Cover art and design by Bee of Bitter Sage Designs

Edited by Nevada Martinez

Proofread by Kayla Davenport

Special thanks to Jean McConnell of The Word Forager, Malorie Cooper of The Writing Wives, Kate K., Elisabeth J., Kara M., Elizabeth L., Kaitlin S., Erin G., and Erin D.

Contents

AUTHOR'S NOTE

THIS NOVEL CONTAINS ON-PAGE descriptions of disordered eating, including binging, and references to past incidences of abuse and domestic violence.

CHAPTER 1

Zita

I F I PEDAL HARD enough, I can turn my brain off.

I wish the bike's display had a reading for that—it's got calories burned, speed, distance, resistance. There's a leaderboard that I ignore. I bought the heart rate monitor, and I never look at that either.

It's supposed to be all about calories burned, right?

But if there were a metric for time remaining until I stop thinking, my eyes would be glued on that, counting down.

I've been doing a climb ride for almost an hour. My thighs burn, my calves are cramping, but my brain's still gnawing away.

Paul was short with me on the phone tonight. I know he's struggling with pathology. He sucks at rote memorization. He's always been a hands-on kind of guy. That's why he loved gross anatomy, and that's why he's going to be an amazing pediatric surgeon. Or orthopedic surgeon. Whichever path he chooses, he's going to be the best. That's Paul. The best.

Ever since junior high, he's been top of the class. Popular without trying. Most likely to succeed.

Maybe I'm not prom queen anymore, but we still complement each other. Right now, he needs my support. I can do that.

What do I have to bitch about? Living at home again? A stocked fridge and a laundry machine that doesn't take quarters?

It made sense to move back home after college. Mom's still reeling from being alone for the first time in her adult life, and even though Mattie's a senior, he still needs someone at home looking out for him. And Paul needs to focus on med school. The professional relationships that he's building with his roommates are invaluable. That's what he says whenever I bring it up.

I need to stop bringing it up.

Just because I'm sleeping in my old bedroom again doesn't mean I've regressed. I'm sacrificing for my family and our future. Paul appreciates that. He says it all the time.

I tighten my grip, and my engagement ring clinks against the handlebars. I might need to get it resized. It's getting loose.

All couples go through periods of time when one partner needs to hyper-focus on their career. If I knew what I wanted to do with my life, I'd be grinding, too. I'm not afraid of hard work.

I press a button and increase the incline.

It's not like I'm slacking. I'm sending out resumes, going on interviews. It hasn't happened for me yet, but it will. I'll find a job that I love.

I'll *figure out* what I love.

My legs pump, my lungs burn, and sweat trickles down my spine.

What do I love?

Over my vanity, there are still the sparkly gold letters that my mom stenciled during one of her crafting phases. *Dream big.*

Oh, the irony. Daniella Graziano only ever wanted to have a richer husband than her sisters, more followers than her sisters, and a tighter ass than her sisters. Her husband's dead, but two out of three ain't bad. She's not complaining.

That old, cold fear sloshes in the pit of my stomach, so I stand on the pedals and push harder. I don't listen to an instructor or music. I listen to my thoughts. I let them drive me crazy as I watch the calories burned tick higher and higher. I didn't mess up today, so it's money in the bank. Insurance against future fuck ups.

Crap I can't control ricochets around in my skull, generating kinetic energy.

Paul.

Mattie.

What happened to Dad.

Dad's not just dead, he was executed. Dumped in the Luckahannock. Or buried under fresh concrete somewhere. Or dissolved in lye and rinsed down a tub drain.

We don't know how it happened, and we never will. We don't know who or when or why, but we can guess, and we can't ever, ever say it out loud.

Lucca Corso and his men killed Dominic Renelli, my dad's boss, and while they were at it, they killed my dad, Vittorio Amato, Frankie Bianco, Joey Zito—more guys I didn't know that well—and we can think it, but we can never let on that we know.

In exchange, Lucca Corso pays Mom's mortgage and the car notes, my brother Tony Junior keeps his job managing Sugarbits, and life continues on like usual. Tomorrow, I have a hair appointment. Afterwards, I'll stop by Paul's place. Cook him dinner. Suck him off. He always appreciates a home-cooked meal.

Everything is fine. Things could always be worse. I increase the incline again and pump my legs until my exercise shorts are plastered to my ass with sweat. My brain finally, finally disconnects.

For a few blessed minutes, I'm floating in nothingness. I'm lungs and muscles and nothing else.

I'm jerked back to reality by a thud on the stairs. I freeze, straining to listen past the blood rushing in my ears. There's silence except for the wheels spinning to a halt. I slowly release my breath. It was just the house settling. Water in the pipes.

Something slams into the wall right outside my bedroom. My heart jumps into my throat.

It's two o'clock in the morning. Mom's asleep.

Mattie cannot be this stupid.

I get off the bike, stumble over my feet to get to the door, leap into the hallway, and grab him, pinning him against the wall before he can slide into a heap on the carpet.

He laughs as I drag him into my room. Halfway to my bed, I lose my grip and trip over him, and we end up tangled on the floor.

"You're drunk." I roll him so he's not breathing on me.

"And stoned," he giggles, struggling to sit upright.

"You're gonna wake Mom up."

He shakes his head, pursing his bright red lips. "She's high, too. She's not waking up 'til noon."

"Oh, Mattie." I hop to my feet and offer him a hand up. It must have been a rough night. His mascara's smeared, and he lost an eyelash. "Let me get you cleaned up."

His big hands envelop mine. I remember when they were tiny, and he'd curl them around my pointer finger.

I have to lean all the way back so he doesn't topple me forward as he regains his footing. At least he had the wherewithal to change before he came home. He's in sneakers, jeans, and a navy hoodie.

"Sit." I shove him toward the bed and grab my makeup case from the en suite.

"You gonna make me pretty, big sister?"

"You're already pretty."

He's going to be maudlin. I hate him like this. I hate that there are things in the world I can't begin to fix for him.

I drag my vanity stool over and grab his chin. Somehow, he scraped his jaw. He jerks his head back. "Ow, Z."

"I need to get some alcohol. Hold on."

"I don't see how you can drink at a time like this," he calls after me, snickering at his own joke.

"Very punny." That's the Mattie I know. He might be down, but he's not out. If you've given up, you don't tell dumb jokes. Right?

I settle back on the stool and begin to dab dried blood with a cotton ball. He hisses. "Do I need stitches?"

"No." I learned how to do stitches from my mother, and between Tony Junior and Mattie, I've had plenty of practice. That's what Dani Graziano taught me—how to do makeup and first aid and keep my damn mouth shut. And one short summer, how to use a Cricut machine.

"How'd you do it?" I ask.

"Damn curb moved when I went to step up on it."

"Is this my mascara?" I ask while I switch from isopropyl to witch hazel and swipe under his eyes.

"I don't borrow your makeup anymore."

"You're all grown up." I tousle his dark brown hair. He's left it down and curled it in fat waves. We have the same hair, the same natural highlights, thickness, and shine. It's our crowning glory as Nonna would have said. "Do you want to get the eyelash, or do you want me to?"

"You do it." He braces himself. We both hate peeling eyelashes off. It squicks us out. I take my time running a

Q-tip soaked in coconut oil along the adhesive so it'll come off clean.

I was six years old when Mattie was born. I doubt he was planned. I think one of Dad's girlfriends got pregnant, and Mom was worried he was looking to leave, so she got herself knocked up too to keep him home.

Tony Junior is a god in Mom's eyes, but I swear, she only sees Mattie when he screws up or annoys her, so he was mine almost from day one. I heated his bottles and tested them against my wrist like I saw my aunts do. I changed him. I went to him when he cried in the middle of the night, and I sang him Kidz Bops because I didn't know the words to the Italian nursery rhymes that Nonna had sung to me.

I kept his secrets before he knew how to keep them himself.

We do this dance, where I know, and he knows that I know, but we haven't ever said the words out loud, not even to each other, because if we did, I would be the one who begs him not to tell because I can't bear the thought of him being hurt, of losing him.

Because I'm the coward.

Once I get the eyelash off, I grab one of my last cleansing cloths, the organic, compostable kind that costs thirty dollars a pack.

"Close your eyes." I wipe his face. I can still see the baby in the shape of his nose, and the little boy in the tilt of his chin. He's eighteen now. He'll be graduating from St. Celestine's in a matter of months.

I'm so lost in worry that I don't notice that he's looking at me.

"Who worries about you, Zita?" he asks.

"No one needs to worry about me. I'm fine." I boop his nose with the cloth. He swats at me and misses, clearly no more sober than when he stumbled upstairs. "If you drove tonight, I'll kill you."

"I took a ride share."

I don't say the other part. If they catch him like this out in the clubs, they'll kill him. He knows it as well as I do.

In our world, it's still the 1950s. Lucca Corso may wear slim-fit suit pants, but he might as well be a reincarnation of Dominic Renelli. Say hello to the new boss. Same as the old boss.

Mattie sighs and flops back onto my comforter, and I return my makeup case to the vanity. When I turn around, he's riffling through one of my wedding binders.

I climb on the bed, and we lie on our stomachs side by side, shoulder to shoulder, flipping idly through venue brochures tucked in plastic sheets.

"What was wrong with this one?" he asks.

"The botanical gardens? Too expensive."

"Don't the bride's parents pay for the wedding?"

"I'd ask Dad, but—" I bug my eyes and grimace. "Too soon?"

Mattie cracks up. "Oh, that was dark."

"It made you smile."

"I always smile."

He does, and he always did, even as a baby.

"Okay, what was wrong with this one?" he asks.

"That one?" I squint at the photo of a rustic barn strung with fairy lights. What did Paul say about that one? "I think it was too historic?"

"That's a thing?"

I shrug. We exchange looks and dissolve into giggles.

"Paul is too picky."

"Who says it's Paul being picky?" It is, but why shouldn't he be? His parents stepped up when Dad died and said they'd take care of the wedding. Dad didn't exactly have life insurance.

Mattie rolls his eyes. "Come on. You do whatever Paul wants."

"Not true." I just don't have many preferences. It's not a shortcoming.

"Bullshit. Name one time you've gotten your way. Just one."

I don't want my way. I want family dinners where the women wear pants if they want to and no one swears in front of the kids. I want a man who asks me to help him study for pharmacology instead of demanding that I tell anyone who asks that he was home Saturday night.

"I love Paul."

"I know. I don't know how you'd put up with his smug ass otherwise." Mattie smirks.

I nudge his bony shoulder with my own. "I'm picky too, you know."

"Yeah? You're picky?" He grins and pinches my middle. I yelp. Then I'm trying to pinch him back, and he's drunk and stoned, so he falls off the bed and knocks the lamp off the nightstand. He stays down there between the bed and the wall, catching his breath through his laughter.

I'd do anything in the world for this kid, and there is nothing I can do for him.

"Get your ass to bed," I tell him. "And drink water and take an aspirin before you go to sleep."

He returns the lamp to its place with exaggerated care and hauls himself up using the side of the bed, his lips still curved into a dopey smile. "Okay, Mom."

It's my turn to roll my eyes.

"Leave the bike alone," he says over his shoulder on his way out. "Give it a rest. Go easy on yourself for once."

I wait until the door's shut to go back to my ride. I can't fall asleep now. If I do another five-hundred calories, I should finally be able to pass out.

I'm almost right. When I fall into bed at three in the morning, I've burned seven-hundred calories, and it only takes a half hour or so to crash.

W

HAT FEELS LIKE MOMENTS later, a voice jerks me from a deep sleep.

"Rise and shine, princess."

I startle awake as rough hands tear me out of bed. My head bounces off the carpet. I scream and kick, my legs tangling in the gauzy white canopy. I'm torn free, my arm almost yanked from its socket.

I see a man's legs. Joggers. Black rubber clogs.

My hip knocks my dresser. Lotions fall over, perfume bottles cracking against the mirrored tray.

"Stop." The word sticks in my throat.

The man drags me to my feet, slamming me into the door frame.

My mother's screams rise from the ground floor.

Oh, God. Mattie.

I lurch toward his room, but the man is too strong. He pulls me in the opposite direction, and I trip and fall. He doesn't let me up again. He drags me down the hallway toward the top of the stairs, and I flail, scrabbling at the walls with my left hand, breaking my acrylics.

He keeps going. My tailbone smacks against a wooden step so hard that my eyes water. The man yanks me along, and I slide behind him, colliding with his shins.

"Fuck." He hops out of the way, and I tumble into the landing, hitting the wall with a thud.

"Watch it," a cool, deep voice warns from below.

The man in rubber clogs was reaching for me, but he stops, straightens, raises a thick eyebrow, and gestures for me to go down the last flight of stairs.

I know him. Vinny Bianco. Frankie's cousin. Frankie was killed with Dad. Vinny must've picked the right side since he's still alive.

I push up to my knees, dizzy, my hair in my eyes. My PJ shorts are twisted, and the V-neck of my top is yanked down almost to my elbow. I fix myself while I stand, legs wobbly, fingers shaking uncontrollably.

I've had nightmares about this all my life, and now it's happening. And like in the nightmares, I'm paralyzed. Mute.

Vinny shoves me to keep going. I clutch the railing and hobble down. I hurt. My butt. My hip. My ankle.

Why is this happening now?

Dad's dead. We were told that if we keep our mouths shut, and if Mom keeps Tony Junior in line, we'll be fine.

Shit.

Tony Junior stepped out of line.

That fucking idiot.

I cross the foyer, round the corner to the kitchen, and as soon as Mom sees me, she sobs and snatches me to her chest, hysterically smoothing my hair, her rings catching strands and stinging my scalp.

I pull free and wrap an arm around her, tucking her to my side so she's not blocking my view. My heart stops midbeat.

In the middle of the open floor, between the breakfast nook and the island, Furio Renelli, Tony Junior, and Mattie are kneeling in a line, hands behind their heads.

Mattie's crying softly, a black streak running down his cheek. I missed some.

He won't look up at me. He's staring at the tile floor, rigid. Terrified. Like me.

This is bad. Really bad.

Dad coming home covered in blood and yelling at Mom to bring a garbage bag to the laundry room.

Mrs. Amato coming to mass with her jaw wired shut and a pinky missing.

Uncle Arturo disappearing one day and no one ever speaking his name again.

That kind of bad.

Tony Junior is gritting his teeth, his nostrils flaring. Furio is running his mouth, wheedling, saying let me explain, it's not what you think. No one's listening. Lucca Corso and Tomas Sacco stand to the side, turned toward each other, conferring like they do in low, clipped words and speaking glances.

Lucca wears a pressed, gray wool suit with a blue accent scarf. His streaked-blond hair's styled and highlighted, his nails buffed and polished.

He's pretty enough to be a model—for editorial work. Tomas is his dark side. Swarthy, shaved head, nose like a beak broken too many times. A pretty man and an ugly man. Two sides of the same coin. The whispers say that they mowed down half the made men in the Renelli organization in a matter of seconds. Dad included.

Dario Volpe, the money man, is sitting at the dinette table, legs crossed like one of my professors, scrolling on his phone. His man, Ray, looms behind Tony Junior, a gun in the hand hanging loose at his side. Vinny goes to stand next to him.

Ray's wearing rubber shoes, too.

Dear God.

There's no one blocking Mom and me from running to the front door, but we're not going anywhere, not with Mattie and Tony Junior on their knees. They know it, too. Men like my father—they always know.

There's another man. I didn't notice him at first. He's off to the side by the French doors. He's familiar, but I can't place him.

He's wearing a suit like Dario and Lucca. Dark. Buttoned. Sharp pant crease. Shiny black dress shoes. Not rubber shoes like the men standing behind my brothers, guns in their hands.

My heart slams in my chest. I clench my back teeth to stop them from clattering.

The man by the French doors is watching me. He's motionless. Almost casual. Not bored. He's alert, but unconcerned. He's not wearing the cold and menacing mask that the other men wear. And he's staring.

I don't dare stare back at him, but I also can't stop my gaze from flicking over. How do I know him?

It doesn't matter—only Mattie and Tony Junior matter—but my brain won't quit puzzling it out.

He's not in charge. He's not the greatest danger here. That's Lucca Corso without a doubt.

But still—I know him from somewhere.

His people have to be Italian. He has the dark brown, almost-black hair and eyes and the olive skin. Despite a slightly crooked jaw, he's handsome. Built. His hair's trimmed and styled, his shoes are polished, but somehow, the look isn't quite right. It's like there's a mafioso filter on him.

He scares me, more than I already am. Everything else makes terrible sense. Tony Junior fucked up. Lucca and Tomas found out. Vinny and Ray are here as the muscle. So who's the man by the door?

It feels like forever, but it's only been maybe a minute or two. Mom and I startle when Lucca finishes whatever he was saying to Tomas and stalks across the kitchen to the pantry.

Lucca points to the door. "This where you keep the buckets, Mrs. Graziano?" he asks, flashing his bright white veneers. He doesn't wait for an answer. He flings the door open, rummages around, and comes out wheeling a red bucket by the handle of the mop inside it.

Mom snuffles back snot and manages to moan, "Lucca, please—"

He cuts her off, raising his hand. "One minute, Dani." He takes out the mop and hoists the bucket into the sink. "May I call you Dani, Mrs. Graziano?"

Mom doesn't answer, but he's turned on the faucet, so he wouldn't have been able to hear her anyway.

Mom is shaking so hard that she's almost convulsing in my arms. She's going to collapse. She's not a hard mafia wife. She was raised in Indiana. She likes the money and the cars and the lifestyle, but she's always pretended to herself that Dad was an ordinary businessman.

If Vinny put his gun to her head now, she'd swear my Dad was in sales, and she'd believe it. She's not going to be able to get us out of this—whatever it is. Pretending won't make it go away.

Lucca has filled his bucket with steaming water, and he sets it back on the floor. Using the mop as a handle again, he rolls it over to the kneeling men—if you can call them that. Furio is my age—twenty-four. Tony Junior is twenty-two. And Mattie's just a kid.

Whatever they did, Mattie had nothing to do with it. He doesn't want to be a made man. He wants to draw and watch anime and steal my clothes and worry me to death. Paul promises that once we're married, he'll let Mattie move in with us. We'll give him choices.

But first we have to get out of this kitchen alive.

"We had an agreement, didn't we, Dani?" Lucca stops next to Furio who's lapsed into silence.

Lucca poses, leaning on the mop like that old dancer with his umbrella in *Singing in the Rain*.

"Dani?" he prompts.

"Y-yes." Mom raises her eyes. "I'll do anything. Don't hurt my boys."

"Relax. I don't need you to do anything."

He smiles, winks at Vinny, and Furio's skull explodes. There was no gunshot, but wet flecks of red are splattered up and down the side of Lucca's suit, and a puddle of blood is creeping across the tiles away from Furio's slumped body.

Mom screams. Vinny raises his gun, topped with a silencer, and levels it at her. I shove my hand over her mouth and pin her against me, using all my strength to keep her upright.

"Mom, shut up, shut up," I mutter, forcing my throat to cut off the surging acid from my stomach. Mattie's shoulders heave. Half of Tony Junior's face is covered in blood splatter and brain, but he doesn't move an inch. There's a dark stain spreading at the crotch of his joggers.

The man by the French doors watches me.

It hits me in between waves of panic. I do know him.

Nicky Biancolli.

We went to school together. He came to St. Celestine's in eighth grade. He followed me around until I told my cousin Tino that he was making me uncomfortable.

His pants never fit. They were too high. What my Nonna called floodwater pants. He always reeked of cigarettes. Even his backpack. He had that dirt-smudge kind of mustache boys had when they first grew facial hair.

After Tino talked to him, he left me alone. I stopped noticing him after a while, and I don't think I've seen him since graduation.

My dad never mentioned him. Neither did Tony Junior. He can't be that high up in the organization, but he's my age, and he's not wearing rubber shoes. He's checking a Rolex, waiting by the door. Waiting for what?

Lucca sloshes the water in the bucket, and my attention falls back to the scene in front of me. He wrings the mop and sloshes it through the blood, smearing it in arcs across the white tile.

He grins at Mom as he does it. "I was raised to clean up my own messes, Dani. I'm sure you taught your boys the same, eh?"

Mom whimpers. "Don't hurt them."

He stops mopping and leans on the pole again. "Well, that's entirely up to Zita here, isn't it?"

What?

My blood freezes at the same time baseless guilt floods my face with heat.

I didn't do anything. I keep my mouth shut and my head down, but that doesn't matter. I'm good at guilt and shame. A natural.

Mom glares at me, lips peeled from her teeth. "Zita," she hisses. "What did you do?"

Mom's a natural at blame.

"Now, now," Lucca tuts. "Don't get the wrong idea. It was Furio here who fucked up. He didn't like what happened to poor Uncle Dominic, and he thought he could get some of his boys together and do something about it." Lucca flashes a smile as if something just occurred to him. "Mea culpa. I guess I'm sort of an inspiration to the kids."

He sniffs and glances at Tomas. Tomas doesn't blink. He stands with his bulky arms crossed, his craggy face blank.

"No?" Lucca says to Tomas. "You don't think so?"

Lucca doesn't wait for a response, and Tomas doesn't give him one.

"Well, notwithstanding that imitation is the sincerest form of flattery, we can't have people talking that kind of shit. Or entertaining that kind of shit." Lucca transfers his sharklike gaze to Tony Junior. Tony Junior drops his head.

What does Mattie have to do with this? He doesn't work for the organization. Dad never brought him into the business like he did with Tony.

"Now, I'm a simple man. I like a simple solution." Lucca knocks the mop against the floor for emphasis, and Mom startles. "I think we should put a bullet in every Graziano, starting with Tony here, and be done with it. I like a clear message, you know?"

He pauses like he's waiting for someone to agree with him. Mom moans in fear. The only other sound is Tony's ragged breathing.

"But Dario thinks we should use a more subtle approach."

Dario lifts his eyebrows, barely acknowledging his name. He's still scrolling on his phone.

"So here's what's gonna happen. Zita, you want your little brothers to walk out of this kitchen, right?"

I don't hesitate. "Yes."

By the doors, Nicky's shoulders square. It's a small movement. I wouldn't have noticed if my nerves weren't stretched almost to the point of snapping. I can't lose it, though. The knees of Mattie's jeans are soaked in blood.

"Good girl. And Tony—" Lucca toes Tony Junior with his wingtip. "You wouldn't do anything to get your big sister hurt, would you? I mean, that'd probably kill your mother, right?"

"This shit was on me, man. Leave them out of it." Tony Junior isn't smart enough to dial down his usual dick-swinging tone of voice.

Lucca kicks him in the ribs, and Tony Junior folds in half, groaning and clutching his sides.

Lucca exhales and takes a moment, straightening his cuffs. "So here's what we're gonna do. In honor of Tony Graziano's close relationship with my mentor Dominic Renelli, may they rest in peace—" Lucca crosses himself. "We're gonna build a new relationship. A marriage. Between your family and mine."

What is he talking about? A literal marriage?

"What do you say, Zita? Wanna get married?"

No. This is crazy. I'm engaged. Lucca's with Tomas, right? Even though no one would ever say it out loud?

I look at Tomas. His face doesn't give anything away.

"To you?" I ask Lucca, because I can't say no.

Lucca's eyes round. "Oh, no. Not me, honey. I'm not the marrying type. But lucky for you, he is." He jerks his thumb toward Nicky.

Nicky steps forward, his hands clasped in front of him, his spine ramrod straight, watching me. His face is unreadable. Shivers skitter across my clammy back.

"You become Mrs. Biancolli, and we,"—Lucca gestures to his other men—"have the reassurance of knowing that the Graziano family won't be giving time to any more motherfuckers who think things were better before." He claps his hands together. "It's a win-win."

Lucca cocks his head expectantly.

I can't marry someone. I'm engaged to Paul DeStefano.

I've been in love with him since tenth grade when he took me to the movies at the Rotunda and whispered, "Can I kiss you?" during the previews, and I said yes, and he did, and then he held my hand for three hours, and never even tried to cop a feel.

I'm going to marry Paul. That's the certain thing in my life. Since the missed period freshman year of college when he went out for a test and came back four hours later with a small velvet box, too.

The next week, when my period finally came, he didn't ask for the ring back, and I knew. We went to Sunday dinner at his parents' house, and his mother saw the ring, turned gray, and gasped, "Oh, Paulie, no. You're too young."

Paul said, "We're older than you were when you married Dad. Pass the bread, please?"

He didn't blink then. I'm not giving him up now. I'm not letting them take this from me.

They don't get everything.

Lucca clears his throat.

All eyes are on me. Except Mattie. His pupils are huge, and they dart from the mop in Lucca's hand to the gun at Ray's side. Oh, Jesus. He's gonna try something.

His fingers twitch, and his muscles tense. I see it in slow motion—every ball that slipped out of Mattie's glove from tee ball to Little League.

He's going to get himself killed.

He draws in a deep breath.

"Yes." It's out of my mouth before my brain can catch up.

Lucca's eyes round in surprise. "Really? Honestly, that was a little easier than I thought it would be. Aren't you engaged to the Italiano's Pizza Grille kid?" Paul's parents own the Italiano chain.

Nicky moves forward, and Lucca punches his shoulder. "Watch out for this one. She's easy come, easy go."

Nicky ignores him. He comes to me, careful to step around the blood. He stops about a foot away, his gaze raking down my front, not cold anymore. Smoldering.

"Where are your shoes?" he asks.

I have to swallow spit before I can answer. "Upstairs."

"Go get her shoes," he says to Vinny. "And pack her a bag."

"Where's your phone?" he asks me.

"In my purse."

He tilts his head slightly. Waiting.

"It's upstairs. On my chair."

"Get her charger, too," he tells Vinny.

Vinny doesn't make any move at first. He looks to Lucca and cocks an eyebrow. Lucca smirks, and after a beat, inclines his head. Vinny heads toward the stairs with a sigh.

"Take your fucking shoes off," Tomas calls after him right before he leaves the kitchen. "Don't track that shit onto the carpet."

There are big red footprints tracked across the tiles. Almost comically big. Like clown shoes.

A wild laugh bubbles up my throat. I screw my eyes shut, willing it back down, balling my fists, tensing my muscles as if I can make myself heavier somehow so I don't go flying off into hysteria.

A hand brushes my shoulder. My eyes pop open. How could I close my eyes on these motherfuckers for even a second?

Delayed panic roars through me.

Nicky is standing there, staring down at me. He was lanky back in school, but now he's solid. At least six foot three, two hundred and twenty pounds. I wouldn't have a chance against him.

I *won't* have a chance.

I can't do this. I can't breathe.

He places his hand firmly on the small of my back, and even though I can't work my arms and legs, even though there's nothing in my brain except the whomp whomp sound when you roll down the back window in the car and leave the front windows up, I let him lead me into the foyer, and I stand next to him, waiting for Vinny to bring down my University of Pyle duffel bag, the red satchel purse Mom bought me for graduation, and a pair of sliders.

Nicky slings the bag over his shoulder. I clutch my purse to my chest. He opens the front door. I can't leave Mattie here with the men and the guns and the blood on the floor. I freeze in place on the threshold.

Nicky's hand goes to the small of my back, and he leans over, saying so low that no one else can hear, "Lucca won't hurt them." He pauses, a split second, but enough so I understand this is a threat and not reassurance. "If you come with me now."

He urges me on with the hand at the base of my spine, and I walk out.

Behind us, Mom collapses to the floor with a heavy thud, and Lucca Corso says, "Damn, Dani, you're getting that shit all over yourself."

There's a black Mercedes S-class parked on the street in front of the house.

Nicky leads me through the front yard. My feet get wet from the dew in the grass, and I slip in my sliders. Nicky glances over his shoulder. I drop my gaze to the ground.

His eyes are terrifying. Black. Blazing.

He continues to the car, and I scrunch my toes so I don't slide out of my shoes. He opens the passenger door, and I get in. He tosses the bag in the trunk and gets in the driver's seat, adjusting the rearview.

He glances over at me. There is a long moment in the silent car, in the breaking dawn, when he searches my face for something and my brain races, scrambling to hold a thought like Lucille Ball in the episode with the chocolates on the conveyor belt.

The Mercedes still has a new car smell.

Nicky smells like nice cologne and blood.

His knuckles are scabbed like he was in a fight a week or two ago. Tony Junior and Dad would come home with swollen, bloody knuckles all the time. But never Mattie.

Oh, God.

Mattie.

I can't leave him. My hand flies to the handle just as Nicky pulls away from the curb.

Nicky accelerates, and so does the panic thrashing in my chest. I dig my fingers into the armrest, my gaze flying wildly around the car's interior. The dashboard lights. The glovebox. Is there a gun? Dad always kept a gun in the glovebox.

I pop it open, but there's nothing but a manual and a pencil gauge.

Nicky glances over again, but he doesn't say anything. He doesn't stop me. He knows he's stronger than me. He knows I'm powerless.

I unclick my seatbelt. When did I put it on? I don't even remember.

Nicky's hands tighten on the steering wheel, his fingers blanching so the red scrapes on his knuckles stand out.

"Don't do anything crazy," he says, staring straight ahead.

"*This* is crazy." My voice is strange to my ears, shrill and echoey.

He doesn't answer. He turns on the blinker, eases to a complete stop, and then makes a right onto the bridge over the river.

"Where are we going?"

"Home."

I scoff, and it comes out as a high-pitched yelp. The sound boomerangs. The silence in the car is tearing at my nerves, conjuring pictures in my head.

Furio's temple exploding, the whites of his eyes huge in the instant red splatter exploded in the air and fell to the tiles. It was like when a bus speeds through a puddle. The same wet plops.

Mattie kneeling in blood, his pants soaked so dark the denim was almost black.

Mom mewling, helpless, mindless with terror, not posing or faking for once in her life, huddled against me as if I could protect her.

Furio face down on the kitchen floor.

Furio and I aren't close. *Weren't* close. But I've known him my whole life. He's a cousin the same way every kid with an Italian last name at St. Celestine's is a cousin if you go back far enough.

He *was* a cousin.

He'd always ask me to get him a Coke when he was over at the house hanging out with Tony Junior. He'd try to slap my ass and miss five times out of ten from pure laziness, and now he's dead by our breakfast bar, slivers of his skull stuck in my brother's pomaded hair.

Oh, Jesus.

Oh, God.

Puke surges up my throat. "Pull over."

I tug at the handle, but it's locked—of course, it's locked. We're speeding down Wiltmore Boulevard like nothing's wrong, like it's any old day. Acid burns my esophagus, and I wretch, clamping my hand over my mouth.

"Pull over!"

Nicky eases the car onto the shoulder, and I throw open the door, barely making it out before I bend over and hurl on the asphalt next to the tire, my hair dangling in my face. My stomach keeps casting up air well past the point that there's anything left in it. My eyes water as I spit and gasp for air.

A car driving past honks.

Shaky and rubber-kneed, I slowly straighten, shoving my hair behind my ears. By some miracle, I don't feel anything wet.

I suck in the early morning air thick with humidity and gas fumes.

Nicky's standing by the open passenger side door, staring at me. A shiver jolts down my spine and every muscle in my body contracts.

What is happening?

He's not pissed. Or concerned. Or grossed out. He's—fuck, I don't know what to call it. He's fascinated.

His gaze rakes down to my cold feet still stuck with a few blades of mowed grass, and moves caressingly up my bare legs, lingers at the juncture of my thighs, and continues over my belly to my breasts, then to the pulse fluttering at the base of my throat, my mouth, my hair.

He seems in no hurry to leave, unaware of the cars speeding past. Frozen.

Lost in looking at me.

I should be squirming. My sleep shorts are barely long enough to cover my ass cheeks. My nose is running. I'm standing next to a puddle of puke. And a man in an impeccably tailored suit is looking at me like I'm the only thing in the world.

I should cross my arms. Yank my top down as far as it'll go.

Get mad.

Get scared.

But my brain is pudding. He looks at me, black eyes blazing, and I stand there and let him, shivering in the chilly and damp air.

What the fuck is he looking at?

Later—maybe seconds, maybe minutes—a siren wails in the distance. I startle. Shit. I don't want to explain to a cop what I'm doing in my pajamas, puking on the side of the road.

Nicky inhales a visible breath and holds the car door open wider.

I wipe my mouth with the back of my wrist and get back into the passenger seat. Nicky waits until my feet are inside, and I'm buckled before he calmly shuts the door.

He crosses in front of the hood, slides into the driver's side, turns on his blinker, and eases back into traffic.

He doesn't drive like Paul.

Paul likes to slam from gear to gear like he's in an arcade racecar, riding people's asses to see if he can annoy them into moving over, passing any guy in a real nice ride, accelerating quickly and cutting in with the bare minimum of space.

Nicky drives an automatic. He obeys the speed limit. When a lady in a minivan hesitates to change lanes, he flashes his lights to assure her that she's good to get over.

I don't know why it amplifies my freak out, but it does. It's like every uneventful second that passes dials up the tension, winding me tighter and tighter.

My mouth is bitter. I fill my mouth with spit and swallow, but it does nothing. I crack the window. Maybe the wind on my face will help.

Nicky reaches over, and I jerk, the seatbelt pulling taut, digging into my boobs. He freezes a second, hand midair, and then he continues for the glovebox, rooting underneath the manual. He takes out a red pack of cinnamon gum.

I used to chew that kind all the time back when I was making bad choices. I don't do that anymore, and I can't stand the taste now.

He offers me a stick. I shake my head. He shrugs, tosses it back, and clicks the box shut.

Early morning sounds filter in through the window. Cars shushing down the boulevard. Sirens in the distance. Inside my belly, the ratchet turns. Finally, when we hit downtown, I can't take it anymore.

"I remember you," I say, breaking the silence. It sounds like an accusation. I guess it is.

His gaze flicks over and immediately returns to the road.

"From St. Celestine's," I go on. "You used to follow me around."

He slows the car. My heart bangs. No, he's not stopping. It's just the light. It turned yellow.

"My cousin Tino made you stop."

The corner of his mouth twitches. That amuses him? I'm pretty sure Tino beat his ass.

It's almost impossible to jive that kid with this man. The boy was the kind you felt sorry for, the ones who wore stained uniforms from the hand-me-down bin and got called down to the office the afternoon before Christmas and Easter breaks and came back to class with gift cards to the grocery store and shame on their faces.

The kids who tried not to take up space, who drifted to the back of the room, who the teacher would call on, and you'd think for a split second—even though you'd known them for years—who's that again?

There's no trace of that boy in this man.

He's the kind of man you look at.

He's not just cut, he almost doesn't fit his seat, his muscular thighs surpassing the edges, his shoulders broader than the back. His hair is shaved into a neat fade on the sides and brushed back on top, styled perfectly. His face and neck are smooth, not a hint of stubble, no nicks, no bumps. His nails are clean and filed.

It's clear that he takes care of himself, but there's no obvious vanity to him like Lucca Corso or Tony Junior. Nicky hasn't adjusted himself once—not his hair or his cuffs or the lay of his jacket. His focus is entirely on the road. And me.

He's terrifying, and not just because of what happened to Furio, but because he isn't like the others.

I know how to deal with the others. I was raised dodging my father's fists and tiptoeing around his temper, ducking and laughing off my "uncles'" groping hands. I know what men like that want.

Something easy. A woman who knows how to keep her mouth and legs shut unless he wants them open. They don't want to be bothered.

They want to drag you along their lives like an undertow, and if you drown, they don't notice—and if they did happen to notice, they sure as shit wouldn't care.

They don't watch you. Not unless you're bending over or showing off your tits.

"What do you get out of this?" I ask when his eyes shift to the road.

They're back on me in an instant.

He shrugs.

I wait.

He checks the rearview.

"You're not going to tell me?" I ask.

"You're fuckin' in charge here, then?" he says in an almost wry tone, his voice gravelly with its thick working-class Pyle accent. It's not a warning. It's a throwaway line. A dodge.

Maybe he's just a soldier, doing what he's told. Maybe he's as trapped as I am.

"Are they making you do this?" I don't know why, but I lower my voice to ask.

"No," he replies without hesitation.

Impossibly, my stomach sinks. My body's so bruised, so wrung out and strung out, I don't know how it's reacting at all. When does this end? How?

This is insane.

"We can't get married. I'm engaged." I hold up a trembling hand, showing him my ring.

He grunts, but doesn't look over.

"I've been engaged for almost five years," I go on.

He doesn't respond. He drives at a constant speed, hands at ten and two, a tic in his cheek beginning to pulse.

"Did you hear me?"

"Five years is a long time," he says to the windshield.

"Paul is in med school."

"Yeah? You can't get married in med school?"

He sounds like my mother. My puffy, sore eyes tingle with the threat of tears. I cross my arms and slump back into the seat.

Men like him don't understand how the real world works. They all get married young so that their wives are virgins, and then they fuck around and make the women miserable for the next fifty or sixty years. They don't have partners; they have women with credit cards in their name who make sure their houses are clean and dinner is on the table at seven.

"You can't force someone to marry you, you know," I say.

He's silent.

"It's not a thing. This isn't the olden days."

He glances over—he can't seem to stop doing it every few seconds—but he doesn't reply. I guess I'm worth looking at but not speaking to.

"What are you anyway? Some errand boy? Lucca's bitch?"

His lips curve. "Gonna be your fuckin' husband. Maybe you show some respect, eh?"

His impassive face breaks into a full smile, flashing bright white teeth. My breath catches at the same time my blood runs cold. He's not just decent looking. He's beautiful. And he's not the least bit pissed off at me for questioning him.

That means he's not an errand boy.

He's not worried about his pride. In this world, that means he has a body count. He's earned a reputation.

Fear takes control of my mouth again, and I keep it shut for the rest of the drive. It's a short one. Five minutes later we make a left onto River Street, and a few blocks later, he turns into an underground parking garage. It happens so suddenly, I don't get a good look at the building, but it must be a nice one. This is prime real estate, across from the promenade that runs along the Luckahannock.

Nicky pulls into a space marked 4B. Without a word, he gets out, grabs my bag from the trunk, and opens my car door. Everything is moving too quickly. Whatever happens next, I'm not ready for it.

I numbly walk with him to the brass elevator. He swipes a keycard before pushing the button for the fifth floor.

We stand side by side, facing the doors as we go up, our reflections blurry in the brass. A tall, imposing man in a suit, shoulders squared. A shivering woman with limp hair in pink pajama shorts and black sliders.

There must be dozens of people in the building. Hundreds on this block. My phone is in my purse. But I can't scream, and no one can help me.

My heart pounds harder in my chest.

What is he going to do when he gets me alone?

I know what he's going to do. The way he looked at me by the side of the road, and earlier, in the kitchen. I *know*.

I'm going to fight. I'll lose, but I won't just give in.

But they say don't fight. Do whatever you have to do to save your life. To get through.

I'm going to throw up again.

The elevator dings and the door whispers open. Nicky takes my elbow and leads me down a wide hallway with a brushed concrete floor. The building is modern—exposed ductwork, a floor-to-ceiling window at the end of the hallway with steel grilles.

There are two doors. Nicky stops in front of the one on the right. 5A.

He sets my duffel bag by my feet and steps back. He doesn't reach in his pocket for a key. He stands there, tense, and for a second, his expression seems to waver, but the doubt is gone in a second, his face blank again except for his burning eyes.

"This is Lucca's place," he says. "He'll be back soon. Tell him that you changed your mind. Tell him you won't do it."

He draws in a breath through his nose, and then, straightening, he turns and strides back toward the elevator, no hurry, no hesitation. No backwards glance.

He's leaving me. On Lucca's doorstep. To tell him I won't do what he wants.

I can't do that.

Nicky knows that.

Lucca will kill my family. He'll kill me. Even if I do this thing, he'll probably end up killing us all. No loose ends. No witnesses.

Panic roars in my ears.

I hate Nicky Biancolli. I hate him, I hate him, but I sprint down the hall, catching him by the door to the stairs. I stop short and slip all the way forward in my sliders, wobbling. He halts mid-step, gazing down while I steady myself, his fingers twitching at his side. It takes him a moment to tear his eyes from my face and stare back toward Lucca's apartment.

"You left your bag," he says. He gently rests his hands on my shoulders and moves me aside, side-stepping me to go back for my duffel. I wait in place, a tornado inside me, a roar that won't let me think. I'm spun up. Twisted. Debris whirling in the funnel.

How is this my life?

I never chose this. I did everything right. I studied hard. Kept my legs closed. I was a good girlfriend. A good fiancée.

Nicky comes back, striding past me through the fire door. He doesn't take my elbow this time. He leads, and I stumble after him down a flight of stairs and along another brushed concrete hallway to apartment 4B. This time he opens the door and gestures me in. My hip grazes his thigh, and I scuttle inside, the only thing in my mind to put space between us.

The dead bolt slides home with a thunk, and in that moment, reality hits me like a punch to the gut.

I walked myself right into the trap. This is my new jail. This terrifying, silent man is my new jailor, and there's no way out.

CHAPTER 2

Zita

Nicky's place is huge and empty.

The ceilings are high, and the wall of windows opposite where I'm standing overlooks the Luckahannock. It's an open floor plan with hardly any furniture to mark off areas. To my right, across from the kitchen, there's a dining room table with two chairs. Further inside, there is a black leather sofa and a widescreen TV mounted above a modern steel fireplace.

That's it. No rugs. No stools at the kitchen island. No art, lamps, armchair, coffee table, or bookshelves. The counters are clear except for what looks like a menu from a pizza place.

There's no dish rack, just a loose roll of paper towels next to the sink.

"Do you live here?" I ask.

Nicky grunts and drops his keys on the island countertop. He disappears down a short hall with my bag and comes back a minute later without it.

The space yawns.

I can't help but talk to fill it. "You live in the same building as Lucca?"

He grunts again and goes to the table, pulling out a chair. Then he holds out his hand. "Purse."

It's a demand.

I don't have anything left in me to argue. I give it to him and sit.

The table seats six, but there are only two chairs, the one at the foot that I'm sitting in and another next to it. That's where Nicky sits. His knee bumps mine. I scoot back an inch.

He unzips my purse and pushes it at me across the table. "Get your phone."

"Why?" I ask, but he doesn't answer, so I go ahead and take it out. My brain's too mashed not to question, but I understand. He's in charge. I'm fucked.

I just want this to be over. I want to fold myself into the smallest possible size and tuck myself away where none of this is reality. I want to be alone.

"Call Paul," he says. "Tell him the wedding's off."

"What?" Again, the question is a reaction.

He plucks the phone from my limp hand, taps a few times, and places it on the table in front of me. Paul's contact info is pulled up.

"How do you know how to unlock my phone?"

"The letter Z? Wasn't hard to guess, *Zita*." His voice is dry. Unaffected.

He's unbuttoned his jacket so it hangs neatly as he props an ankle on his knee, leaning back in his chair.

My toes barely reach the floor. My sliders slip off my feet and thwap the polished concrete. The apartment's cold. My arms and thighs are covered in goosebumps.

I catch a faint whiff of puke. I must not have missed all my hair. Or is it on my clothes?

My eyes burn, but I can't cry. If I let anything out, even a tear, I'll crumble.

Nicky nudges the phone toward me. "Call him now."

"Tell him what?"

Nicky lifts a shoulder. "Tell him you don't want him anymore."

Paul would never believe that. I've never *not* wanted him, and he knows it. That's why he's with me. The ultimate ego boost for the strait-laced student government president—the mobster's daughter is in love with him. She'd do anything for him. He's right.

I can't give him up.

My nose tingles. "It's not even six in the morning. He'll be asleep."

"Then wake him up."

"I can't do this." The words hardly make it past the lump in my throat.

"You don't have a choice," Nicky says, taps the call button, and puts the phone on speaker. The rings are impossibly loud in the empty, silent apartment.

Paul picks up on the fourth ring. "Z?"

"Paul."

I didn't wake him up. There are voices in the background. A woman murmuring. A man barking a laugh.

"What's up, honey?" He's irritated, but he's a good man, so he's concerned. That's Paul. He's a *good* man.

I can't let on that something's wrong. I can't drag him into this. He doesn't belong in this world. He's better.

I press my palms on my thighs to steady myself. "I need to talk to you."

"Now, baby? It's six in the morning."

"You're awake." And he's not alone.

"We're pulling an all-nighter tonight. I told you that."

No, he didn't.

He knows he didn't, too, but that's how he's always been. Sometimes things he wishes he did or said become things he did do or say. As a fault, it's nothing. Not compared to a broken jaw. Not compared to a pool of blood on the white kitchen tile.

Mattie's blood-soaked knees flash across my mind.

"I have to say something."

"Okay. Let me just—" There's a rustling, and the voices in the background fade. "What's going on, baby?"

I lick my dry lips, and beside me, Nicky's eyes dart down. His hands rest lightly on the table, but every muscle is tight. Veins show in his neck. Does he think I'm going to tell?

I know Paul DeStefano can't help me now.

I swallow and say, "P-Paul, I can't marry you."

There is a long silence. Nicky turns to stare across the room. I reach for words, for something to say, but there's nothing—only my heart aching and the feeling that everything I always wanted is slipping through my fingers, and I'm paralyzed. I have to watch it go.

Please don't let him cry. Oh, God, please.

"P-Paul? Are you there?"

He coughs. "Uh. Yeah. Sorry, Z. I'm just a little bowled over. I figured I was going to be the one to have to call it, but I guess you beat me to the punch." He laughs. It's a strangled, awkward chuckle, but still—it's a laugh.

Why is he laughing?

He does it again. "I guess I'm surprised." There's a pause. I can hear the woman's voice again, but I can't make out what she's saying. A man answers her, teasing. They're having a good time. They're not studying.

"I have to say, I'm relieved," Paul goes on. "It's been a long time coming. I didn't think you were ready to face it yet." He blows out a breath, and he laughs. Again. "This is good. Good." His voice trails off.

It's good?

We're going to get married. Live in a cute apartment in a reasonably priced, liberal city. We're gonna get Mattie out of Pyle and raise our children in a place where no one's ever heard the name Renelli.

Under the table, my hands shake like I've got the DTs. My ring twists to the side. Nicky is watching me again—I know, even though I'm staring at the phone—but he can't see my hands.

What is happening here? Two nights ago, Paul was coming in my ass. The next morning, he stopped by the coffee shop during his run to buy me a mocha, and I promised I'd pick up his dry cleaning. It's still in my trunk.

We're good.

In the background, a woman calls Paul's name. He says, "I'll be there in a sec."

In a sec.

"Listen, Z. Obviously, we'll need to talk. I want to be friends, really, I do, but I think right now, it would be best for the both of us to take a breather."

A breather?

I can't take a breather. I can't even take a breath. My lungs don't work. Nothing is working. I'm only upright because of the chair.

This isn't happening. It's a bad dream set in a cold apartment with no furniture and a man in a suit with tiny pinpricks of blood splatter on the front of his white dress shirt.

Paul keeps going, gearing up like he does when he's about to lecture me about something he knows a lot about, and I'm not interested in at all.

"I'm really happy that you've come this far on your own," he says. "I honestly thought you'd need intensive therapy before you'd get to this point. Actually, I was, well, scared if we're being frank. But it's so great that you're finally ready to figure out who Zita Graziano really is. Be your own person. Follow your own dreams, right?"

He's downright enthusiastic.

"Codependence is very understandable coming from the kind of upbringing you've had—the neglect and trauma, everything you've seen—and I'm just so proud of you that you're taking this step. And Zita—" He lowers his voice, taking on that confidential, caring tone he uses when people ask him for his medical opinion at parties. "I hope that now you'll also take another look at treatment for the—"

My hand flies out from under the table, and I stab the end call button.

Before he can ring back, I snatch up the phone and quickly power it down, accidentally dropping it against the wood with a clatter.

Nicky and I sit in silence, staring at the new crack in the screen.

I feel worse than naked. I feel splayed. Sandpapered.

I want to tear out everything I am and shove it down the trash compactor.

If Nicky's staring at me, I'm going to snatch his eyes out. But I can't.

And even though I can't bear to look up, I know he's looking, and there's nothing I can do.

My hand reaches for the phone on its own, picks it up, slams it against the table, screen down, once, twice, harder, until pieces of screen crunch against the wood. The meat of my palm hits the table, and it stings, but I need to burn.

Into a crisp.

Into ash that blows away.

I shove the phone away and slam my palms down again and again. I want to shatter the bones. I want the roar of pain to shut up Paul's words that are ringing in my brain.

"Stop." Nicky lunges, grabs my wrists mid-air, pins my arms to my chest. His grip bites, but not nearly enough. I fight him, and he shoves harder into my chest until I can't draw in a breath. Good.

I stop struggling. If this will end it, okay.

He's bent awkwardly over the table, panting, a lock of hair falling across his forehead, searching my face. His eyes are pitch black, but somehow, they shine like liquid even though the recessed lights are dim overhead. How does that work?

"Are you done?" he asks.

Yeah.

He doesn't let go right away. He waits a beat and then loosens his hold. My arms drop to my lap.

Shame creeps through my veins.

Who cares what Nicky Biancolli knows? Who gives a shit what he thinks? I don't. He's Lucca Corso's pawn—just like the rest of us.

I don't care, but like always, I'm powerless against the feeling. It whispers in my head with the undeniable ring of truth.

You're garbage, and everyone knows it. Worthless. No one expects anything from you, and you can't even do that. You're only a body, and not even a good one.

Disposable.

Forgettable.

Nothing.

"You smell like puke," Nicky says as he straightens. "You need a shower and some sleep."

He turns and heads down the hall where he took my bag. There's nothing else to do, so I follow him. I do stink.

He gestures me into a room. It's as bare as the rest of the place. A queen-sized bed with a navy plaid comforter. Night tables on either side with nothing on them. No rug. No windows. No pictures.

My bag's sitting on the floor by the far wall.

"Bathroom's over there," Nicky says, loosening his tie.

Is this when he rapes me? I guess he'll wait until after I shower. When I don't smell like puke.

I need to pull it together. So I can defend myself. Fight. Argue. Plead. I can't just let this happen, right?

I'm so tired. Even without windows and the lights out, the room is gray. The sun has come up, and it's filtering through the open door.

But I turn my back on him and wander over to the bathroom. I hear his footsteps as he retreats down the hall.

I peel off my pajamas and kick them into a corner. The bathtub has a clear sliding door that doesn't lock. If he comes back, nothing's stopping him.

I stand in front of the bare sink and squeeze my eyes shut. Locks. Curtains. What could they do? He can have my family killed with a word.

I pull down my panties and kick them over with the rest of my clothes.

There's nothing I can do but what he says. It doesn't matter that I don't have the energy to fight. I can't.

I step into the shower. There's a bottle of three-in-one. An expensive brand. I turn the water as hot as I can take it and scrub hard. My palms are red. There are fingerprint bruises on my arms and bigger marks on my hip and legs. My nails are a jagged mess. I nick my scalp as I wash my hair.

I realize my mistake when I get out and wrap a thick terrycloth towel around myself. My bag's in the other room.

Maybe Nicky's sleeping somewhere else. This feels like a guest room.

I crack the door and steam escapes. Immediately, my stomach sinks. He's back, lying in bed in a white ribbed undershirt, propped on a pillow, arms folded behind his head.

Of course, his gaze is riveted on me.

He tenses. His bunched biceps twitch, and his throat bobs as he swallows. He doesn't say anything. Except for the twitching muscles, he doesn't move. He just gorges himself with his eyes.

I know what starving looks like, the hunger you can't feed. I know that no matter how tightly you hold on, eventually, you can't stop yourself.

He's watching me now, but it's only a matter of time.

My damp arms pucker with goosebumps. This towel covers more than my pajamas did, but I feel uncovered. Exposed.

Is it because I don't have anything left—not even the energy to lie to myself that I'll put up a good fight?

I dart out and snag the strap of my duffel bag, dragging it into the bathroom. I prop it on the closed toilet seat, and when I unzip it, a hysterical giggle flies up my throat.

Vinny must have gone into my closet and took the first things that came to hand. There's nothing but a folded mass of summer sundresses. No pants. Shirts. Socks. Underwear.

I peel off the outer dress, a pale-yellow skater dress with spaghetti straps and slits up the thighs. I pull it over my head, and then I tug the towel off. My hair is wet and knotted. I check the medicine cabinet. There's toothpaste and men's deodorant. I use my finger to clean my teeth and rinse the taste of stomach acid out of my mouth.

There's no comb in the vanity, and Vinny didn't pack one. I run my fingers through the clumps and end up with broken strands stuck to my wet skin.

I don't dig my nails into my scalp and tear, rip chunks out by the root, scalp myself until my brains leak out, and I'm not afraid anymore. I gently pluck the strands from my shoulder, drop them in the toilet, and flush. Then I calmly leave the bathroom.

Nicky hasn't moved, but his eyes fly open. He wasn't sleeping. He's not the least bit disoriented. He's lounging there, the comforter pulled to his waist, his steady breaths raising and lowering the tank top that clings to his sculpted abs.

I take a step toward the bed, and he tracks me. His hair's damp. When did he shower? He must have done it when I was in the bathroom.

Is he wearing anything under the blanket?

It'd be weird if he wasn't. My father wore an undershirt with tighty whities to bed. Before Lucca Corso killed him.

Was Nicky there when it happened?

Was he one of the gunmen?

My stomach heaves.

"Get in," Nicky says, breaking the silence. He nods at the other side of the bed, the one further from the door.

If I ran, how far would I get?

The hallway? The kitchen?

How horrible will this be?

I can keep my eyes closed. Breathe through my mouth. Bury my head in the pillow. Pretend he's—

Pretend *I'm* someone else.

Nicky flips the comforter down, and I catch a peek of light blue boxers and dark hair on muscled tan thighs.

"Now," he says.

I stumble on numb feet toward the bed. Sit. Raise my legs. Lie back on the two fluffy pillows. The sheets are clean and crisp, and they smell like fabric softener. He smells like soap.

He breathes out very slowly, beats his pillow, resettles it under his head, and his eyelids drift shut. He has long, dark eyelashes. Like a woman.

I turn and stare at a bare, eggshell-white wall. Except for our breathing, the room is quiet. I can hear the air like I'm listening to a seashell.

"Go to sleep," Nicky says without opening his eyes.

I can't. I ball my fists to feel that sting where I slapped my palms raw. For a while, we lie there, two feet between us, both motionless, in a gradually lightening room. Strangers. But not. Enemies. But not.

Finally, Nicky exhales and turns onto his side, propping his head in his hand.

"Zita—"

"I can't sleep."

He stares at me, his hand resting on the mattress between us. I'm so tight, my shoulders are cramping.

"Stop looking at me," I hiss.

He lets out a short laugh. It echoes. "You don't call the shots."

I know. I know, I know, I know, I know. Rage rises inside me, a sad little flash of temper, what's left after this never-ending night, thin and weak like the air that splutters out when the whipped cream can is empty.

"Is this when you rape me?" I squeeze my balled fists tighter, so hard my knuckles ache.

He rolls onto his back and stares at the ceiling, his mouth twisting in the corners. "Not tonight. I got a headache," he says.

And then he closes his eyes and doesn't say another word.

I lie there forever, the room dim, but not dark enough to escape any of it. The man. The flashbacks. Furio's blood. The black streaks on Mattie's cheeks. Mom shaking in my arms.

At some point, I drift off, not to sleep, but into some kind of in-between place where I know I have to pee, and I'm too scared to get up and go, but otherwise, there are no thoughts in my head, just a thick numbness.

I don't know how long I'm like that, but I'm only jostled into awareness when a heaviness settles on my chest. I blink awake, but I don't react as Nicky finishes covering me with a weighted blanket, bamboo like the one I have at home.

He tugs it to my chin and says, "Sleep."

Then he leaves the room, firmly closing the door behind him, and finally, I let go and sink into nothingness.

S OMETIME LATER—MAYBE AN HOUR, maybe three—motion drags me out of a deep, sweaty sleep. I struggle to sit upright, scrubbing my face. Nicky's a few steps into the room, straightening his cuffs under his jacket sleeves. He's facing the bed, watching me.

He's wearing a different dark suit with the same sharp cut and fine white shirt. He hasn't tucked the tail of his tie into the loop, so it swings loose when he bends to tie his shoes.

"I gotta go to work," he says, straightening.

I drag the weighted blanket up to my chin.

He sniffs, gaze raking down the mound I make on the bed. There's not much to see but the tops of my bare shoulders, and that's where his eyes linger. I scrunch my neck, trying to make myself smaller. He shakes his head as if to clear it.

"Here." He takes his wallet out and thumbs through it, pulling out a few bills and dropping them on the night-stand. "Go to the store. Get some shit for dinner."

He digs into his breast pocket, slips out a thin white phone, and rests it on top of the cash. "It's a burner. It'll have to do for now."

Because my phone is busted. It broke when I slammed it against his dining room table. The blur in my brain sharpens, and yesterday rushes at me like a train.

I flush hot, my blood draining, while his eyes skim down me again, catching on my hands clutching the blanket.

He moves so quickly that I don't have time to startle. He puts his knee on the bed, leans over, grabs my hand, tugs off my ring, and shoves it in his pocket.

"I like steak or fish," he says, standing, unruffled while my knuckle stings from where he scraped the ring over it. "And get some dish soap. The blue kind."

His gaze skims one last time over my shoulders while he takes a gun from his end table, tucks it into his waistband at the small of his back, and leaves. The apartment is so empty, so echoey, I can hear the front door snick shut.

A sob escapes my raw throat.

Everything hurts. My hip. My head. The nail beds where my acrylics ripped off when I tried to grab the wall while Vinny dragged me down the stairs.

I hold up my hands to examine my palms and rotate my wrist, straightening and splaying my fingers. Even though it's early spring, there's a faint tan line on my ring finger. In summer, there's a white circle as pale as my boobs and ass.

I've stood in front of the mirror in August, hating the parts of myself that I can't change—the curve in my lower belly that I can only hollow by canting my hips backward, the padding on my outer thighs that I can't clamshell or sumo squat away—but I admired the untanned triangles.

I don't have to tan all over like Posy Santoro or Jen Amato. I don't need to pay a girl to bleach my asshole and wax my pussy completely bare.

The differences are so small, aren't they? Between women like them and women like my mother and my aunts.

Between women like my mother and women like Paul's mom.

The more disposable you are, the harder you have to work at your hair, your face, your attitude. The less allowance men make for not meeting standards.

Mrs. DeStefano doesn't even own a pair of heels, and two years ago, she cut her hair short and let it go gray. Mrs. DeStefano's never been backhanded once in her entire life. She says anything she wants to her husband, and if he doesn't like it, he goes and watches TV in the garage.

And Paul doesn't think anything of it. To him, it's normal. He'd never hit me in a million years.

Hot tears leak down my cheeks.

How long had he been wanting to break up with me? When did he figure out that I'm damaged beyond repair? I thought I'd hid it so fucking well. I thought I had it on lock.

He thinks I need help.

I laugh, and it's a terrible sound in the empty room. Dear God, do I need help—and there's none coming. Not anymore.

The blanket's weight is suffocating now. I hoist it off the bed and swing my legs after, forcing myself to breathe through the panic, nausea, and foul taste in my mouth.

I go to the bathroom, pee, and do a better search of the cabinet and drawers. I need mouthwash. They're still empty, but I discover a linen closet behind the door. On the highest shelf, there's a perfectly folded stack of fluffy white towels and an unopened pack of toothbrushes.

And on the shelf at eye level, there's my brand of aluminum-free coconut and vanilla natural deodorant, still in the plastic wrap.

And my argan oil body butter.

My shave cream.

My rose gold razor.

The kind of natural sea sponges I use instead of loofahs.

My shampoo.

My conditioner.

My air dry cream.

My styling balm.

A slender pink bottle with a charm and a purple heart-shaped bottle of perfume, the same ones I have on my vanity. The ones I knocked over when Vinny dragged me out of my bed.

The products are all lined up like in a store display.

I reach for the body butter and unscrew the lid. There's a very slight indentation where someone ran their finger lightly across the top. I skim my finger along the same groove and rub the lotion into my shaking hands.

I am cold to the bone.

My feet are freezing on the tile. Of course, there's no mat on the bathroom floor.

Nicky's been in my bedroom. Or someone told him what products I use. Oh, Lord. He's gone through my stuff.

I sweep the bottles in the front aside, rooting through tubes and sprays, knocking shit over. My hand hovers over the balancing gel cleanser that I stopped using a few years ago when I decided I didn't have combination skin anymore and moved to a gentle hydrating wash. Two years ago. I was at college then.

Until I graduated, I never came home to stay overnight. For Christmas and Easter, I stayed with Paul at his parents'. During the summers I crashed with a girlfriend, worked as a barista, and took easy As like yoga and post-war European cinema.

At some point, Nicky was in my dorm room.

Holy shit.

What do I do with that?

I pick up a bottle that fell on the floor, shove it back onto a shelf, and slide the door closed. A blind panic rushes through me, roaring in my ears, driving me back into the bedroom.

I race for the nightstand where he keeps his gun, hoping against my better sense that there's another in there as I yank the drawer so hard that it slides off the rails. It's empty except for a box of bullets. I toss the drawer on the rumpled comforter and squat, peering under the bed. I don't see anything, but it's dark.

I grab the phone and stab the flashlight app, laying on my side and craning my neck to see the underside of the frame. Dad kept a gun taped under his side of the bed.

No luck.

I dash into the hall, careening through the door across the way. This must be the master suite. It's twice the size of the room we slept in, and the windows offer the same view as the living area—the promenade, the river, and the mansions on the far bluff. He's set it up as a gym.

There is a rack of free weights, a bench, an all-in-one, a rowing machine, and a pull-up bar in the doorframe to the en suite.

There's an exercise bike in the center of the room, facing the wall of windows. Same kind as mine.

With the same heart rate monitor that I bought separately.

I check the bathroom. It has a jacuzzi tub and a shower with two heads. The tile is wet. He got ready in here. Why? To not wake me? So I couldn't sneak up on him naked and bust in his brains with the bedside lamp?

A hysterical laugh slips from my lips.

I could use a hand weight as a weapon. Wait beside the door for him to come home. Catch him by surprise. What would it take? Ten pounds? Twenty?

Could I swing twenty pounds fast enough? He's got at least eight inches on me. I'd have to swing high.

And then what?

Then Lucca Corso has my family killed.

I move more slowly to the main room, sticking my head in the hall closet—empty except for a black wool coat and a baseball bat. It'd be easier to bash him in the head with the bat.

And then my family dies. Corso would make it a message, like Renelli did with the Carbones back when I was in elementary school. Renelli had their house burned down with them locked in the basement. One day, Angie Carbone sat three seats behind me, and the next, she was gone.

There's a weight in my stomach like a bowling ball. I'm trapped. Even though I could walk out the door right now. Even though I could kill Nicky Biancolli—maybe. If I could kill any man, I could kill him. I'm scared enough.

But still, I'm trapped.

I wander into the kitchen. The fridge is mostly empty. Nicky doesn't even have the stereotypical bachelor condiments. There's a half-gallon of unopened milk and a six-pack of beer. The cabinets above the counter have a generic white dinnerware set. Glass tumblers. What look like never-used pots and pans and casserole dishes. He could've gotten the stuff from any box store.

There's a drawer with silverware, and a drawer almost filled to overflowing with an assortment of plasticware and stacks of cheap paper napkins, white and brown.

There are knives in a block. I graze the handles with my fingertips, but I leave them be. It doesn't give me any comfort to touch them. It just makes my stomach hurt worse.

Beside the fridge, there's a folding door. I'm expecting a closet, but it hides a full-sized washer and dryer with an empty shelf above. No detergent, no dryer sheets. Like the cookware, the machines seem new and unused. There are still stickers on the front.

I go back to get a glass of water and realize that I missed a cabinet. I'm not expecting much when I swing it open.

Instantly, my heart bottoms out, and my throat squeezes shut. My face bursts into flame. Out of instinct, I check over my shoulder, but no one's there.

No one can see me ripped naked, strung up. Exposed.

The bottom shelf is completely full. Swiss rolls. Frosted fudge cakes. Peanut butter bars. Strawberry shortcake rolls. Brownies. Coconut snowballs. Crème-filled cupcakes with curlicues and strips of icing. Lemon. Orange. Butterscotch. Chocolate. Frosted apple pies. Cherry pies. Moon pies. Coffee cakes. Muffin bites. Honey buns.

Everything is individually wrapped, exactly like I buy. So I'll stop at one. This time.

The boxes are stacked like bricks, wall to wall.

My hands fly to cover my mouth, and I squeeze my eyes shut. The heat kicks on, and the silence in the apartment is broken by a low hum.

If there was anything in my stomach, I'd puke it up, but since there's nothing inside me anymore, I stagger on my feet. I wish I could melt into a puddle so a man with a mop could come along and smear me across the floor.

I know this isn't the worst thing to happen in the past twenty-four hours.

I *know*.

Furio is dead. I'm a hostage. I've had a stalker for years and years, and I had no idea.

I know this isn't the catastrophe, but it is. It *is*.

But my brain doesn't have any control over the thing that makes me feel this way. That makes me do the things I do.

Mom took me to talk to a shrink once when I was a freshman in high school and the dentist said that I was ruining my teeth. We drove all the way to Shady Gap to see the guy. Mom signed me out of school early so Dad wouldn't know.

He was a psychiatrist, a stick thin man in his fifties. He asked me questions as he scribbled notes on a yellow legal pad.

"How much do you eat when you're 'bad?'" he asked.

"I don't know. A lot."

"What do you eat?"

"Garbage. Junk."

"Like—?"

"Snack cakes."

"How many snack cakes do you eat in one sitting?"

"A lot."

"What's a lot? Three? Four?"

Three.

Hah.

Four.

Hah.

"Boxes," I said.

"You eat a whole box?"

I remember how he sounded. Like he couldn't believe a person was physically capable of doing such a thing. I didn't tell him that I meant three *boxes*. Four *boxes*.

Later that week, Dad found a receipt from a gas station in Shady Gap, Mom ended up with a black eye, and that was the end of that. I heard them fighting. Dad thought she'd gone to meet someone. A man. She denied it, but she didn't tell him the truth, either.

I learned my lesson. I stopped puking, and I started running. Later, I got the bike. Mom never mentioned any of it again.

We all do what we have to do.

I force my eyes open. There are easily twenty boxes of snack cakes filling the entire bottom shelf. They are all my kind. Every single box.

He knows. The shame scalds.

I don't care about him. Fucking stalker. Loser. Lucca Corso's bitch.

Still, the shame scrapes me raw.

I begin snatching boxes, piling them in my arms. They're going in the trash. This place must have a garbage shoot in the hall or a dumpster in the basement.

I'm heading for the door when the thought occurs to me—he'll think I ate them all.

And why should I care?

I know the answer is I shouldn't—I *don't*—but that's not how it works. The thing that makes me do what I do is louder than everything. It can shout down any intention, any resolution. It decides what I feel, and it howls and screams until I do. It demands shame. Despair. Capitulation.

I shove the boxes back into the cabinet, but I can't make them all fit. I throw some on a higher shelf. He'll know I got into them.

Fuck him.

I drag myself into the living room and sit on the cold leather sofa in the middle of the empty apartment. There's a remote on the arm. I turn the TV on and huddle into a ball. The guide scrolls by while an advertisement for lawn treatment plays at the top.

Past the windows, clouds hide the sun and cars zoom noiselessly along River Street. Only a few people with dogs are walking the promenade this early in the day.

No one knows about what I do.

Mom likes to think I'm all better now. She brags to her girlfriends about how health conscious I am. I have my own credit cards now, so she doesn't need to know.

Paul has his suspicions. I don't eat much around him, so he figures that I starve myself. He's always on me about macronutrients and micronutrients. The responsible way to do intermittent fasting. Whenever he gets on a kick about my eating, he eventually comes around to telling himself that I have a healthy BMI, so there's no cause for serious concern. Just side-eyeing my plate all the time.

I'm not Paul's problem anymore, though.

I flip to the home improvement channel. I like watching disasters get plastered over in less than an hour. Something inside me gets off on thinking about how soon all the cosmetic changes are going to start falling apart.

I watch houses get flipped for hours, until my knees ache from tucking my feet under my butt. I don't even get up to pee. Even though I'm totally dehydrated, I'm not thirsty.

A little after noon, a wave of panic breaks through the numbness, and I rush to the bedroom on prickling legs. It takes me forever to remember our home number. I have no idea what anyone's cell phone is. Mom picks up on the first ring, and I can hardly understand her through the hysterics, but she and Mattie are okay. Tony Junior's at work.

She's been trying to call my phone for hours. I told her it broke by accident. We don't say Furio's name or Lucca's or Nicky's.

She says, "Are you hurt?"

I can almost hear her praying that I say no.

I tell her that I'm fine and change the subject to inconsequential things. Can she pack me a bag of shirts and bottoms and underwear? And my makeup? I don't know when I'll get it, but soon.

She makes me promise that I'm okay, and I do.

Mattie's at school. She says she'll have him call me when he gets home.

When I get off the phone, I don't want to watch TV anymore. I get on the bike, crank the incline to fifteen percent, and pedal in my sundress, barefoot and braless. It hurts my soles, but I don't stop until my quads give out. Then I limp back to the sofa and collapse, my sweat slicking the leather, my thigh muscles quivering.

I burned two thousand six hundred calories.

That's where Nicky finds me when he comes back. I don't even startle at the sound of keys in the lock.

My instinct is to straighten up and perch on the edge of the sofa, but I don't have the energy. My head is collapsed against the cushions, and all I do is swivel my neck so I'm facing the door, my hot cheek pressed against the cool leather, arms listless at my sides like a rag doll.

The instant he strides in, his eyes find me. My gelatinous muscles tense. He tosses his keys on the counter and kicks off his dress shoes. He's wearing what looks like black silk socks. His jacket's unbuttoned, and there are creases in his lap. He has a five o'clock shadow.

He didn't last night.

He must've shaved before he broke into my house to kill Furio and blackmail me into marrying him.

My tapped-out brain doesn't know what to do with the realization, so I let it drift away. It's not like knowing that can help me.

He takes off his jacket, shakes it out with a snap, and drapes it over the back of one of the dining room chairs.

If you ignore the gun in the holster at the small of his back, he could be a businessman coming back from a day at the office. I guess. He doesn't have a normal man's eyes, he has an addict's—calculating and fixated and dauntless.

"Where's dinner?" he asks, scanning my body like he's checking for damage.

I just stare back at him. I should be afraid of him. I should muster up my sense of self-preservation, but at some point in the past 18 hours, it broke.

He stalks to the kitchen and swings the fridge open. "There's nothing in here," he says to me over the door.

"There's beer and milk." I brace myself. You don't speak to a man like that in his own home. Not even joking. Dad had to remind Mom once in a while after she had a few glasses of wine. She'd always make him carbonara the next day. Carbonara was his favorite.

Nicky stares a few more seconds before he takes out the milk, unscrews the lid, tips it, and drinks, eyes drifting shut. His throat bobs with each long swallow.

He really should come across as a pretty man. He has the cut jaw and sharp cheekbones and plush lips. That's not the effect, though. Maybe his eyebrows are a little too dark. Maybe his nose is a little too Roman, a little too much like a bust in a museum.

Or maybe it's because he doesn't act at all like a pretty man. He acts like a dangerous one, the walk-softly-and-carry-a-big-stick kind.

He wipes his mouth with the back of his hand and puts the milk away. There's no more than a cup or two left.

"Why didn't you go to the store?" he asks while loosening his tie.

I shrug and turn away to stare at the dark TV screen. Out of the corner of my eye, I see him grab a carryout menu from the counter.

"You like sausage?"

A deranged giggle bubbles up my throat. Forcing it down makes my eyes water. This is beyond surreal.

What do you even call shit this weird?

He doesn't bother asking twice. He calls and orders a large sausage and mushroom pizza with insalata caprese and a side of garlic bread. Carbs with carbs.

At the end of the order, he adds on two root beers.

I watch his reflection in the TV as he rests his phone on the wireless charger and heads down the hallway. He disappears into the gym, and I hear the shower. He's quick. He's only in there about five minutes before he comes out wearing a towel around his waist and crosses into the room we slept in last night.

He emerges not long after in sweatpants and a white ribbed undershirt. Everyone calls them wife beaters, but I don't. To me, "wife beater" always jars. Like it's a little too true.

Nicky comes back to the living room and stops behind the sofa. If I glanced over my shoulder, he'd be right there. I don't. I stare straight ahead.

For a long moment, we look at each other in silence, both blurry on the blank screen. Smudged. We can't meet each other's eyes. The reflection isn't distinct enough.

"What did you do today?" he asks.

"You're looking at it."

"You rode the bike."

"Then why'd you ask me, if you already know?" Shit. Does he have spy cams set up in here?

I scan the ceiling, twisting to look above the kitchen cabinets. "Are there cameras in here?"

"You changed the height on the seat," he says.

"Are there cameras?" Shame makes my voice shrill. Makes me forget that I should tread carefully.

"No."

"Would you tell me if there were?"

"Yes."

"I don't believe you."

He lifts a shoulder. It's not a shrug. It's an acknowledgement.

"What *is* this?" I ask, gesturing around the room. I don't elaborate. He has to know what I mean.

Things happen in our world. People disappear. Dario Volpe married Posy Santoro after everyone in the organization saw a video of her taking it up the ass from another guy. The stories of what Lucca and Tomas have done—they can't all be true, but some must be, and it's wild, psychopathic shit.

But no one's getting blackmailed into marriage, though. Sex, sure. Turning state's evidence—it's happened. Marriage, though? It's not a thing.

Nicky doesn't miss a beat. "What does it look like?"

I can't suppress the cackle. This man will not give you a straight answer. "I cannot even begin to tell you."

"Why didn't you cook?" he asks, strolling to the table and taking the seat at the head. That's where I was sitting last night. When he made me dump my fiancé. Who didn't want me anymore anyway.

"I'm not your maid," I say and stand, a restless energy sweeping away the lethargy I've been sunk in all day. I stalk to the window and give him my back.

"Maids don't cook," he says.

"And you know that how, Nicky Biancolli?" I let him hear the sneer, and I don't turn to face him.

I want him to know that I remember his floodwater pants and the musty stink no amount of body spray could cover. I want him to know that no matter how much he scares me now, I remember feeling sorry for him.

"You want to come over and talk shit to my face?" he says. There's no anger in his voice. Only cautious amusement.

I cross my arms tight against my chest and lift my chin.

"Did you eat anything today?" His gaze roams to the cabinet with the snack cakes. If he mentions that shit, I'll go for the baseball bat.

"Did you kill anyone today?"

His lip curves, and he stretches his legs. They're at an angle, not under the table. His feet are bare. Veiny like his forearms. He pushes the other chair away from the table with the ball of the left one.

"You gonna just stand over there?" he asks.

"Until I work up the nerve to throw myself out."

His small smile fades. "Come and sit."

"Are you gonna make me?"

"Do you want me to?"

Part of me does. Part of me wants to put a match to this thing, so it blows, and the worst is over already. But at the end of the day, I've taken enough blows to have learned not to go asking for it.

I grudgingly make my way to the table, pulling the chair further away before I sit.

"You want a beer?" he asks as he gets up.

"I don't like beer."

He uses the edge of the marble counter to pop the lid off the bottle before he comes back.

"You know that, though, don't you?" I ask.

He lifts a shoulder almost imperceptibly as he takes a swig.

"I'll wait for my root beer." That's what I always order. Root beer in a glass bottle if they have it.

I rest my elbows on the table and lean forward. My muscles won't stay stiff anymore. They've given up.

I prop my chin in my palm and consider the man facing me as he sips his beer. He's maybe hotter and less loud, but otherwise he's no different than Tony Junior or Furio or Frankie Bianco or any other clown from the neighborhood.

"How long have you been watching me, Nicky?"

He raises his eyes to stare over my shoulder at the wall. It's the first time he's stopped looking at me since he got back.

"You really want me to marry you?" I press. "How do you see that going?"

His jaw clenches. He's leaning back in his chair, though, legs stretched again. His free hand rests on the table. His face isn't flushed. He's not gonna hit me. Yet.

So I push some more. "I'm gonna be your maid? Your whore? What?"

He drums his fingers. A tic appears at his right temple. He's still intent on the blank wall.

"You gotta know this is crazy, right?"

A wry smile flashes across his face, and he swigs his beer.

"How's this work? We go to Las Vegas or something?"

His eyes dart back to meet mine. "We're getting married in the church."

"What?"

"Saint Vincent's. Next month."

I didn't think I still had the capacity to be surprised.

Paul nixed the idea of a church wedding early on. He's embarrassed that he was an altar boy back in the day. None of his friends are Catholic, and the priest jokes make him defensive. It was fine by me. I didn't want to start my new life in a place I've been going to for my whole life and never once felt comfortable.

"You're completely fucking nuts," I tell him.

This time, he gives me a whole smile, teeth and everything. They're almost too white and even. I bet they're veneers.

There's a knock at the door, and he rises to get our food. He takes it to the kitchen, futzes around a while, and comes back with slices on paper plates and insalata caprese in paper bowls. He puts the Styrofoam container of garlic bread, stack of white napkins, and plasticware between us.

He opens my root beer, pours it into a glass with ice, and sets it in front of me. Then he sits and eats.

Like a *machine*. Like he hasn't seen food in a week.

His shoulders hunch, and he devours a folded slice while he forks mozzarella into his mouth with his other hand. He's not looking at me now. He doesn't have eyes for anything but his plate.

Maybe two minutes pass before he's up getting more slices. Finally, he notices me. I haven't touched anything.

"Eat," he mutters. "It's good."

It smells good. It's New York style, and the sausage is in rounds, not crumbles.

But I don't want to touch his food. I sure as shit don't want him to watch me eat.

My Dad got pissed if I didn't eat at the table. He'd say, "Not good enough for you, princess? You insult your mother."

Mom got anxious if I ate too much. *A moment on the lips, a lifetime on the hips. Nothing tastes as good as skinny feels.*

Paul would look at my plate, raise his eyebrows, and very obviously say nothing.

Nicky's piling it away, ignoring me. I unwrap my fork and spear a tomato. It's good. Ripe. The perfect amount of oregano and olive oil. There are a few leaves of fresh basil, too, not the shake kind.

Nicky goes back to the kitchen for thirds.

I nibble tomatoes.

The bread is easy to resist. It's the type where the whole loaf is heel. I can get into trouble with bread, but not when it's gross.

I glance over at Nicky. He's still shoveling it in.

I finish the tomatoes, and I'm hungry now. Starving, actually. Shaky and sweating. My pizza is cold, but it looks so damn good, and it still smells melty and toasty and familiar, like it'll make everything better.

I can have a slice.

An average large slice of pizza with one topping is around two hundred and fifty calories, so round up to three hundred to account for the mushrooms. Divide into fifteen bites. Twenty calories a bite. So, let's round up to, say, twenty-five per bite.

Cheese is a hundred calories an ounce, give or take. I've had about a half cup of mozzarella so far, so two ounces, which is two hundred calories. Plus fifty calories for the olive oil. Round up to three hundred to be safe.

I have two thousand six hundred calories in the bank from today's ride, minus three hundred is two thousand three hundred, and if I eat the whole slice, I'm still in a calorie deficit. Two thousand. That's a decent sized deficit.

That feels safe.

Mushrooms are vegetables, and veggie calories are the safest. I pick them off and eat them one by one, slowly, wishing the gnawing in my stomach away. When I'm upset, I can go for days without eating. A bite here and there is usually enough.

My body's on the fritz, though. It's gone the way of my mind. The normal rules aren't applying.

Sausage is nothing but fat. I don't care what they say, fat calories stick faster. My hands tremble as I remove it, slice by slice, and set them in a pile on the edge of the limp plate. I use my fork and knife to cut off the tip of the slice and slip it into my mouth.

Minus twenty-five.

It's so good.

I hate myself.

I cut another row, divide it into even pieces. I peek up at Nicky. He's got a fresh beer, and he's working on the garlic bread.

I take another bite. The cheese is room temperature, but it hasn't gotten rubbery. It's the gooey kind that goes down smooth.

Minus fifty.

Paul is a talker, and not the kind that's happy with the occasional nod and uh-huh, so I always lose count when I eat with him. I end up deducting the maximum and spending an extra twenty minutes on the bike just in case.

Nicky doesn't say a word, and he chews with his mouth closed.

When he finishes, he sighs and gets up, taking his plate and the empty garlic bread container to the trash can.

I freeze with my fork mid-air and lower it.

"Don't get up," he says. "You're not done." And then on his way to the living room, he sets his paper bowl in front of me.

He sits on the far side of the sofa, props an ankle on his knee, flips on ESPN, and proceeds to ignore me entirely.

The bowl is full of tomatoes speckled with oregano. No mozzarella.

He saved me his tomatoes. He was paying attention. Even when it looked like he wasn't.

My belly does a strange flip. From fear? Greasy pizza? I can't tell.

Is he watching me now somehow out of his periphery? There's no way. I think. Where he's sitting, he's totally in profile, and I can see his eyes flick, following the ball in some soccer game recap.

I consider the tomatoes. Am I supposed to eat them? Is he being *nice*? Is it a power thing? *Don't get up. You're not done. Eat this.*

I'm in control. You do what I say.

That's how I should read it, right? That's what's happening here. This is blackmail. I'm a hostage.

That's not how it sounded, though.

There's nothing hesitant or conciliatory about how he speaks, none of the polite, fake-ass due deference that Paul and his friends use when they speak to me. Nicky talks like my Dad and Tony Junior and all my other uncles and cousins. Not much and not nicely. Not unless they want something.

Nicky does want something, though. I shiver. He must.

But here we are. He's engrossed in the TV, and he gave me his tomatoes.

I take another bite of pizza, chewing slowly. Minus seventy-five.

Do I throw the tomatoes in the trash?

That's what I should do, right? You might be completely powerless, but you have to fight, right? You can't give up your pride. You can't give in.

If you do surrender, you've got to make yourself suffer for it.

Right?

I spear a tomato so hard the tip of the plastic fork breaks off. They're fucking delicious. Even better since they've been marinating at room temperature for a while.

I shove a slice in my mouth whole, glancing over at Nicky. He's still intent on the screen.

I eat them all, swirling the last one in the olive oil and oregano, and then I finish the slice of pizza, even the crust. My lips are slick, my belly's full, and I'm going commando in the sundress I slept in, but for some reason, I feel better. Not much. But some.

The TV gets louder. A commercial. Nicky stops watching and turns to look at me. His eyes dart down to my empty plate. My stomach cramps. His gaze rises.

"You didn't fix your hair today," he says.

I threw it up in a ponytail to work out, and I didn't bother to redo it when I was done. No doubt it's a mess.

"Nothing gets past you, eh?" I push up from the table and toss my trash away. I turn away from him on purpose, so I startle when I feel him at my back.

"You wore this to bed." His rough finger slips under a spaghetti strap, tracing a line along my shoulder. I shudder. Shiver.

How do you tell the difference?

"Vinny didn't pack anything but dresses." It's not really an excuse, but I don't need one, and he doesn't deserve one anyway.

And even though he's not touching me anymore, my skin is still prickled with goosebumps.

He takes my elbow and guides me out of the kitchen. I let him. I can't fight him now. I ate his tomatoes. He watched ESPN. And his hold isn't rough, only firm.

When he hurts me, I'll fight. Then I'll go for the weights. The bat. The knives. I have options.

Adrenaline kicks up my heart rate. By the time he leads me through the bedroom into the bathroom, my lungs are tight, and my palms are sweating.

He stops in front of the sink and faces me. It's a decent-sized bathroom, but with both of us in it, it feels crowded. He's a foot away, but he feels closer. Tall and imposing. He's blocking the door.

"What are you doing?" I ask, breathless.

"Take this out." He grazes the rubber band holding up my hair with the back of his fingers and drops his arm to his side.

"Why?" The word gets stuck in my throat. It comes out like a cough.

"If I do it, I'll hurt you."

He's staring again, his eyes like burning coals. The lighting is dimmer in here, and unlike the rest of the apartment, there's a drop ceiling. I can smell him. Beer and faint soap.

He's more real in here, his stillness even stranger. I'm scared.

But not as scared as I should be.

I tug the band out and set it on the sink. My hair doesn't move much. I sweated a lot, and it dried in the ponytail.

I look past him at the closet with the stash of my products, and I remember the gel cleanser that I don't use anymore.

"When did you break into my dorm room?" How did he even get in? There was a swipe card and a front desk. "Or did you get someone to spy on me?"

"Why snack cakes?" he asks, voice gravelly.

It's not the same. That's not his point, though.

"That's fucked up," I say, quietly. We've both lowered our voices for some reason.

I'm not sure if I mean the stalking or the snack cake question or both.

"I know," he says, and almost as if he can't stop himself, he raises a hand and slips a strap off my shoulder. I cross my arms. He slips the other strap off. My breath catches.

I can feel him peering at my face, but I keep my eyes cast down. For a few moments, we just stand there, my dress held up by my folded arms.

I know what I should be doing. Feeling.

I always know what I *should*, and yet—

There's no one else here besides Nicky and me. No one to tell what I did or didn't do. To judge. He sure as hell can't judge me.

Something much too close to excitement stirs in my belly.

"Let the dress go," he says, breaking the silence. It's not an order. Not a request. It's a lure.

My nipples contract, hardening into points that poke into my forearms. I raise my eyes to meet his, and instantly, I'm stuck, a fly in honey. His black, glassy irises are tar. Quicksand. My breath shallows.

He is beautiful. Not almost. *Is*. It's short-circuiting my survival instincts, persuading my lizard brain that he's something he isn't, lulling me out of my fear, and that terrifies me.

"What are you going to do to me?"

"You need to wash your hair."

"Do you ever give a straight answer?"

He tugs one of my straps, gently, nowhere near hard enough to rip it or drag the dress down, not with my tightly folded arms holding it up. "Take it off. Get in the shower."

"And that's all? I take a shower and wash my hair. You don't touch me?"

He nods, the slightest dip of his chin.

Why am I negotiating? I should be saying hell no. Fuck off. Never.

Should, should, should. Who believes in should? Not my father. Not Lucca Corso. Sure as hell not this guy.

He wants this. He doesn't give a shit about should.

He's not even trying to hide how much he wants it. Paul looked something like this at the very beginning when we both hadn't done it yet. We spent hours on the couch in his parents' finished basement, pretending to watch movies, going further and further—no tongue, tongue, over the shirt, under the shirt, my pussy grinding against his thigh in jeans, his fingers against the seam of my shorts.

He was so bad at it—we both were—but once it wasn't like that anymore, it was never as good. It was never like we were in it together again. It became something we did to each other. And then, for the past few years, something I did for him.

But no, thinking back now, even younger, horny Paul never wanted me this bad. I don't think I've ever seen anyone look like they want something this bad.

"You want me to strip for you? You want to watch?" My tone is sharp, but breathy.

A slash of color stains his cheekbones.

"Yes." His voice is even, but the word has weight. Heft.

"And if I won't?"

"You won't."

Another straight answer.

I slip my straps back up on my shoulders.

He doesn't blink. Doesn't move. His expression doesn't change at all. It's still hungry. Ravenous.

I step past him. He tenses.

I open the closet and root through the bottles, taking out shampoo, conditioner, body wash, everything that's in my shower at home.

Brushing past him again, I step into the tub, and slide the door shut. Through the frosted glass, I see him sit on the closed toilet seat. He's watching me, but in the dim light, I'll be nothing but an outline. A shadow.

I don't know what the hell I'm doing, but I'm doing it. I peel off my sundress and toss it over the door.

The porcelain under my bare feet is cold and squeaky clean. My nipples get even harder, my dark areolas puckering. My belly clenches.

I run the water, wait until it's hot, and draw the stopper. The pressure is good, and there's a rain shower head. The glass fogs up quickly.

I can't see Nicky anymore, but I know he's there. I bet he's not playing on his phone, either.

Is he touching himself?

I lift a sea sponge over my head to soak it as the water rolls down the insides of my arms and sides and back. The heat begins to soothe the muscles still sore from my bike ride.

I'm not relaxing. I'm more aware of my body than I usually am, and I'm never, ever unaware of it. This is different, though.

I squeeze a dollop on the sponge, and the scent of wild orange and vanilla fills the air. I inhale and close my eyes as I begin to wash my skin. Shoulders down to my hands. Underarms. Breasts. Under my breasts. Belly. Legs from ankle up to thighs.

I squeeze suds into my palm and stroke it through my folds and up my crack, lungs catching, eyes flying open. There's no way he can see. Does he know somehow?

I scan the tub and white tile walls. There's no place to hide a camera, no matter how small. Not even a vent.

I let my eyes drift closed again and hold my ass cheeks apart, bending slightly so the hot water sluices down the cleft to rinse my pussy.

He wants to see.

I bet he's picturing it.

How long has he been stalking me? I bet he's pictured it a hundred—thousand—times.

Something swirls in my belly, again not quite fear, not quite arousal. Or maybe it's both.

Is this turning me on?

I'm so fucked up.

Was I always?

Have I always been a fucked-up mess stuffed into nice clothes, propped up on a nice boyfriend, like a scarecrow, like a monster from a horror flick that gets stabbed, and its insides turn out to be nothing but cockroaches?

Has my life been a horror flick all along? The first act before the hammer falls, but all the signs are there, and only an idiot would imagine it was going to be some other kind of story?

I straighten, rinse myself clean, and shampoo and condition my hair, not bothering to leave it in for the usual three minutes. I'm done lingering.

I turn the shower off and stick my arm through a crack in the shower door, steam escaping.

"Towel."

A few seconds later, I feel terry cloth against my fingers. I briskly dry myself and wrap it as tightly as I can around my chest. I wave my arm again.

"I need another one for my hair."

Nicky hands me a second towel. I wrap it in a turban.

I don't let myself hesitate sliding the door open. The quicker I finish this, the sooner it'll be over. Then I can get on the bike. I can stop thinking.

It's too swampy in here.

I fling the door to the bedroom open and turn on the exhaust fan. The vent is over the toilet where Nicky sits. If he's got a camera hidden in there, it's not aimed at anything interesting.

I go back to the closet and dig out face wash and styling product. There's a blow dryer—my make and model—and a round ceramic brush.

"You gonna watch this part, too?"

He's resting his forearms on his thighs, and he gazes up at me from under sooty eyelashes, a sheen on his olive skin from the steam. His undershirt is damp and clinging to his sculpted pecs. He's hard. There's a tent in his pants that he's making no effort to hide.

I'm covered from chest to knees in a thick towel. My boobs are one lump.

Every muscle in his body is straining. His biceps. His shoulders. His neck.

The strange swirling is back in my belly.

Yeah, he's watching.

I unwind the towel from around my head. He's rapt. I drop the soggy towel on the floor and toe it into a corner. He doesn't blink.

I spritz pre-styler on and work it through with my fingers. I can do my routine without thinking, but not with him tracking my every move.

I rinse the tackiness from my fingers and do a once over with a heat shield. Then I plug the dryer in, divide my hair into sections, clip it up, and get to work.

It isn't until there's the roar of air in my ears that I realize I could hear his breathing before. Not now. If I focus on the mirror, I can block him out completely.

But I dart glances to the side as I twirl the brush, turning my natural limp waves into big soft curls. When my hair dries, it lightens, and the highlights begin to shine.

Nicky watches like he's never seen anything like it before, and his interest makes me aware of every inch of my skin, every slight movement, in a way I never am.

I drive my body, make it work until it gives out, shove it into shapewear and shoes with narrow, pointed toes. I chemical peel, exfoliate, wax, pluck. I strongarm it into compliance, make it do what I want, be what I need it to be.

But the way he's so close, almost at my elbow, following every stroke of my hand—I slow down.

I gentle my motions so my hair twirls through the brush like in a commercial, lengthening my spine, vertebrae by vertebrae, tilting my chin. Shivers race across my drying skin as Nicky notices.

When I swallow, his gaze falls to my throat. When I inhale deeply, it drops to my chest. I turn my head to work on my right side, and it rises.

It's like there's a thread between us.

My breath shallows, but it's not a panicky feeling. It's an edge-of-your-seat feeling.

What would I do if he touched me now?

What would I *feel*?

My hair is thoroughly dry and styled well before I turn the dryer off. After I apply finishing spray, I take my time combing it through with my fingers, arranging the curls over each of my shoulders and then flipping it back like all the effort was nothing.

My chest tightens.

What is he going to do now?

I forgot to get face wash and a toothbrush. I could drag this out another ten or twenty minutes. Longer if there's a mask in there.

The tension's been ratcheting up every minute in here, though, and I don't think I have the courage to walk past him to the closet.

It's almost a relief when he stands, except my heart starts pounding. He moves behind me, and I freeze. Lungs, limbs, everything.

He's so much taller than I am. He could rest his chin on the top of my head.

Our eyes meet in the mirror. This isn't like the blank TV screen. I can see his blown pupils. The thin band of dark brown iris. The vein in his neck that throbs in time with the whoosh of blood in my ears.

He shuffles a half step forward until his chest is flush with my back, resting his palms on the sink. I'm bracketed between his arms. His thick cock is steel against my spine.

He divides a length of hair, combing his fingers from scalp to ends, and lays it back over my left shoulder. His touch doesn't linger on my bare skin, but it skims. Dusts.

My belly spasms. Low. My breath audibly catches.

He takes another length of hair, and slowly, so slowly, places it over my right shoulder.

Now I look like I usually do. Like I tried, I spent the time, I did all the things to look like I'm supposed to. So I am unremarkable. Faultless.

Nicky bends, and—gently, carefully—presses his lips to my exposed nape, his nose brushing along my neck. Shivers race from nerve to nerve, down my spine and arms, to the tips of my fingers and toes.

I don't mean to, but a sound escapes my mouth. A strangled moan, a smothered whimper.

Nicky straightens, steps back, finds me again in the mirror.

Something hot and mean floods into me as the shivers recede. I reach for the rubber band still on the edge of the vanity and fist my hair into a ponytail, twisting it tighter and tighter until my scalp stings.

I glare at him.

For a second, his lids close, his smoky eyelashes sweeping his sculpted cheeks. Then his gaze returns to mine, and a wry smile plays at the corners of his mouth.

Calmly, methodically, he wraps his fingers around the base of my ponytail, slides his fist to the ends, and then winds my hair around his hand, forcing my neck to crane and my chin to rise. Pulling at my scalp until tears spring to my eyes. I can feel his strength, how much he's holding back.

I reach behind my head to clutch his wrists, but I can't budge him. My back is forced to arch. I sob.

He leans to speak in my ear, his breath hot on my cheek.

"I like it either way," he says.

He lets go, still smiling, and he walks out.

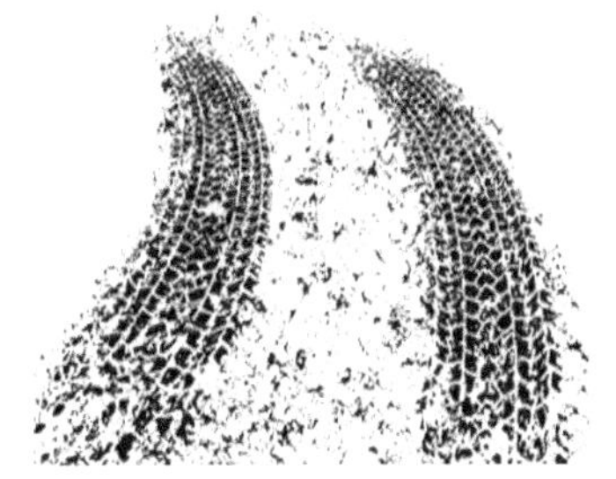

CHAPTER 3

Nicky

Zita's in bed, and her eyes are closed, but she's not asleep.

I don't bother keeping it down while I change into a black track suit and black sneakers. I strap up, tuck a bandana in my pocket, and grab a black beanie. The knit is unraveling where I picked the logo off, and I fucking hate that, but it's a necessary precaution. I haven't done this in a hot minute, but you don't forget the basics. No distinguishing marks or logos, no visible tattoos.

It's almost one in the morning, and Zita's been pretending for hours now.

Before she rolled onto her side and gave me her back, she said, "You lied. You touched me."

She's trying to guilt me. She can't—not over inconsequential shit like that—but I get that she's gonna try. She's a woman.

I don't want to leave her, but I won't be able to settle until I do this thing.

I pause in the doorway and watch her a little longer. It isn't long enough. It never has been. Is there a point when I will get used to her? When my adrenaline doesn't spike and my dick doesn't get hard?

If there is, it hasn't happened yet. She's covered to her chin in that bulky blanket, and I could still pound nails with my cock.

"I'll be back," I tell her.

She doesn't answer, but she can't resist peeping at me over her shoulder with those big brown eyes. My entire body comes to attention.

I knew it would be like this. She's still afraid, but soon, she won't be. Zita's no coward. She's a fighter. I can't wait for her to throw down.

With a last glance, I zip my jacket to my chin and head out, grabbing the remaining root beer bottle from the fridge. When I get to the garage, Tomas is standing next to a filthy white sports car that's at least thirty years old. Someone drew a cock and balls in the dirt on the rear panel by the gas tank.

"Nice dick," I say.

"That's what they say," Tomas answers, deadpan.

"Where'd you get it?"

"The '90s." Tomas gets in and shoves the passenger door open for me from the inside.

"No shit." The interior smells like mold and cigarettes, and the upholstery's damp. I try to roll the window down. It doesn't budge.

"You know where you're going?" I ask as he flies up the ramp and burns rubber turning onto River Street.

"Vaguely." He grinds the gears, trying to get into fourth before he has to stop at a red at the corner.

"You have to drive it like you stole it?"

"Kind of. Yeah." He almost smiles. "This is the dumbest shit I've done since I was a kid."

I can't say the same.

"You're fucking crazy, you know." He actually smiles this time, and it looks weird. He doesn't have the face for it.

Too many bones like my jaw that were broken and mended wrong.

"That's what they say." I smirk back as I finally force the window down a crack. I twist the top off the root beer and take a swig. I don't love it, but I drink it from time to time. It's Zita's favorite.

The light turns green, and Tomas peels out fast enough to leave black marks on the asphalt.

"You know, the whole thing about doing crimes is not to get caught." It's strange having to tell him. Tomas is usually the cautious one. Lucca's the showboat.

"Not seeing what she can do—that would be the crime." Tomas slams it into fifth as we merge onto the highway, and he opens it up. He gets her all the way up to seventy before the body starts shaking like the engine's gonna fall out.

I don't say anything. From his scowl, he knows I'm laughing my ass off at him on the inside.

We don't have that far to go. Pyle's a small city, and all the good neighborhoods are strung along the river.

Tomas slows down to the speed limit as we exit onto University Boulevard, turning on his brights and squinting at the street signs. There's no one out on the sidewalks. It's a Sunday night, and the bars are closed.

"Everything looks the same," he complains.

He's right. In this part of town, the buildings are all ivy-covered red brick, block after block.

"She lives over a sub shop," I say.

"She? Aren't we going after the guy's ride?"

"He's at her place. He's been sleeping there."

Tomas raises his eyebrows. "Does Zita know that?"

"I see no reason why she should."

Tomas exhales in that way he has that makes him sound old as shit. "I still don't get it," he says.

He doesn't have to. Like Lucca and Dario, all he needs to do is keep his word.

"You realize that we own you completely now, right?" Tomas glances over, trying to read me. I face forward and drink my root beer.

That's the worst thing he can imagine—being in debt to another man. And yet, that's how we got here. They all owe me. Zita is my payment.

"When you wanted her, we had leverage, but *now*—" Tomas shakes his head. "You know this game. A man will do a hell of a lot more not to lose something he has than he will to get something he wants."

Yeah, I know the game. They think she's their leverage. They're wrong, but if they're smart, I'll never have to disabuse them of the notion. A man will do anything to keep what belongs to him.

After a few more glances, I realize Tomas is waiting for a response. Zita's right—I don't give straight answers.

"But aren't we brothers?" I toss back, arching an eyebrow.

That's Lucca's line. We're the new generation, closer than blood because we've fought side-by-side in the trenches, overthrown that bastard Dominic Renelli to drag the organization into the modern era. We're not gangsters anymore, we're tycoons, 'cause what's the difference nowadays?

Lucca saw a movie about Henry the Fifth a few years ago, and now he always talks like he's giving a speech from on top of a horse. If I get paid in cash, and he leaves Zita to me, he can talk however he wants. If he reneges on our deal, he'll see how many shits I give about brotherhood.

Tomas shakes his head. "You're a smart man, and clearly, you're not averse to doing crazy shit. Why didn't you just take her? Nobody would've said shit."

He's really bothered that he doesn't get it. Makes him nervous. He reads shit he can't understand as a threat, but he could never understand, even if I explained it to him.

"I'm touched that you care so much about me. Love you too, man." I clap my hand over my heart, middle finger raised.

Tomas snorts and refocuses on the road. "Hope she's worth it," he mutters.

She is. Everything I've done. Everything I would do. Worth it.

We pass a dark sandwich shop, and Tomas slows down. "Here?"

"Yeah."

Paul DeStefano always parks on the street to the east of his side chick's building. There's no entrance on this side. No dumpsters or fire escapes. A windowless telephone company building runs the length of the other side of the block.

He's made this very convenient.

"What does he drive again?" Tomas asks.

"Audi SQ7."

He whistles. "Nice ride."

"Mommy and Daddy bought it for him."

"You know what I don't get?" Tomas says as he goes to circle the block. "You want this woman so bad, but you let this douchebag fuck her?"

I scan the neighboring buildings for CCTV. "Pussy's a renewable resource, man. She's not gonna run out."

"Fuck off with that man. It's gotta kill you."

No, it's gonna kill Paul DeStefano. One day when Zita doesn't give a shit about him anymore, I'm going to decapitate him with a hacksaw and punt his head off the Widow's Bluff overlook into the Luckahannock.

I drain the last of the root beer and put the bottle in the cup holder. "Women aren't action figures, man. They don't lose value 'cause someone got in their box."

He snorts a laugh. "Where do you get this shit?"

"TikTok."

He's cracking up when I say, "Pull over."

Paul parked right under the streetlight. It's a V8, 8-speed in Daytona Gray. I know for a fact he takes good care of it. Much better care than he took of Zita.

"Meet at the bottling plant?" Tomas asks, slowing to a crawl.

"The bottling plant," I confirm as I jump out, trotting two steps to the vehicle and busting out the driver's side window. You don't go for subtlety at this point; you go for speed.

Stealing cars is like riding a bike. I disable the alarm, start the engine in under sixty seconds, and head north toward the bridge, obeying the speed limit and all traffic laws. Except for a few beads of shattered glass, the interior is immaculate. Even the floor mats are pristine.

DeStefano likes his shit to look perfect.

The first time I saw Zita, her face was dirt streaked, she was barefoot, and her hair stuck out from her lop-sided ponytail like dandelion fluff.

She wasn't pretty. Not back then. She was skinny as a stick with eyes too big for her face.

But from that moment on, it's been Zita Graziano.

That's the answer. A shrink might be able to explain it, but I can't.

Some men have Jesus. God and country. A dream. Ambition.

I have Zita.

Tomas doesn't understand? Neither do I.

It's as inexplicable as the mystery of faith, but it's real. Physical. Inside me like my heart or my liver.

Tomas follows me at a distance as I take an indirect route to the abandoned industrial zone we use for shit that's gonna be loud or messy. The city doesn't maintain the roads anymore, and the streetlights that aren't broken are dim. I do my best to avoid the potholes, but I land in a few before I get to the old bottling plant, a five-story windowless brick building along the river.

I drive around to the back, and Tomas pulls in a yard behind me. He pops his trunk and takes out two bottles of lighter fluid.

I roll down the SUV's windows. A flicker of excitement makes my dick twitch.

"There's more in the back," he tells me as I hop out.

It's a velvet black night, no wind, no rain in the forecast. Perfect.

I grab two more bottles, and Tomas and I work quickly to douse the seats. I'm careful to drench the steering column, gearshift, and driver's side door handles.

We toss the empties in the back seat, and I go back to Tomas's ride for the root beer bottle and the last container of lighter fluid.

"Hold this." I hand Tomas the bottle and carefully fill it halfway. Then, I take the handkerchief from my pocket and twist it, threading it into the mouth of the bottle, and giving it a few seconds for the fluid to wick up the fabric.

"You've done this before, eh?" he says.

I shrug and take out my Zippo.

"Are you actually smiling, Biancolli?"

I thumb the striker. The flare lights up Tomas's craggy face. I absolutely am smiling as I toss the flaming bottle into the driver's seat.

The show isn't instantaneous. The Germans make a quality automobile. It takes a minute to catch. At first, there's nothing but a snake of smoke rising from the seat and the smell of charring upholstery, but eventually, the interior catches, and then—

The whole damn thing explodes. A fireball shoots into the night sky. Scraps of metal fly.

Tomas drops flat in the dirt, and I laugh. Flames lick out the open windows.

"You could've warned me it was gonna blow," Tomas bitches as he hauls himself back to his feet, dusting himself off.

"I asked if you wanted to blow up a car," I remind him. "What did you think was gonna happen?"

He's got nothing to say to that, so he curses under his breath and trudges back to his borrowed ride. He drives the speed limit all the way back to the chop shop. We take the bus back downtown, and it's five in the morning before I get back to the apartment.

Zita's asleep, but she rouses when I lie down on the covers and exhale.

"You smell like smoke," she mumbles, so I drag my ass into the shower before I pass out beside her.

CHAPTER 4

Zita

A SOFT CLICK WAKES me up. Nicky's standing by the nightstand, loading brass bullets into a solid black revolver.

I struggle to sit, fighting the weighted blanket. My heart pounds. I'm sweaty, and my eyes are blurry.

There's another click as Nicky pops the cylinder back in the frame. He holsters the gun behind his back and gives himself a once over, straightening his starched collar, tweaking the sleeves of his white dress shirt, and smoothing his slicked-back hair. He slips on the pressed black jacket that was laid on the bed.

He smells like fresh cologne. When he came back last night, he reeked of smoke and gasoline.

I shake my head to clear the fog. "Is my family okay?"

I reach for my phone. Nine in the morning. No missed calls. Panic still punches my chest.

He gazes down at me, concern or confusion creasing the bridge of his nose. "They're fine."

"What did you do last night?"

There's a second when he decidedly doesn't answer me.

"Will you go to the store today?" he asks, taking out his wallet from his back pocket.

"I don't want your money." I swing my legs over the side of the bed, shoving the blanket aside as his eyes track the movement. My sundress worked itself up to my waist while I slept, and the way I'm sitting, my thigh is exposed all the way to my hip. I stumble to my feet and yank the dress down.

I look past him. If he's got a hard on from the show, I don't want to see.

"There's no food in the house," he says.

"Not my house. Not my problem." I'm spitting words this morning without a second thought. The stress and sleeplessness are catching up to me. I need to chill out.

Drawing a deep breath, I force myself to meet his eyes. "Where did you go last night?" I ask again.

"You don't have to worry about that."

"I'm worried about everything." I didn't mean to say it. It just came out.

He exhales and carefully sets another stack of bills on the night table. Then he makes his way to where I'm standing on the far side of the room in the narrow aisle between the mattress and the wall.

He stalks closer until we're toe to toe, his body blocking me in, the nightstand at my back. I could scramble across the bed, give up all dignity and maybe get a few feet before he catches me and does whatever it is he wants to do.

A surge of irritation sweeps the cobwebs from my mind.

I step toward him, closing the short distance between us until my braless breasts brush his crisp cotton shirt. I tilt my chin, blink the remaining sleep from my eyes, and glare at him.

"Where did you go last night?" I ask again.

"I won't tell you."

"Did it have to do with my family?"

"No."

"Would you tell me if it did?"

His eyes drop to the carpet, and because the thread I've been hanging on to is gone after lucid dreaming for hours about fire and blood and shards of white skull stuck in my brother's black hair, I grab his jaw, dig my nails into his smooth-shaven face, and make him look at me.

"Would you?" I ask as fear belatedly floods through my veins, and my fingers shake.

His dark eyes widen, as thrown by my audacity as I am.

He raises a hand, slowly, and he wraps it, gently but firmly, around my wrist. I can't let him go now if I wanted to. Out of self-preservation, I ease up with my nails. I've made little red half-moons in his tanned skin.

"I won't hurt your family," he says, using his hold on my wrist to compel me backwards, pivoting me, pressing my back against the wall, rendering my arm useless, pinning it flush to my chest. But gently. Slowly.

"I won't let them get hurt," he adds.

"That's not what I asked," I say, but I'm breathless, and my momentary insanity is gone, my courage gone with it. He's so much bigger than I am. So much stronger.

So strange.

But he's not hurting me. He draws my arm down to my side and shifts forward until his pelvis presses against my lower belly. Every time his chest rises, it compresses my breasts, but lightly. I can feel him breathe.

His hard cock prods my hip bone. He winds the fingers of his free hand through my mussed-up hair. When he hits a tangle, he skims past, leaving the knot.

Like he doesn't want to hurt me.

The irritation surges back, hot and wild now. I haven't felt this way for a long, long time. Since before I learned how thoroughly a smaller, weaker woman can be made to regret losing control of her temper.

I raise my face to his, and I lick my bottom lip, dragging it between my teeth. His eyes blaze. I shift my hips into his and plunge my fingers into his combed and moussed hair, urging him to bend.

He does.

I part my mouth, and he moans as he takes it, wrapping me in his arms, crowding me, demanding I open to him.

For a split second, I forget myself, and I let him in. Mint. Hunger. *Starvation*.

A blazing want that is sharp and unrepentant and some-how, somehow *familiar*.

But I'm not like him. This life isn't mine. This isn't what *I* want.

I sink my teeth into his bottom lip, biting as hard as I can until I taste copper. He grunts. I smile with my mouth full. He has to jerk his head back to free himself, using his forearm to pin me to the wall.

I'm panting, and his lip is snarled and dripping blood. A growl sounds at the back of his throat.

Excitement sparks inside me, so raw, so unrestrained, I hardly recognize it for what it is.

He lunges a knee forward, forces my thighs apart, and with his chest holding me in place, he shoves a hand between my legs, finds my pussy and spears two thick fingers inside me. He goes in easy. I'm dripping.

I beat at his upper arms, but I'm trapped. Splayed. And his fingers slide in and out, making wet, squelching sounds in the silence, his forehead pressed to mine, hard, bone to bone, our ragged gasps mingling.

"You're wet," he says, so close I feel his warm breath on my lips.

"You're bleeding."

"You like it."

"Fuck you."

His rough thumb finds my clit, and he flicks. I whimper.

I can't tell if I'm turned on, or if I'm being pumped full of impotent rage, stretched, until I'm fearless and stupid. I can't tell if there's any difference between the two.

"I'm not afraid of you," I say, fisting his hair again and pulling.

"I don't want you to be." His deep voice rumbles in my ear, and he finger-fucks me harder, watching my face like a creep. Like an addict. A trail of reddish-brown blood drips down his crooked jaw to his corded neck.

This is wrong. *I'm* wrong.

My pussy spasms. My clit throbs. He won't rub it like I need. His thumb circles, strums, pissing me off, making me squirm and buck.

He doesn't get to be in control.

I clutch his shoulders and climb him, wrapping my legs around his hips, throwing him off balance. He staggers as he scrambles with both hands to grab my ass and hold me in place so I don't knock us both backward.

I want to fall onto the bed on top of him. I want him under me.

He's got me, though, his hands spreading my bare ass cheeks, urging my pussy closer, pressing my mound into the hard bulge in his pants. His leather belt cuts into my pubic bone as I grind and he thrusts, slamming my back into the wall, snapping my teeth shut.

If I open my eyes, his will be right there, skewering me, black and bright, like he can actually see into me, like he actually cares what I am, what I'm feeling. So I keep them screwed shut, and I get myself off, working my hips, mindless.

This is a dream, a fever dream. I don't know who I am. I'm someone else, someone mean and wild. Fearless.

Shameless.

I drive my heels into his taut thighs, spurring him on, his groans and jagged pants music in my ears.

He wants me so fucking bad, worse than I've ever wanted anything, except the closer I get to hurtling over the edge, the louder my moans become, overpowering his.

"Oh, fuck, Zita," he says, ripping a shoulder strap, baring my breast, grabbing it, squeezing, rough and clumsy, and then he ducks his head and shoves it in his mouth, suckling hard, no finesse, teeth scraping my nipple, tongue lapping.

It's not a performance. His moves aren't rehearsed. He's feasting, eating me up all at once, gorging himself, and I'm doing the same, and I'm terrified. Out of control.

High.

He bites down on my tit like an apple, my adrenaline rockets through the roof, and I come, screaming and shaking. For a second, my ears ring. My mind goes blank.

My mind goes blank.

And then it all rushes back, a crashing tsunami of garbage thoughts. Slut. Crazy bitch. Foul trash.

I slam my palms into his chest and contort my spine, trying to draw back and get enough room to head butt him. Break his fucking nose. Fight now that it's too late.

He steps back. I catch myself from falling by slumping against the wall, chest heaving, struggling for breath.

What did I do?

Fucking *why*?

"You bit me," I say between pants. It has to be his fault. I'm not this—thing.

He glances down to where I'm covering my bare breast with my forearm. "I didn't break the skin."

His bottom lip is puffy. His tongue darts out to dab the cut. My fingers fly to brush my own swollen lips. His hungry eyes follow. My pussy flutters. An aftershock.

"I shouldn't have done that," I say. I'm not sure if I mean biting him or dry humping him or what.

"You do what you want."

I don't. I so obviously don't.

His hands go to his belt. I freeze. "What are you doing?"

He glances down at his lap meaningfully. "Changing my pants." The corner of his mouth quirks. "You made a mess."

My face erupts in flames. The wool tented over his still hard cock is dark. Soaked. He turns and strides off into the closet, no rush, no shame.

I dive back under the covers, haul them to my ears, and curl up, facing the wall. I ignore him when he comes back out and says, "Have dinner ready at six. We've got a thing tonight. We need to leave by seven."

He doesn't wait for an answer.

I lie there shivering, watching the minutes pass on my phone, listening to the quiet grow bigger, something inside me sinking. It's like the carnival ride that spins faster and faster until the floor drops, and you're left stuck to the wall. "Weightless" they call it, but you're not. You're plastered in place, utterly dependent, and if anything breaks, you're utterly and completely fucked.

I can't stay here anymore. I heave the blanket off and stand, my decisiveness fleeing as suddenly as it appeared. There's nowhere to go.

I peel off the sundress, drop it into the bathroom trashcan, and put on another one—pink with a cherry pattern and wide straps. No bra. No underwear.

Panic and unease rise inside me, driving me out of the bedroom where the scent of sex and Nicky's cologne lingers, to the kitchen, to the cabinet with the boxes.

I don't make a decision. That capacity is offline. I slip my finger under a cardboard flap, unsealing it like an envelope and take out a crinkly cellophane package. I pluck it open at the seam, calm, methodical, as if I'm not about to fuck up big time.

I slide out the cupcake, peel off the piece of cardboard underneath, and set it on the counter.

I do it again. And again. I open all twelve, lining them up, shoving the trash into the box, crushing the box, shoving it into the trashcan, rummaging to hide it under the folded pizza box from last night. And then I eat each one, icing first. I break the cake in half, tongue out the filling, chew, swallow, and then I eat the next.

Around the fourth, I stop to pour myself a glass of water, rinsing the clump of chocolate sponge down my throat, and I keep going, strung out with the fear of getting caught, flinching at every sound, the air kicking on, the ice maker dumping ice. I'm terrified, and I'm ashamed. That's all I feel.

I eat past fullness. I eat past being able to taste it. I eat, and I hate myself.

I'm the guitar solo in "Freebird." I keep going because I started, and now I can't stop. I don't have brakes.

I finish the last cupcake, and I grab a box of peanut butter bars, refill my water, and slump to the couch. For the next hour, I let the home improvement channel run in the background as I unwrap bar after bar, shoving the wrappers in the crack in case someone comes, the box hidden between my side and the arm. My body is wired, and my brain is thick with sugar and shame.

I am trash. Weak. Hopeless. Disgusting.

I force more and more into my stomach until it aches. I'm bites away from puking, but also—

Everything is far off now. Paul. Furio. Mattie. The kitchen. All the years of shit that came before, that I've shoved down deep, that I have to keep burying, day after day, hour after hour, or it'll rise up and drown me.

My thoughts are woozy. They can't catch me. I can float in my shame, and I don't have to worry. I've already fucked up. I'll have to pay later. But not now. Nothing can hurt me. I already hurt myself.

I can just stare as pretty people demo walls with sledge-hammers and lay tile. I don't need to figure out what happened in the bedroom. Or what I'm going to do.

All I have to do is lie here and be a disgusting pig.

I beat myself with the words. Not like a boxer. Like those priests in the Middle Ages who whipped themselves and burned witches. You can't be a masochist without having a little sadist in you, right? Part of you has to get off on hurting yourself, or you wouldn't do it.

You'd want help.

I don't. I hide the second empty box with the first, and then I return to the couch and float along in a sugar coma, drifting off for an hour or so. I go longer than usual before it starts.

What word is stronger than regret? Like regret but with teeth. Acid. Boiling oil.

Maybe terror describes it better.

I can't get fat.

Fat is beautiful. Yumi Nu is beautiful. Ashley Graham. Precious Lee. So beautiful. I *know* this.

But *I* can't get fat.

Existing is too dangerous as it is. The leers. The contempt. I'm worth nothing now. I can't be worth even less.

And I know there's a world out there where none of this is true. Where Paul's mom grabs a handful of her own chub, joking, and her husband laughs with her and kisses her mouth. I was there. I was *so close*.

But I don't live there. I never will now.

If I'm not pretty, I'm nothing. Not nothing like something you don't care about. Nothing like someone you can do anything to, and no one will care.

I know exactly how fucked up it is and how there is absolutely nothing I can do about it. So I count.

Cupcakes are one hundred and seventy calories a piece. That's two thousand and forty for the box. One hundred and eighty calories per peanut butter bar is one thousand four hundred and forty calories. Round up to be safe. That's three thousand five hundred total. Three endurance classes. Three and a half hours on the bike, in the saddle, with high resistance.

I can't do that, but I don't have a choice, do I?

I scrape myself off the couch, pee, and get on the bike. It's almost noon. I'm slow to start. My limbs feel heavy, my clammy thighs chafe, and my brain spews garbage. The seat is hard on my bare ass. I'm not exactly sore between my legs, but I can feel that I've been touched.

I let myself be touched.

I don't want to think about that.

I pump harder. A former professional cyclist talks enthusiastic, sincere nonsense. I break a sweat, pedaling until the bloat goes away, until the distension of my belly disappears. Until my brain shuts the fuck up.

I watch the sun glitter on the Luckahannock and the office workers buzz along the sidewalks on their way to lunch, and then I watch them stroll back to the buildings they came from. Cars speed silently down River Street. A man in a straw hat sells roses at the intersection. Along the promenade, older folks walk their dogs.

The ordinary world.

I watch it go by, pedaling in place in an empty apartment. Fixing my fuck up. Protecting myself.

Somehow.

From something.

For some reason.

I can't do three hours. My legs give out after two. I have to sit for a while, but I manage to take a shower and change into a white puff-sleeved sundress with an oranges and lemons print.

I'm zoning out in front of the TV when there's a soft knock at the door. I hobble to the peephole, and there's Mattie with a piece of my mom's luggage, glancing nervously down the hall. I fling the door open and drag him into my arms.

"Zita, let go." He wrestles me off, fixing the neckline of his teal scoop-necked T-shirt, smoothing his hair even though I didn't muss it at all.

"Is that my shirt?" I ask.

He smiles brightly and raises the suitcase to his chest. "I brought some shoes and shit."

"Underwear?"

"Yeah."

My eyes prickle. "Thank you."

He squirms and looks over my shoulder, lowering his voice. "Is he here?"

"No."

"He left you alone?"

"Where am I gonna go?"

Mattie leans over and rests his forehead against mine like he's been doing ever since he was tall enough. He's wearing my amber body mist. For a second, my arms have the overwhelming urge to scoop him up, hug him tight to my chest while he clings to me like a monkey, and tuck his face in the crook of my neck as I rock from foot to foot. I long for that comfort.

"Let's run away," he says. "Let's just get the fuck out of here."

We could. The door's open. I could go to Paul, swallow my pride and ask him for money. Drive to a big city where no one's ever heard of the Renellis—Los Angeles or Houston—and disappear.

How long would we last? Dario Volpe found Posy Santoro in weeks, maybe two months on the outside, and as far as the rumors go, she ran over a sex thing. She wasn't a witness to murder.

It would be a matter of time, and if they knew Paul helped me, they wouldn't overlook it. Whatever I feel about yesterday, I don't want him dead.

"We can't." I force myself to stand back and paste a calm expression on my face. "We just have to let things blow over. Go along for now."

Mattie lifts a sculpted eyebrow. "Blow over?" He knows I'm full of shit.

"Yeah."

He blinks his big, liquid brown eyes. "Don't do this 'cause you're scared for me."

"I'm not," I lie. "Don't worry about me. Worry about you, okay?"

"Okay," he lies back to me and toes the suitcase. "Text me if you need something. I'll bring it over."

"Don't be using this as an excuse to ditch school."

He raises both brows.

I sigh. "Please?"

He gives me a quick smile and a quicker hug. "I love you, big sister."

"Love you, too," I say, and much too quickly, he's hurrying down the hall on his own, and I'm left alone. Scared. Wrung out.

Lonely.

I go back to the couch, and that's where I still am hours later when Nicky gets home. I startle out of my skin when a key clicks in the lock and the front door opens without warning. Nicky locates me, and immediately dismisses me, dropping his keys on the counter, kicking off his shoes, and taking off his jacket. His five o'clock shadow is back, but otherwise, he's clean and kempt.

What does he do all day?

My father spent most of his time at Maggio's, the supper club where Dominic Renelli held court. At least that's where Mom called when she wanted to find him, and he wasn't answering his cell phone. I heard Maggio's went under, though. Paul's mom was stoked about it. She wanted to buy their walk-in freezer from their fire sale.

I can't see Nicky hanging out at a bar. I can't picture him doing anything. He just doesn't fit right.

He's got these custom-tailored suits—really expensive suits—but he's my age. When Paul dresses up, he wears the light blue dress shirts and tan slacks that his Mom bought him for church back in high school. He does own suits. His college interview suit. His cousin's wedding suit. The med school interview suit.

Nicky has a closet full of suits. I snooped after my shower. They're Armani, Zegna, Tom Ford. He has a Brioni, and it's made to measure.

He has drawers full of brand name athleisure wear, a dozen pristine pairs of sneakers, cuff links in boxes, a full tie rack, a belt rack.

No books. No décor. No clock. I'd say he just moved in, but I knocked the bike by accident, and I saw it had made a deep impression in the low pile carpet. Besides, as weird as it sounds, the place feels lived in. Even though the washer and dryer still have stickers on them, there are easily fifty dry cleaner hangers in the closet.

Clearly, something is wrong with him, but what? He talks like the men in my family, tough and monosyllabic. He likes to eat. Watch sports.

Have sex.

I sit straight and scoot to the edge of the couch. Nicky stares balefully at the stove before transferring his black gaze to me.

My dad would have lost his shit by now. Then again, my mother would've never dared not to have dinner ready.

I tense.

He strides toward me, and I instinctively huddle back against the cushions. Trapping myself. He leans over, bracing his arms on the back of the couch. I tuck my knees to my chest, balling my hands.

He leans closer.

His clothes smell faintly of cigarettes. Not like he was smoking, but like he was around it. A vein pulses in his neck. The top three buttons of his shirt are undone, and the collar's gaping, revealing a smattering of black chest hair and the tattoo across his collarbone. I've caught glimpses of it, but not enough to make out what it is. From what I can see now, it's a beaded chain.

I kind of want to push the shirt aside, see the whole thing. I squeeze my fists tighter.

I don't look him in his face. I know he'll be staring straight into my eyes, searching for whatever the fuck it is he searches for there.

"I didn't make dinner," I say to his Adam's apple.

"I noticed." His voice is low and close to my ear.

"I'm never going to make you dinner."

"I can't cook for shit."

I can't help it. My eyes flicker to his like this is some kind of reverse staring contest, and I lose.

I was right. He's watching. My smartass retort flies out of my head.

The corners of his eyes crinkle like he's amused. Like he's happy. The lines are faint, fainter than the scent of cigarettes and what's left of his cologne. But he's not mad, and that's confusing, and it pisses me off.

What am I if I'm not angry and scared?

Deluded. That's what I would be. Prey. A natural born sucker. Like Posy Santoro. Like my mom.

"Let me up." I tilt my chin and glare past his ear.

He straightens, but he doesn't move back. He grabs my left hand and smooths my fingers, intertwining his, splaying them. Then he slips a ring over my knuckle. It's a perfect fit. He drops my hand into my lap and strides off down the hall.

"Be ready to leave when I get out of the shower," he says over his shoulder.

It's a three-stone ring, round diamonds, yellow gold. It's old-fashioned like my Nonna's.

I loved her ring. She used to let me try it on, and I'd hold my hand up to the window to catch the light. I thought it was the most beautiful thing I'd ever seen. We buried her with it. She told Mom it'd be hers when she died, but we decided she wouldn't want to be without it.

Paul and I picked out a platinum solitaire that we could upgrade when he was established in a practice.

I hear the shower start and become restless. I click the television off, go to the window, and watch the gridlock on River Street as folks head home. I hold this ring up to the light. The sun's low over the bluffs on the far bank of the Luckahannock.

Nonna was my father's grandmother. She'd had her children in her teens, so she wasn't much older than other grandparents. She came to live with us when I was born—to help my mother—and she kept to her bedroom, the kitchen, and the laundry room. Mom was happy to leave her to it.

Nonna came from Salerno to Pyle by way of New York. She never bothered to learn much English. She never bothered herself about anything besides church, food, and the kids. If she knew what her husband or her sons and grandsons did, she probably prayed for them and put it out of her mind.

When I was a little girl, before Mattie was born, I thought the world she made was real. A pretty white dress for confirmation. Soft amaretti warm from the oven. Her AM/FM radio tuned to the Mets games as she scrubbed pots.

It wasn't. It was glass waiting to shatter.

But the ring was pretty, and so is this one. I'm still admiring it when Nicky returns, changed into nice jeans and a casual black button down with the sleeves rolled twice, baring his tan forearms sprinkled with dark hair.

My nerves scramble. He is impossibly hot. And this morning, he had his fingers inside me. I came on his pants. My cheeks blaze.

I hustle past him toward the bedroom to get my shoes and quickly tug on a bra and panties. I did not get ready to leave like he told me to.

When I come back in my sandals, he's polishing off the milk with the refrigerator door wide open. Nonna would've whacked him across the back of the head for that.

He wipes his mouth with the back of his hand. I lick my dry lips. He grabs his keys.

I cough to clear my throat. "Where are we going?"

"Saint Vincent's."

"Church?" It's a weekday night.

"We've got Pre-Cana," he says.

"Are you shitting me?"

"I told you we were getting married in the church." He holds the front door open for me. I walk out, trying to process.

Paul would've never even considered Pre-Cana. He'd never sit there and let people act like they know better than him. He was a relationship expert; he always had pointers for me.

"It's like pre-marriage counseling, right?" My cousins all did it. They have great stories about sneaking off to bone during breaks for prayer and contemplation. "How do you think this is going to go?"

Nicky shrugs and presses the button for the elevator. "Don't say I'm forcing you to marry me, and it should be fine."

I snort.

His lip twitches.

Our gazes touch, the barest brush, an exquisitely raw split second.

We freeze, our mouths clamping shut. We stay that way during the ten-minute drive to Saint Vincent's, and we continue in silence as Nicky leads me to the church hall basement where a circle of metal folding chairs have been set up. The three other couples make awkward conversation in the echoing space and help themselves to the coffee and cookies.

This church is a different breed than Saint Celestine's. Saint C's was built in the sixties, so it's almost a church in the round. Lots of light wood, tall windows, and a blocky, almost impressionist rendition of Christ on the Cross.

Saint Vincent's is old school. Jesus is three dimensional, emaciated, nailed and contorted in agony.

We're not in the burbs. We're downtown in Little Italy. The hall was probably redone in the seventies, but it's at least a hundred years old. The tilted floor is cracked green linoleum. The wood paneling has black lines between the planks and a bold use of knots and swirls.

It's squeaky clean, swept, polished, mopped and glowed, and it's falling apart.

I haven't been here since a mother-daughter fundraising tea in elementary school. It's exactly the same.

I take it in, ignore Nicky, and pray that none of the others try to talk to me.

Eventually, ten excruciating minutes past seven thirty, an older man in a checked shirt and pleated corduroys joins us. He makes his way around the circle, shaking hands and making small talk.

To Nicky, he says, "Good to meet you in person, son."

To me, he says, "Have you helped yourself to a cookie? They're sinful." And he laughs.

He's like the other men I'd see at mass with Nonna, passing the collection plates and handing out the bulletins at the end, the gray-haired men with pot bellies and bifocals who do the readings and sell Christmas cards and Easter lilies for the Knights of Columbus. They might as well have been a different species than the men I knew. They were harmless.

"Well, you all know me," he says, settling in his own squeaky metal chair. "I'm Deacon Dan. Usually I do this with the wife, you know, but she's in Tampa with her sister, so you'll have to make do with me. I brought the cookies and got the coffee going. I think I'm doing all right so far."

Everyone politely laughs with him. Not Nicky, not me. But everyone else.

The other three couples are versions of Paul and me. Clean cut and cookie cutter. We go around the circle and introduce ourselves. I learn that the bottle blonde and the guy in boat shoes are Emma and Noah. The two in corporate casual are Liv and Jake. The nervous woman with the vaguely irritated guy in a hockey jersey are Ava and Maddox.

Emma and Noah are holding hands. Maddox's arm is propped on the back of Ava's chair. Jake's holding Liv's water bottle so she can dig something out of her purse.

Nicky and I sit beside each other like strangers. Nicky makes no move to touch me. His spine is ramrod straight, his hands resting on his thighs, like he's waiting to be interrogated.

The others suspect something. Liv and Ava give us side eye. They probably figure we're fighting.

There's a brief conversation about wedding and honeymoon plans. Nicky and I keep quiet.

Deacon Dan smiles at me more than the other women. His attention skips over Nicky. The other men miss Nicky with the bro things they do with each other, the brief nods, the commiserating smirks. By instinct they must know not to engage him, that he's not like them.

I'm not like these people either.

Except for the hair color, Emma and I are the exact same type, but you can just tell from how she holds herself that she's comfortable in her body. No one's taught her what happens if she doesn't keep it just so.

When the conversation dwindles, Deacon Dan sighs and says, "Well, shall we begin?"

He bows his head, and we all follow as he draws in a deep breath and begins. The cavernous, dim basement creaks and hums while we pretend to pray. He rambles about the sacrament of marriage and the Church as the bride of Christ, the God of endurance and encouragement.

I furtively watch the others.

Jake squeezes Liv's hand. Maddox shifts impatiently in his seat. Emma and Noah sneak a smile like they're sharing a joke.

I don't look at Nicky. From the corner of my eye, I know his head is bent. I can't see it, but I know he's watching me. A strange thought pops into my brain.

He's here for me. All this is because of me.

Deacon Dan opens his Bible and begins to read from Ephesians. He skips the part about wives submitting to their husbands and starts with "...husbands love your wives just as Christ loved the Church." I've heard it often enough at cousins' weddings.

He stops at "This is a great mystery" and lets the line linger in the silence for a while, I guess so we can reflect on the mystery. It sure baffles the shit out of me. Every married man in my family has stood in front of the altar at Saint Celestine's and made vows that likely didn't last the week.

Father Dominic surely knows they're lying, as did Father Bernard before him, and Father Leo—retired now—who gave Nonna the Anointing of the Sick in her bedroom and shook Dad's hand afterwards, as if Mom didn't have a shiner, and Dad didn't have busted knuckles.

I don't fault Father Leo. I kept my mouth shut, too. Everyone does. Yeah, humans might all be sinners, but we're habitual cowards, too. If we don't have to see it, we look past.

I guess it's not really a mystery after all. The fact that we pretend there is good in the world, and that we're trying to do it—that's the mind-boggling part. How do we keep up the act?

After I've gotten myself thoroughly depressed, Deacon Dan claps his hands, and says, "Who's ready for some fun?"

Maddox exhales gustily and stretches his arms over his head like he's waking up from a nap.

Deacon Dan bends over and fishes a milk crate out from under his chair. It's filled with dry erase boards like we used in elementary school. He passes them around the circle along with a baggie of markers and miniature erasers.

Noah starts doodling a dick on his. Emma yelps and swipes his board with the side of her hand.

There's a pit in my stomach. I hated this kind of crap in school. I'm not the raise your hand and volunteer type.

Nicky uncaps his marker, all business.

"You guys are too young to remember *The Newlywed Game*, right?" Deacon Dan grins, clearly relishing the anticipation of whatever awkwardness he's about to put us through.

There's a confused mumble from the group.

"It was a game show from *my* parents' day," he says. "Classic TV."

"Like *Seinfeld*?" Emma asks.

Deacon Dan is thrown for a second before he plows ahead. "Basically, I ask a question, you answer on the whiteboard, and if you show that you know each other, the couple earns a point. Simple. Ready folks?"

I can't help but glance at Nicky. He seems unconcerned. The pit in my stomach grows.

"We'll start with an easy one." Deacon Dan shuffles through index cards until he finds one that amuses him. "Well, in my day, you wouldn't admit to knowing this, but times change, so—who spends the most time in the shower?"

There's a general tittering. My face bursts into flame. I remember Nicky's hand twisting my hair. His lips against the nape of my neck. His dark eyes in the mirror. A shiver zips down my spine.

I'm the last to finish. I'm still scribbling on my board when Deacon Dan clears his throat.

"All right, Emma and Noah, you two go first." They flip their boards, grinning. They both wrote *him*. Everyone laughs.

"One point for the Romanos!" Deacon Dan makes a tally mark on his whiteboard.

"Okay, Mr. And Mrs. DeLuca. Your turn."

Liv and Jake flip. He wrote *Liv*. She wrote *Jake*. There is general groaning.

"But what about when you trim your beard?" she argues.

"Well, yeah," he admits, and we chuckle. It's all nice, polite fun.

"It's the Sullivans' turn," Deacon Dan says.

We all kind of hold our breath. When Ava and Maddox both flip boards that say *Ava*, we relax.

"Okay, Biancollis. What do you have?"

My brain snags on "Biancollis," and Nicky has to reach over and prompt me to show my whiteboard. It says *me*. His says *Zita*.

Everyone claps politely.

"Let's kick this up a notch." Deacon Dan shuffles. "This is a fun one. This time you have to answer for yourself *and* your partner. Ready?" Everyone nods except Maddox. He's fiddling with his phone in his lap like we can't see. "Okay, if your partner had five extra hours in the day, what would they do with it?"

I have no idea what Nicky does with the twenty-four hours he has. Goes somewhere in a suit. Eats. Watches TV.

I'm the last to finish again. I scribble *TV*.

Deacon Dan goes around the circle again in the same order. Emma and Noah get a point—Emma would shop, and Noah would go to the gym. Liv and Jake also get a point on the board. She'd work around the house, and he'd sleep. Ava gets that Maddox would chill, but Maddox doesn't get that Ava would read.

The pit sours in my gut as our turn gets closer. I got the directions wrong. I only picked for Nicky. I didn't say what I would do.

He goes first. His board reads *work out*.

"Is that for Zita or you?" Deacon Dan asks.

"Both of us," he says.

"Fitness fanatics, eh?"

Nicky grunts.

I go ahead and show my board. We're not getting this point. Except Maddox, the couples tut or groan in sympathy.

"You'll get it next time," Emma says brightly.

I doubt it.

"Okay, round three." Deacon Dan clears his throat. "What makes your partner laugh?"

Yeah, I'm screwed. I've never seen Nicky laugh.

If I write *jokes*, will I sound like I'm being a smartass? Deacon Dan's on Maddox by the time I think of something. I write *The Big Bang Theory*. Everyone loves that show.

Nicky's flipping his board when I realize I did it wrong again and only wrote an answer for him.

"Zita's into funny animal videos, eh?" Deacon Dan says.

That's what Nicky wrote. My skin breaks out in goosebumps. He's right. I used to watch them with Mattie all the time. When he was little, it was the only way to calm him down when he got upset. Monkeys riding pigs. Cats scared of cucumbers. We'd snuggle and watch for hours.

"And you like animal videos too?" Deacon Dan sounds dubious, but like me, Nicky only wrote one thing.

"Yeah," Nicky says.

"What's your favorite animal video?" Deacon Dan prods, getting pushier as the vibe in the room mellows.

"Dogs scared of cats," he answers without missing a beat. Deacon Dan's laugh is nervous, a little too high pitched. I understand where it comes from.

Nicky is so stoic and reserved, his quiet lulls your normal defenses into relaxing, and then, like it's startled awake by a disturbance in the force, your intuition sputters and your survival instinct freaks out. You'd have to be utterly oblivious not to recognize at least on a subconscious level that this man is dangerous. More so because he's in complete control of himself.

What did he do to get the apartment in Lucca Corso's building and the five-thousand-dollar suits? To get me?

"Zita? What do you have?" The way Deacon Dan says it, he must be repeating himself. I drifted off.

I smile apologetically and flip my whiteboard. There's a collective murmur of appreciation when everyone reads *The Big Bang Theory*.

Deacon Dan clicks his cheek. "Sorry, guys. No point this round."

How many more rounds are there going to be?

It turns out—a lot.

Ideal date?

Nicky says *the Wade Arboretum*. He's right again. When Mattie was younger, I'd take him to feed the koi and run his energy off. In college, I'd take my books and a blanket and study on the rolling lawn, anonymous in the middle of normal couples in love and families having picnics. I never once ran into anyone I knew. It's my favorite place in the world.

I write *coffee*, though.

I say *dinner* for Nicky, and he says *the movies* for himself. No point.

Silliest fear?

Nicky says *creepy dolls* for me. Yeah, I hate them. Ever since I saw *The Conjuring*.

I say *spiders* for Nicky. Nicky writes *heights* for himself. I can't imagine him afraid. I can't be certain, but I'm ninety-nine percent sure that he's lying. Regardless, no point.

Sure-fire way to get on their nerves?

Nicky says *kicking her chair*. I say *people who don't look where they're going*, but the chair thing does drive me nuts.

For Nicky, I say *bad driving*. He says *dropping weights at the gym*. No point.

It becomes a joke how bad Nicky and I are at this—well, how bad *I* am.

What does your partner consider his/her best physical feature?

Nicky says *hair* for me. So do I.

I say *arms* for Nicky. He says *legs* for himself.

Favorite movie?

Nicky says "*The Perks of Being a Wallflower*" for me. So do I.

I say "*Avengers: End Game*" for Nicky. He says "*It's a Wonderful Life*" which I would not have guessed in a million years.

It sucks so much that I'm becoming numb to it when Deacon Dan says, "Favorite junk food."

Instantly, my heart lurches, and my palms break out in sweat. Next to me, Nicky doesn't react at all, but I know he's thinking about the boxes in the cabinet, and it kills me, stabs me in the gut.

This time, it feels like it's our turn in the blink of an eye, and my hand's still hovering over the whiteboard when Nicky flips his.

He wrote *popcorn* for me.

I don't notice what he says for himself, I'm scribbling popcorn so quickly—I don't care if it's cheating and everyone will know it. Then I try desperately to come up with another food of any kind to write for him.

Turns out he said his favorite junk food is wings. I ended up dashing down *pizza* for him.

"Almost got that one," Deacon Dan says, and everyone laughs. Even Maddox. Our abject failure has loosened up the crowd.

"Last one," he says over the chatter. "This one's for no points. Do your partner only. Ready? Best trait or quality." He smiles benevolently.

There are a lot of dopey smiles, and everyone takes a long time to write their answers.

My mind is blank. It's like the file for any trait or quality—good or bad—is empty. Is "fit" a trait? The question paralyzes my brain. I can't ask Deacon Dan for clarification, that's for fucking sure.

I can't write fit, but I literally cannot think of any other adjective or noun in the English language.

Emma and Noah share. There are tears and a quick peck that turns into a long hug, but too soon, Deacon Dan is calling on Liv and Jake.

My heart pounds harder and harder, and my brain hysterically catches on snatches of Liv's answer—he's a truly good person, great sense of humor, he'll make such a great dad one day. I can't wait to spend the rest of my life loving this man, my best friend.

What the hell do I write?

He hasn't hurt me yet.

The way he stares at me—it's like he's been missing me forever, and if he looks away, I might disappear, and he'll never let that happen, not in a million years.

He drives responsibly. He shares his tomatoes.

He's so beautiful that sometimes you forget what he is. What he must have done. What he's capable of doing to you. And you don't realize you've forgotten until you suddenly remember, and it's terrifying, every single time.

Ava shares while Maddox sighs and slouches in his seat. Time is running out.

In pure panic, I scribble whichever words are jumbling around in my head and sink back, exhaling. Maddox is already done. I don't know what he said, but my sense is that it wasn't much. The temperature in the room has cooled off quite a bit.

"Nick. You're up, my man," Deacon Dan says. He leaves the "well, moving on" unsaid, but it's there.

People have been ad-libbing, not reading from their whiteboards, but Nicky just shows his. The women "aw" in unison.

She's perfect.

My face burns, and my hands curl into fists. Asshole.

"Would you care to elaborate?" Deacon Dan prompts.

I expect him to decline, maybe mutter some terse bullshit, but he glances over at me and says, "She doesn't believe it, but she is. She always has been. She's a good thing in an ugly world, you know?"

Nicky's mouth closes like he didn't mean to say that last part. His jaw clenches, and he swipes at his nose.

Liv and Emma grin fondly. Ava smiles, too, but it's strained. Jake and Noah nod. Maddox cracks his neck and glances down at his phone.

Deacon Dan's eyes mist up. "For thou wilt light my lamp: my God will lighten my darkness,'" he says, approvingly.

I don't know where—or how—to look. My nose tickles. I am not crying. Not here. No freaking way.

I flip my whiteboard, and for a second, I have no idea what I wrote. I read it upside down.

He's fearless. Strong. He's in control. He's very generous.

Maddox snorts at that. You can hear him affirming to himself that all women are gold diggers.

I sense Nicky tense beside me, but I keep my eyes down, erasing the edge of the word with the tip of my pinky finger.

Deacon Dan sighs contentedly and slaps his thighs. "I think after that it's time for a break before we dive into our next agenda item, right?"

Thank the Lord.

We all stand and stretch, returning the whiteboards and markers to the milk crate. Emma and Liv venture off together to the bathroom. Noah and Jake get on their phones. Ava chats with Deacon Dan and organizes the markers in the baggie so they all go the right way.

I arch over the back of my chair to crack my spine. It's eight-thirty. How late is this thing going to run?

Maddox saunters off to the folding table with the cookies and coffee. I'm surprised when Nicky gets up and follows him.

Maddox is a mean-looking guy, buzzed brown hair, pale complexion, jeans a little low and loose, but not baggy enough to cross the line. He's got a wallet chain and a class ring. He's the type I wouldn't make eye contact with if he held a door.

He fixes himself a coffee as Nicky goes to stand beside him. Nicky's taller, but not by much. It's obvious that they both work out. There's no big weight difference. But as I watch them from behind, something weird happens.

First, Maddox tenses, his chest puffing, his shoulders squaring. He sets down his cup and the coffee sloshes onto the plastic tablecloth.

Nicky takes a napkin from the stack and blots up the spill. If he's saying something, I can't see or hear.

Then, Maddox just stops, his hand freezing mid-gesticulation and falling to his side. His shoulders lower.

Nicky reaches across him and takes two rainbow cookies and a pignoli.

Maddox's head drops. His neck turns crimson red.

Nicky claps him on the back. Maddox flinches.

When Maddox goes back to stirring the creamer in his coffee, his hands are shaking.

Nicky makes his way back to the circle of chairs and sits, calm and cool.

"Want one?" He holds out the cookies. I shake my head. He shrugs and eats them all.

Maddox abandons his coffee and heads off in the direction of the bathroom. No one seems to have noticed the interaction at the refreshment table.

"What did you say to him?" I hiss under my breath.

"I told him what I'd do if he disrespected you again."

For a second, I don't know what he's talking about, but then I remember the snide snort when I said "generous."

I sink into the cold back of the metal chair, cross my legs, and fold my arms. I should drop it. Shut my mouth and get through the rest of this farce.

I swing a leg, letting my strappy sandal dangle from my foot, and under my breath, I ask, "What would you do?"

"You know," he says without hesitation.

"Why? Your pride?"

He finishes swallowing the last bite of cookie and crumples the napkin. "I think I've proved I have none when it comes to you." His lip quirks, he winks, and he gets up to throw his trash away.

For the next two hours, we "work through" the first third of a fifty-page, stapled packet with Deacon Dan. We do worksheets on finances and children interspersed with clips from VHS videos and Deacon Dan's personal anecdotes. When nine thirty rolls around, we haven't gotten to housekeeping, friendships, families of origin, or faith. Apparently, there are two more evening sessions.

It becomes a running joke—with everyone except Maddox who keeps his mouth shut and his eyes on his phone—that Nicky and I are hopelessly on the wrong page.

Deacon Dan tries to prove a point by having everyone share their number one financial priority. I say buying a house. Nicky says savings.

During a story about the time Deacon Dan's oldest boy—at six years old—rode his bike with training wheels across four lanes of traffic to a convenience store, he asks us all to say what we think a reasonable consequence would be. I say ground him. Nicky said he'd spank his ass and take the bike.

Not even Emma or Liv dare give him stink eye for saying it, either, and you can tell they're the type that normally would.

I just can't make him out. It's like the memory of the scrawny, smelly kid got in the way of my ability to judge the man, and I can't nail down my impression of him. It's not my imagination that he intimidates people. I don't know if it's because they can sense that he's dangerous, or if it's because he's beautiful and quiet, and that combination is unsettling. So, yeah, for either reason, I should feel intimidated.

I don't.

I'm not unafraid—I'm not stupid enough to think I'm safe with him—but I don't think he's a scary man. I know scary men. I was raised by one.

He's something else, but I have no clue what.

By the time the end of the evening rolls around, Noah and Jake are bros, and Liv and Emma are besties and a little punch drunk to boot. After the final prayer, we help Deacon Dan return the folding chairs to the rack and straighten up. Ava wants to stay, but Maddox drags her out as soon as we cross ourselves and say "Amen."

Liv, Emma, and I pack up the refreshment table. Nicky hangs nearby, checking his phone.

Liv and Emma tease each other.

"Want to take these cookies home so Jake doesn't starve?" Emma jokes. It came out during the worksheet on parenting that Liv doesn't cook.

"I wouldn't talk, Miss Can't-Mow-Because-She-Can't-Start-the-Lawnmower," Liv shoots back. They both laugh.

"Hey, it's a complicated piece of machinery." Emma catches my eye and grins at me in complicity. I return the smile politely and continue wiping down the tablecloth.

Liv catches the exchange, and her face flickers. "And then there's Zita here. Do you even know Nick? I mean, did you meet on the way here?" She laughs, and there's an edge.

There's a second when Emma's not sure how to respond. Her porcelain cheeks pinken.

I could give a shit. I was cheer captain and student council secretary. Senior year, I was prom queen. In college, I was Theta Beta Upsilon. I know how women like Liv work.

I smile politely again and sweep crumbs into my palm. Emma busies herself with the coffee urn.

Liv decides to double down. "It's like you ran into each other in the parking lot and decided, 'Let's crash Pre-Cana. Free cookies!'"

Emma flashes me an embarrassed glance.

If it were me, I'd ignore it. I've never had time for mean girls. I was always much too busy tormenting myself. I kind of feel bad for Emma, though. She's sweet.

"Oh, I know Nicky well enough," I say, hoping Liz will realize I'm not a soft target and back off.

She doesn't. Her eyes light up. She's down to get dirty, this one. And in the church hall basement.

"Do you really? Remember the game? It seems like you don't know that man at all." She laughs to make it seem like she's joking, even though she knows—and I know, and Emma knows—that she's not.

I'm about to walk away, but before I can, Nicky speaks up from over by a pillar concealed in wood paneling.

"She knows what she needs to know," he says. He's put his phone away. He's speaking to Liv, but his eyes are on me.

"Yeah?" Liv says. "What's that?"

"She knows what I'll do for her," he says, and he holds his hand out to me. His black eyes burn. Shivers zing down my spine.

I take his hand. He draws me toward the stairs.

Liv says something else, but I don't catch it. Deacon Dan calls from the kitchen, "Bye! See you next week!"

Butterflies batter my belly, a pulse starting between my legs.

Nicky leads the way up the narrow stairs through the dark hallway and out a side door to the parking lot. It's the kind of spring night when the sky is dark denim-blue, you can see the craters on the moon, and the air smells like it's been rinsed clean.

For some reason, we both come to a stop on the sidewalk, tilting our heads to look at the moon. He's still holding my hand, his grip firm, assured.

"You know, none of this is real," I say.

"Isn't it," he says. It's not a question.

"You don't really know me."

He doesn't answer.

"Whatever you think I am, I'm not."

He's silent, but he tightens his hold on my hand.

"When you realize that, what happens? Do you kill me then?"

"I'll never hurt you."

This time, I don't answer him. I stare at the moon and think about how there are seas with no water up there, and how human and stupid it is that we named one the "Sea of Clouds" when it isn't and never will be.

The flutters have dissipated, replaced by a chill breeze in my chest and a rawness in my heart.

Gradually, I become aware of voices in the darkness, between Nicky's car and the one beside it. A man and a woman. Her voice is too soft to make out her words, but he's getting louder and louder. It's Maddox.

"No, *you* listen," he's saying. "You owe me."

She murmurs, breathy and anxious.

"You think I wanted to waste my night like this? For your fucking mother? Goddamn, Ava." He spits. "Give me the keys. I'll drop you at the house."

She pleads.

"Just give me the—" There's a strangled curse and a thud, flesh on flesh. Ava cries out.

I take off toward their voices.

Nicky tightens his grasp and doesn't move, forcing me to careen to a halt mid-step.

I glance back over my shoulder. He's unconcerned.

I try to jerk my hand free. His grip doesn't give at all. He looks past me to the sounds of a scuffle, and then he raises an eyebrow, as if to ask if I'm sure.

I consider his cold face, his flaming eyes. I clench my teeth and raise an eyebrow back.

In the darkness, Ava whimpers, "Maddox, please."

This time, when I take off, Nicky lets me.

They're next to a souped-up Honda Civic. Ava's hunched against the driver's side door. Maddox is looming over her. He has the keys.

"Ava?" I call from a yard away. She twists her head to hide her cheek.

It's a motion I've seen a hundred times. The tilt left or right. The duck so your hair will fall in your face. That instinct to hide something you can't, to will everyone to ignore something that they will regardless.

Mattie and I were going to escape. We were going to leave all this ugliness behind, but it's everywhere, and for once, I'm not tired, I'm not barely holding on—I'm furious.

We're in the goddamn church parking lot.

I stalk closer. Nicky's let me drop his hand, but he's on my heels. I can feel him.

"Ava, what's going on?" I ask.

"Keep walking," Maddox snaps. "This isn't your business."

I don't answer him, expecting Nicky to tell him to shut up, but he doesn't. He stands at my elbow, shoulders square, arms loose at his side. Cool, alert, and not the slightest bit intimidated.

Now that Maddox is only a few feet away, I can see he's amped up. His hands shake, and his jaw tics. I'd say he came out here and smoked up, but I've seen rage and ego have the exact same effect on a man.

"Do you want to come with us, Ava?" I ask.

"Didn't you hear me?" Maddox answers for her. "Keep walking, bitch."

I can feel rather than see Nicky tense, but he doesn't say anything.

But I think he would.

If I asked him.

If I just said his name.

A trickle of heat begins to flow through my veins. It's not excitement exactly, not anticipation, but it makes shivers dance across my skin.

"Ava?" I prompt. She's pushing herself upright against the car door, sniffing, wrapping her cardigan across her chest, thumbs poking from the slits in the cuffs. For some reason, in this moment, in this light, she reminds me of Mattie.

"I'm fine," she says. "I just tripped."

I've acted this scene so many times with my mother. My next line is "Are you sure you're okay?"

She'll say yes, and I'll stare piercingly into her eyes before I walk away, not for reassurance but for absolution for my cowardice. My powerlessness.

I'm not powerless now. The trickle in my veins swells into a rush.

When I speak, I'm looking Maddox straight in the eye. "Did you hit her, you asshole?"

He did. We all know he did.

I don't wait for his denial. "You're a real big man, aren't you? What is she, a hundred pounds soaking wet?"

Ava mumbles excuses, reaching for my arm, but I don't want to help her. I want to fight *him*.

"What the fuck is wrong with you?" I stalk into his space. "Why are you such a pathetic piece of shit?"

My heart pounds. I've crested the top of the roller coaster, and I'm rushing down, and whatever is going to happen will happen.

His face darkens, the veins in his neck bulging. "You better come get your bitch before she gets herself hurt," he snarls over my head.

"I'm not his anything," I sneer up at him. "And you're the only bitch I see, smacking around women half your size."

"You let her talk like this?" Maddox asks, but as his gaze rises from my face to Nicky's, the bravado in his voice wobbles.

The wild thing inside me thrashes, tightening my muscles, tunneling my vision. I want to hit him. I want to knock him down. I want *him* to lower his eyes because he doesn't want to see us witness his shame.

"I talk how I want," I say, and it's such a bare-faced lie, but in this moment, it *feels* true.

I hardly register Nicky stepping in front of me, gently prodding me aside. Without signaling his intent, totally unhurried, he buries a fist in Maddox's gut.

Maddox folds, air whooshing from his lungs, and he collapses on his side on the asphalt, groaning and clutching his belly. Ava shrieks and falls to her knees beside him.

I'm still standing with my chest puffed and my hands balled. It happened so quickly. He dropped like a brick.

"Is that enough?" Nicky asks me, considering his handiwork dispassionately, as if he's turning up the heat or pouring a cup of coffee.

Maddox grunts, scrabbling to sit upright, to recollect his dignity, and as I watch, the rage inside me burns itself out, sweetening like the char on a toasted marshmallow.

I glance up at Nicky. His eyes are on me. Of course.

If I said, "Kick his ribs in," I bet he would.

I gnaw my lower lip, my brain scrambling to remember what's right. Who's good and who's bad. Which one I am. The world is upside down.

I take in a shuddering breath, force myself to walk away from the edge I'm dancing along.

"Are you okay to drive home?" I ask Ava.

She mumbles yeah, she's fine, it's all a misunderstanding, while she works her arm around Maddox's waist to help him to his feet.

"This just got out of hand," she says as she hauls him up, and he staggers around to the passenger side. "It was no big deal. Seriously."

She gets him in the seat, and as she's driving off, I hear him start to yell through the closed car windows. I watch the taillights disappear down the boulevard, and then we're alone.

Thank goodness we were the only two cars in this lot. Everyone else must have parked out front on the street.

Nicky holds out his hand. I slip my palm into his. He clicks his key fob, opens my door, helps me in, and waits until I'm seated and buckled before he carefully shuts it.

We drive home in silence, obeying the speed limit, indicating all turns and changes of lane. My mind zooms in circles.

I tear my gaze away from him time and again, but I can't stop it from darting back, as if there are magnets in the line of his extended arm, his wrist resting on the top of the steering wheel, his cut jaw, the sharp planes of his cheeks.

He's a dangerously beautiful man, and that's before you consider the cool competence and effortless assurance.

Why is he obsessed with me?

Granted, I'm considered hot. I'm fit. Groomed. I make damn sure of that. I'm smart enough to earn a degree in business administration. Not smart enough to have earned a scholarship like Paul or to score a job in the field. Not in this labor market. When it comes down to it, I'm no different than Jen Amato or Dita Bianco or any of a dozen girls from the neighborhood.

There's obviously something wrong with him. What happens when he realizes I'm not whatever ideal woman he's constructed in his head?

What right does he have to put all that shit on me, anyway?

I turn to stare out the passenger side window. I can feel his eyes track the movement, and it pisses me off.

"You can stop watching me now. We're in the car. It's not like I can go anywhere."

In the periphery of my vision, I see him face forward.

"What made you mad?" he asks.

I cross my arms, hugging them to my chest. It's cold now that it's getting late, and Nicky didn't turn the heat on.

"Maybe I don't want to be stared at all the time."

For a second, he's silent, and I think he's not going to respond. But then he says in a light, gentle voice, "You were staring, too, Zita."

Angry prickles heat my cheeks. I was. Fuck him. Fuck all of this. I shut my eyes and drop my head back against the rest.

"You're in control, Zita."

"No, I'm not."

"You can be angry if you want."

"No, I can't." In the quiet cab with my eyes closed, his voice deep and low, it almost feels like a confessional.

"You can be whatever you want to be," he says.

My bitter laugh is too loud.

Nicky doesn't say anything else until the car stops. We're back in the basement garage of his building. I don't wait for him to open my door. I get out and make for the elevator, stabbing the button. Like a good little hostage.

He follows.

Inside, I push the button for his floor. He stands a bit further away from my side than usual.

When the doors slide open, I sail out and down the hall. He keeps up easily. We get to the apartment door, and I have to step aside so he can unlock it, but as soon as he shoves it open, I sweep in.

I head straight down the hallway to our bedroom, slam the door, and come to a sudden halt in the middle of the room, the bang echoing in my ears.

What am I doing?

My lungs are heaving. My face is flushed. What is wrong with me? Am I throwing a temper tantrum? I've never—*never*.

I press my hands to my head, rubbing my temples, racking my brain for a plan, when the door flies into the wall. I stumble as I turn.

Nicky fills the frame, top and sides, his chest rising and falling, too.

"I—" I don't even know what I was going to say, but my voice is a starter pistol.

Nicky comes for me. He seizes me, grabs my waist, and throws me on the bed. I bounce.

I'm flailing for words, scrambling at my dress to pull it down, and he's standing at the foot of the bed, methodically undoing his shirt buttons, one by one.

My mouth waters. My breath is ragged. I stop trying to smooth things out, to cover myself. I still, and I watch.

He shrugs off his shirt and peels off his white undershirt over the back of his head, one-handed, biceps flexing. There's a tattoo around his neck. A crucifix. It's familiar. I try to place it, but then his hand is at the button of his jeans, and there's a zip, and his thick, reddish-purple cock thrusts in the air, flush with his sculpted abs.

He kicks his jeans aside and stalks onto the bed, prowling up my body, knocking my knees open with his hard thighs.

He doesn't give me a second to think, to react.

He grabs the collar of my sundress in two hands and rips it neck to hem, and then I'm naked under him in pink silk panties with little bows on each hip and a matching bra, my aching, hard nipples poking through the lace cups. Covered by him completely.

Bare.

Trembling.

Overpowered.

He stares down at me, *feasting*. Instinctively, I clench my thighs, flexing against his tensed quads. A pulse beats between my legs.

"I'm in control?" I say, my voice husky, the taunt uncertain. I don't think I really care about proving myself right. Not anymore. Not with his thighs forcing me open, his eyes devouring—memorizing—every inch of me.

Men look. I don't like it. I don't angle for it like some women do. In the end, though, it's safer to be worth looking at than to be worthless. Better to be my mother who got a new handbag and flowers for a black eye than my Nonna who had to stick to the kitchen and her bedroom until all was forgotten.

Paul thinks I spend so much time on my body because I'm superficial, but he likes—*liked*—that I made him look good. That other guys envied him.

My body isn't me. It's the puppet at the end of the string. It's the car I drive, the safest, most popular model I can achieve.

Nicky narrows his eyes. "Get out of your head, Zita."

A dozen retorts come to the tip of my tongue. *Fuck off. Get off me. Go to hell.* But I don't say that.

"Make me," I say, and a growl sounds in his throat.

He seizes my wrists, pins them over my head, wrists crossed, elbows bent. The tips of his rough fingers bite into my tender skin. His nose nestles in the crook of my neck, and he inhales.

"Leave them where I put them," he says, his lips brushing the hollow below my ear. He tightens his grip once, hard, and I can feel how easy it would be for him to crush the thin bones.

He looms above me, and I leave my arms on the mattress above my head. His smoldering eyes meet mine. I don't look away. And in that moment, we both know—I'm complicit.

I'll pretend I have no choice, and he won't ask me to make one.

He pushes my knees back until my hip sockets ache, wedging his hip to keep one leg in place, his hand forcing the other back, spreading me open as far as I can go, until my pussy gapes, and I feel cool air in my hole.

And he looks, stroking his thick cock with his free hand, working glistening pre-cum over the head, staring inside me, and I leave my arms where he put them, my breasts heaving as my breath quickens.

He drags his eyes up over my belly, the skin that stretches taut over my ribcage, the slight shadow under my arms that I've tried everything to get rid of—spot corrector, microdermabrasion, baking soda and rosewater.

Thwack. I jerk. A sting erupts between my legs.

He just slapped my pussy. Hard.

Thwack. He slaps my breast, grazing the aching nipple. I cry out.

He slaps my pussy again, leaving his palm cupping me. I pant for breath.

"Get out of your head," he says, grinding the heel of his hand against my beaded, needy clit.

"You can't make me," I gasp.

He smiles.

Like I made him do it. Like we're sharing a joke.

I feel a layer stripped from me, an eggshell cracking, a cocoon crumbling, and I'm afraid, but also, I can *feel* my skin for the first time in my life.

He takes his cock in hand, and before I can tense or refuse or prepare, he spears into me to the hilt, splitting me, and it burns, it burns so fucking good. He pulls out and slams home again, battering my G-spot, and I spasm, and now it's an even more impossible fit, but it feels amazing, oh God, so amazing.

I cling to him because he's in charge. He's driving. I'm riding along.

I couldn't think if I wanted to. I can only let him piston into me, shoving my knees back, no gentleness, no hesitation.

A sheen of sweat appears on his chest, his upper lip. His eyes are closed—finally—in concentration, so I can watch him fuck my pussy like he's driving the devil out of me, watch his cock plunge in and out, flushed and slick with my juices.

His beautiful face is strained, a lock of black hair falling on his forehead, and somehow I know he's not lost in this either. We're both still here.

He knows what he's doing.

So do I.

We're hurtling toward the end, throwing ourselves over an edge, running and leaping because everything else in the world hurts. Everything else is cold and impossible and empty, and this isn't.

I move my hands, reach for his shoulders, and he lets go of his painful grip on the insides of my thighs. He lowers himself closer, bracing over me. I curl my fingers around his bunched biceps, and he buries his face in my hair, and I wrap my legs around his waist.

And we're doing this together. I'm terrified and naked and something inside me is erupting, knocking everything over until all I can feel are the spasms, the clenching, the rush. My pussy clamps down on his cock, and he drives into me so hard that he shoves me up the mattress, the sheet burning my back.

He grunts and shudders as he comes, triggering aftershocks that leave me quivering and limp. When his hips slowly cease their rocking, he pushes up on his arms, easing his weight off my chest, but he doesn't pull out.

While I gasp for air, he kisses my lips, softly, as he gazes into my eyes.

And I am afraid.

Because he's not smug. Not self-satisfied, not done and over it until he wants it again.

He's *here*. With me. *Me.*

Floodgates open and panic roars into my chest, muffling my ears. What have I done?

Nicky grunts, rolls off me onto his side, and gathers me to his chest.

"You don't have to beat yourself up," he says, quietly, into my hair.

Yes, I do.

He sighs. "Rest," he says.

My muscles bunch, my fingers curling into a fist, short nails biting into my palms.

He holds me. Quietly.

When my skin cools and his breath evens out, I try to pull myself loose, but he still doesn't let me go. He traces curlicues on my bare hip, down my thigh to the outer edge of my knee, until I feel a poke against the small of my back. And then, with no fanfare, he lifts my leg and sinks into my swollen pussy from behind, our combined fluids easing his way, and he thumbs my nipples and clit until I come again.

All night long.

I drift off, and he wakes me up, rolls me onto my back, my side, urges me up onto all fours, and he fucks me over and over until he needs to get lube from his nightstand to even get his cock inside my tender, swollen pussy. I'm raw and sore, but I come, over and over, although it takes longer each time.

In between, Nicky keeps me tucked against him, and he strokes my hair, my arms, down the valley between my breasts to my belly. My muscles ache, my limbs are weak, and my brain is numb. Quiet.

The fear is muted and far away, and whenever it swells, Nicky flips me over and fucks me until I'm floating again.

At some point, I remember birth control, and I mumble that I have an IUD. Nicky smooths my hair and whispers hush. I drift off.

Sometime near dawn, when daylight from the hallway turns the bedroom gray, Nicky lays on his back, propped by a pillow, and I curl into his side, as if we were any couple. As if we know each other. I finally get a good look at his crucifix tattoo.

The oval beads are different shades of brown from tan to mahogany. The "Our Father" is a square silver medal of the Holy Family, and the crucifix is Jesus on the cross with Mary Magdalene at his side, catching his blood in a chalice.

The realization comes slowly, as if through a fog. I press the pads of my fingers to the beads.

"I had a rosary like this." My Nonna gave it to me for my First Communion. It was her mother's.

His pecs tense under my hand.

"I lost it once."

In high school, I kept it in a pouch in my purse. One day in tenth grade, I noticed it was gone. My purse had been locked in my locker. I hadn't left it anywhere. No money was missing. Sister Gerard said I must have left the crucifix at home. She didn't want to hear anything about stealing at St. Celestine's.

I was so upset that I cried in the girl's bathroom, and I was never one of the girls who did that.

Nicky stares at the ceiling, his jaw locked.

"You took it," I say.

He swallows, and his throat bobs. "I gave it back."

A few days later, it showed up at the bottom of my locker. Sister Gerard said, see, I told you so, better clean that locker out. I kept my locker neat, though, and I'd checked it a dozen times.

I should be mad. I should be reminded of how fucked up this is, but instead, I feel the gentle twinge of old grief. I miss my Nonna.

I splay my fingers, cover the Holy Family with my palm. "It was my great-grandmother's. She was from Salerno."

His chest dips slightly as he exhales.

"Where were your people from?" I ask.

His lip lifts, wry, not quite a smile. "New York."

"Before that?"

He shrugs.

"I lost it for good in college." It got misplaced somewhere in the moves from dorm to dorm. "I don't suppose you have it?"

He shakes his head.

"Why'd you take it in the first place?" I trace the cross.

He takes my hand gently by the wrist and places it on my stomach. "Go to sleep," he says.

I roll to my side to face him. "Why'd you give it back then?"

He covers his eyes with a forearm. "Go to sleep," he says again, resettling himself. "I have to be up for work in an hour."

My brain wants to twist itself into questions. They're bubbling, waiting for me to open my mouth, to pick one out of the hundred, but my thighs are shaky and my abs are Jell-O, and in this strange twilight, my fucked-up head doesn't rule me.

I almost let it go, but then, when drowsiness has muted everything, I mumble, almost without thought, "Did you hear me crying about it in the bathroom?"

There's silence, long silence, and just before I slip under, he says, quiet and deep, "Yeah."

CHAPTER 5

Zita

WHEN I WAKE UP, Nicky's messing around in the closet, and I feel like I've been run over by a truck. Every muscle screams as I roll over and flop onto my back like a starfish. No, a jellyfish.

It feels like I've done three hours on the bike. How many calories did we burn? At least two thousand. At least.

Nicky comes out, buttoning his white dress shirt.

What does he do all day?

Dad was slow to leave the house. Mom cooked breakfast. He'd have a few cups of coffee, a few loud conversations on his cell phone, and then he'd take a long shower, fuss with his comb-over, holler for Mom at least a dozen times to get him something or the other. He was consigliere, though. Whatever Nicky is, he's not that high up in the organization. I don't think.

I'm less certain than I was. Dad and Tony Junior get—got—calls all the time. Nicky doesn't seem to be at anyone's beck and call.

Nicky interrupts my thoughts. "How do you take that thing out?"

"What?"

He nods at my belly. "That thing. The IUD."

I'm so tired, and my head is so foggy, that Nicky has his jacket on and is taking cash from his wallet before I wrap my brain around what he's asking.

"Why do you want to know?"

He sets some cash on the night table and takes out his gun, checking the clip and sliding it back in place. "Why do you think?"

"No." I scramble to sit up. "No fucking way. We're not bringing a baby into this mess."

He tucks the gun into the back holster and goes back into the closet, reemerging with his watch. He looks at me as he straps it on.

"Do you have to go to the doctor?"

I tuck my knees to my chest. "There's no fucking way in hell, Nicky."

He doesn't answer. He fiddles with his damn watch.

"I won't let you. I *won't*." If he thinks I won't fight since I let him fuck me, he's wrong. I'm not bringing a baby into an empty apartment with a crazy mother and a father who does God knows what. Never. Not in a million years.

I cling to the fierceness and screw my eyes shut against the other feelings beating around my chest.

Finally, he buckles the watch and twists it to face out. He moves further toward the door, putting distance between us. I'm huddled against the headboard, shoulders square, spine stiff, head high. He's giving me space.

But his eyes—

They're dark and raw and wild.

His jaw tics. His gaze flicks to the blank wall above the bed. When he speaks, his voice scrapes.

"Why can't we have what we want?" he asks.

I blink, pressing my spine into the hard wood.

He raises his firm chin. "The house, the yard, a dog— Why can't *we* have that?"

And I don't know how, but I understand he doesn't mean why can't *he* have that with *me*. He means why can't *he*, Nicky, and *me*, Zita, why can't *we* have what other people have.

For him, I don't know. For me? Because my father is Tony Graziano. Because there are two worlds, and I was born into this one. Because by the time I can remember, I'd already seen too much.

"I almost did," I say, quietly.

"It would've been a lie."

"A lie's not the worst thing." I don't know his story, but there's no way he hasn't learned the truth of that.

He doesn't say anything to that. He buttons his jacket and tugs the cuffs to straighten the sleeves. "There's cash on the table. Get groceries."

I lift my chin and stare straight ahead at the closed closet door.

I hear his steps head out the door, but before he leaves, he pauses. "I've gotten us here, Zita," he says. "I'll get us the rest of the way."

I don't know what he means, but it's not a threat. More like a promise. A vow.

He coughs once, and then he leaves, shutting the door behind him.

For a long time, I huddle, cold despite the weighted blanket, every muscle aching, torn between hating myself for what I did last night and hating Nicky or the organization or this life or whatever did this to me.

I think about the cabinet, the boxes, the cellophane, the icing and cake and filling. The bike.

And I get tired.

I'm so fucking tired of being tired.

I'm so tired of riding in place, the same cycle over and over. So tired of this weight on my chest.

So I do what I do every morning. I hoist it off. Haul my ass out of bed. Drag myself into the shower. I turn the heat as high as it'll go, and when it scalds me, I dial it back to bearable and let the stream unknot my shoulders.

I wash and blowout my hair, do a soft, smoky daytime eye and a nude lip. I take time fixing the quick file job I did the other day and swipe on a coat of clear nail polish.

Then I go looking for my luggage. At some point, Nicky moved it into his closet. He didn't unpack. He set the suitcases and duffel on top of the shoe shelf on the empty right side. The left side is full of his stuff. In the back, there's a safe. It's big, the kind that sits on the floor, way bigger than you'd need for papers. He keeps his gun in his nightstand drawer.

What's in the safe?

Probably more guns and cash. I wander back and idly try opening it with my birthday as the combination. It doesn't work. I'm almost surprised. I can't think of any other number to try.

Last night, I let him do whatever he wanted to my body, and I know nothing about him. Except that he can be rough and gentle, and it doesn't feel like he's faking either.

And he has scars. Straight. Round and puckered. Some white against his tan skin, others a darker brown. His skin looks like footage on the evening news of pock-marked walls in war torn cities.

Oh, and *It's a Wonderful Life* is his favorite movie.

Is it really? He can't possibly see himself as George Bailey. The stand-up American family man. Maybe he likes the idea of a do-over.

I know that he's obsessed with me. That he's been stalking me for years. I know that he fucks me like a starving man, reverent while he crams me in his mouth.

Paul was fairly insatiable when we lost our virginity to each other, but he never fucked me like that.

Like he'd been waiting his whole life.

Shivers skate down my spine.

I can't sit in this empty apartment with nothing but a cabinet full of garbage. I pull on a silky cream-colored tank top and peach capris, strap on a pair of sandals, and on a whim, scoop the cash off the night table.

No one stops me from leaving the building. The sidewalks are busy with lunchtime traffic, so I cross at the corner to walk the promenade instead.

There are fewer people strolling along the river. A few bicyclists. Dogs on leashes. A roller skater in high-waisted cut-off jean shorts and big ol' headphones. She looks happy. Blissed out, actually.

I slow my pace. The sun is bright, the air almost no temperature at all. The Luckahannock glitters blue and silver. I'm not sure where I'm going, or what I'm doing, but it feels better out here. It feels better to be doing something.

So I walk, and it takes a few blocks before I become aware that my brain has wrapped its tentacles around something—

Nicky's question.

Why can't we have what we want?

I'm not interested in the reasons we can't, or even the wild concept of "what I want"—I'm captivated by the question.

I like how it hits the bloodstream like a bump, how it feels like the kind of danger that wakes you up, clears your sinuses.

Why can't I have what I want?

What if there was a world where I *could* get what I want? What if that existed?

I play with the idea, hold it up, turn it so it catches the light, squinting, admiring it, all the way to the south end of the promenade where the walk ends in a shopping plaza. There's a fancy organic market anchoring one end. There's nothing at the house but junk.

I could pick up a few things. I've got nothing else to do. I'm a housewife for the moment, I guess. More or less.

I'm aware that it's a half hour hike back, so I just pick up a few fresh plum tomatoes. Onion. Garlic. Butter. Olive oil. Fresh basil. I get a box of whole wheat rotini, a bunch of bananas, strawberries, and red grapes. Avocados. Walnuts. A loaf of multigrain bread. White tea. I stop when I figure I have enough to fill two bags.

I don't even walk down the snack aisle.

It's not until I'm handing over the money to the cashier that I realize how much Nicky gave me. It's probably a thousand dollars, mostly fifties. A thousand bucks doesn't stack nearly as thick as I'd have figured. I go ahead and buy two reusable bags.

I misjudge, and although everything does fit in two bags, the plastic straps are digging into my shoulders by the time I'm halfway back to Nicky's. The late afternoon sun's gotten hot, and the promenade is filling with the post-work crowd stretching their legs or grabbing tacos and smoothies from the trucks before happy hour. I cross over River Street to go the rest of the way on the sidewalk.

I'm lost in thought—whether I'm really going to make dinner, last night, what it all means—and I don't notice at first that a man has fallen into step alongside me until he says, like he's repeating himself, "Need a hand?"

"No thanks." He's innocuous-looking enough, a forty-something banker bro in khakis and reflective sunglasses on a cord. I give him a dismissive smile.

My brain's already wandering off again, figuring the interaction's over, when he says, "What's for dinner?"

Ugh. He's that guy.

I keep my eyes straight ahead and pick up the pace, hoping he takes the hint.

He actually peeks into a bag. "Tomatoes, eh? Italian?"

I tug my bag higher onto my shoulder and keep walking.

"Taco Tuesday?" His voice oozes. "Gonna make it spicy?"

It's like the less reaction you give them, the grosser they decide to go.

"Listen," I say. "I'm just walking here."

"Whoa, honey," He puts his hands up mockingly. "I'm just being friendly."

How come it never registers with these guys that no one who's actually being friendly has to tell you?

"Well, I'm just minding my business." I refuse to speed up. If I do, I'd be slow jogging, and we're on a busy street in the broad daylight. All he can do is make an ass of himself.

"You don't have to be a stuck-up bitch," he says.

I look up at him, out of shock more than anything, and then everything happens so quickly, in so many directions, it's like a Guy Ritchie movie sequence.

I trip on a crack where a tree root has busted the concrete, and the man grabs my upper arm to steady me.

Tires screech.

The bag on my right shoulder begins to slip down my arm, and I lurch to keep it from falling.

A Mercedes drives up on the curb ahead. The driver's door flies open, and Nicky exits at a dead sprint toward me while the other three doors burst open in unison.

Men in suits leap out. Jackets flap as they chase Nicky, leaning forward, arms outstretched, close on his heels.

"You don't fucking touch her!" Nicky shouts as he wrenches the man away from me and flings him into the tree that tripped me.

I clutch my arm where the man's fingers dug into me reflexively when Nicky tore him away, and at the same time, I try to keep the bags secure in the crooks of my elbows. I gape at Nicky's stark, terrifying face. He hulks over me, his gaze raking from my head to my feet as if he's accounting for all my parts, assuring himself that I'm intact.

He sees the red fingerprints the man left on my upper arm. He turns to the man.

"I didn't mean to!" the man cries as Nicky drives his fist into the man's jaw, slamming his head into the tree trunk.

Nicky's black eyes are on fire. He's not there. His stony control is gone, and he's not a guy in a suit. He's an avenging angel, St. Michael from the mural on the ceiling of St. Celestine's, the beautiful monster that strikes terror into the hearts of men.

He draws his fist back again, and in that same instant, like choreography, Tomas hooks his right arm, and Dario grabs his left, shoving his shoulder into Nicky's chest, barreling him backwards. Nicky fights like hell, and he almost wrenches himself free, but Tomas and Dario have too much mass and momentum. They wrestle him into the back seat of the car and pin him with the full weight of their bodies.

When the car door slams shut, Ray goes toe-to-toe with the banker bro.

"We gonna have a problem?" Ray asks, opening his jacket and flashing his gun in its holster.

"No, man." This time, when the guy holds up his hands, he means it.

"You know who we are?" Ray lays his Sicilian accent on thick.

"I can guess, yeah." He gasps for air, propping himself against the tree, bent over, bracing his hands on his knees.

Ray stares him down. Lucca Corso leans idly against the driver's door, a bemused smile playing at his lips.

Ray nods and offers the banker bro his hand. "Lemme walk you where you're going. Buy you a drink. No hard feelings."

"That, that's n-not n-necessary." The guy straightens, trying to fix his sunglasses, but they're busted beyond repair. The entire left side of his face is turning a deep red.

Ray tuts. "Oh, we insist," he says, slings an arm around his shoulder, and begins to walk him away.

I stand there like an idiot, my grocery bags hanging from my elbows.

By some miracle, no one stopped to record us. Folks are moving along, minding their business. I guess it happened so fast that no one saw much of anything.

While I'm willing my heart out of my throat, the Mercedes drives off, too quickly for Nicky to be driving. A couple passes me, heads together, oblivious and laughing.

I drag in a shaky breath and hoist the bags back on my shoulders.

"Allow me," a smooth voice says, and I startle.

Lucca takes advantage and scoops up the bag that slips down my shoulder. "Tomatoes? Making Italian tonight?"

I swallow a giggle. The question doesn't sound the least bit like a come-on from him. It sounds like a threat. Everything about the man is a threat.

He gestures for me to walk. I do, and he falls in beside me. It's an entirely different sensation.

The banker bro creeped me out. Lucca terrifies me. My muscles tense, and my mind sharpens. With the shot of adrenaline, I can easily keep up with his long stride.

My dad hated Lucca Corso. He called him "that pretty pansy boy." He should have been watching over his shoulder. Everyone was busy dismissing Lucca while he collected enough favors to take down a don. And when the smoke cleared, where was my dad?

I don't know, but Lucca Corso sure as fuck does.

When we get to Nicky's building, Lucca holds the door open for me. He greets the woman at the front desk. She replies, "Good evening, Mr. Corso."

He calls the elevator and leads the way to Nicky's apartment. He opens the door with a key on his own key chain.

He gestures for me to enter first, and he takes the bag I've been carrying and sets them both on the counter.

"Have a seat," he says, unpacking the tomatoes. "Do you have anything perishable in here?"

"No."

I wander to the table and sit. It feels like there's a tiger in the kitchen. My instincts scream to remain calm, make no sudden moves.

"I guess a fruit bowl would be too much to ask for," he mutters, opening drawers. He pauses when he gets to the cabinet filled with snack cakes, and my stomach clenches, but he keeps rummaging. Eventually, he huffs a sigh and puts my fruit in a big stew pot.

He rinses the tomatoes and leaves them in a colander by the sink.

Finally, he strides over to the table, takes a seat, crosses his legs, and considers me, that strange smile on his lips, his eyes as cold as ice.

He tilts his head slightly. "You don't play chess, do you?"

I shake my head. Paul tried to teach me, but I never got past memorizing what the pieces do.

He nods. He doesn't seem disappointed. More like I've confirmed something.

"Posy does."

I've heard that. The women in our circle whisper that that's why Dario Volpe married her. I don't believe it. I've seen him look at her, how his eyes turn almost human.

"I never learned," I say.

"It's good you don't. You'll live longer." He bares his perfect, even teeth in an approximation of a smile.

I wait. Men like my father—and despite the modern fit of his sharkskin suit and his artfully messy hair, Lucca is most definitely a man like my father—that kind of man doesn't need your cooperation or consent to continue.

"How's your cousin Tino?" he asks.

"Fine, last I heard." Tino was sent to Chicago shortly after Lucca took over. Tino's loyal to his wallet, so we figured it wasn't so much to get him out of the way as to discourage anyone from looking at him to avenge Dad.

Like Furio.

"You talk to him much?"

I shake my head. Tino's four years older than me. Four years was a lot when we were kids growing up. It wouldn't be now, but we have nothing in common but blood.

"So did he ever tell you about Nicky?"

"What about Nicky?" Tino was the one I complained to about Nicky creeping back in school. He handled it.

I *thought* he'd handled it.

Lucca's fake smile melts into a genuine smirk. He relaxes in Nicky's chair.

He chuckles. "I guess he wouldn't have been spreading that story around."

I wait. He'll tell me what he wants me to hear.

I don't play chess, but mobsters aren't as complicated as all that. Money, pride, and their own personal ease. That's what they give a shit about, in that order. Take away any real capacity to love or feel compassion. They're predictable as shit. However convoluted the delivery, this is a threat. Lucca doesn't require anything but my attention and—once he's done amusing himself—my compliance.

"You remember running to Tino about Nicky staring at you?"

I nod.

"And you never heard the story?" He raises his eyebrows.

I shake my head. Growing up, men told stories at the dinner table after the plates were cleared, drinking, laughing and talking louder while we played in the family room until Mom sent us kids to our rooms. She'd go hide in the kitchen with the other women, open a bottle of wine, and linger over drying the dishes, gossiping amongst each other with the door firmly closed.

Women didn't listen in. You didn't even *look* like you might be listening. It was a sure way to get backhanded.

Even if I'd heard the story, I wouldn't admit that I did.

Lucca narrows his eyes and folds his hands over his waist. "So this is how it went—Tino asked Tomas and I if we could take care of something on the way to—conducting some business. We said sure. Anything for cousin Tino, right?"

He pauses expectantly. I nod. He goes on.

"Maybe if I'd known we were gonna hassle some junior high kid, I would've said no, but Tino, he's a man of few words, yeah?"

He stops again. I nod.

"So we drive all the way to the old neighborhood to intercept this kid walking home from school. Did you know he lived all the way over there?"

I shake my head.

"Why would you, right? He was just some charity case. His mom was a junkie, his dad was a wannabe hustler, but his grandfather had been connected back in the day. Never more than a soldier. A no one, really."

It's not an insult the way Lucca says it. More a statement of fact.

"Anyway, we had to go way out of our way. It was a hassle, right? So when we block Nicky in this alley, I figure I want to have some fun. Make it worth the trip to the shitty side of town."

Little Italy is coming back now that they've run out of riverfront to redevelop, but yeah, ten years ago, you didn't go there unless you had a reason.

"I made Nicky a deal. If he can fight Tino and win, he can watch you all he fucking wants."

My stomach turns.

"Now, you know Tino—big guy—at the time, he must've had at least seventy pounds on this kid, and Nicky, he wasn't eating like he does now. A stiff wind would've blown him away. Tomas bet me twenty that Nicky'd win. I thought he was fucking with me."

I'm picturing them in my mind. Tino has always been a meathead, and even back in school, he lifted, and it showed. In retrospect, he was probably juicing. Nicky was thirteen, maybe fourteen, the kind of lanky that boys get when they shoot up in height and haven't evened out with the weight yet.

It would've been nowhere near a fair match, but that was why I asked Tino, right? I figured that Tino would rough him up a little. No big deal. We all took our licks. At least boys had a chance when they fought back. I can't remember whether it bothered my eighth-grade conscience. I doubt I lost any sleep over it.

Lucca gazes hazily out the window, lips curled. "Last time I ever bet against our man Nicky. I've still never seen anything like it. Tino put him on the pavement again and again, and he kept getting up like he was a fucking reanimating zombie. Shirt ripped, face busted beyond recognition. His arm was hanging weird. Couldn't put weight on an ankle. But he kept getting up."

For some reason, in my head, I can't picture Nicky as a kid anymore. I see Mattie, and like always, my empty arms ache for wanting to wrap him tight, keep him safe, even though it wasn't him, and it all happened such a long time ago besides.

"I told Tino to put him out of his misery." Lucca's smile widens. "Nicky must've figured time was up, so he did this move—never seen it before, never seen it since. At first I thought he'd gotten the good sense to run for it, but he was backing up. He comes at Tino at a dead sprint—fuck the ankle—and he leaps at the last minute and throws his whole body into Tino, knocks him clear into a wall, slamming the back of Tino's head into the brick. Tino went"—Lucca snaps—"out like a light."

Lucca's full-on grinning now. "Kid was barely standing, dripping blood, clutching his ribs. I told him he could fuck you if he could take Tomas down too. He tried." Lucca laughs. "Got himself knocked out cold right next to Tino."

Lucca's looking at me like he expects a reaction. Appreciation? Awe?

Or maybe he wants to see exactly what he gets—me sitting obediently in my chair, choking down the fear, blanking my face, so very obviously hiding my shaking hands in my lap.

His lips curve higher and the corners of his eyes crinkle. "If you're wondering if I'd have let him, if he'd done it—I would have." He winks.

I have no doubt.

A footstep sounds in the hall. My fucked-up lizard brain perks up, and for a split second, all I want is for Nicky to walk through the door. He doesn't. It's a neighbor. Lucca sees my gaze leap to the door, though, and he's pleased, so damn pleased with himself.

"But that's not the end of the story. Far from it." He stands and strolls back into the kitchen. He breaks off a cluster of grapes from a bunch in the pot, rinses them in the sink, and grabs a paper towel.

I know I'm supposed to be sweating. Panicking.

Lucca's a different performer than Dominic Renelli was, but I've seen the act before. Dominic was a prop man. He'd shuffle into a room, taking his time, leaning heavily on his ivory cane. He'd sit with a gusty sigh, take out a cigar, snip the end with his silver cutter, and make a show of patting down his pockets for matches until my dad or one of his lieutenants offered him a light.

It was all to waste time, to put you on edge. I think they picked it up from watching Scorsese.

I've lived on edge my whole life. I feel it, but it doesn't fuck with my head.

I'm the one who messes with that.

Lucca returns to his seat, plucks a grape from its stem, and offers it to me. I take it. Slip it into my mouth.

Lucca smiles and puts the fruit down between us on the table, gesturing for me to help myself.

"Do you know how I got where I am?" he asks. It's a sudden change of subject, but not unexpected. It's part of his flair.

I nod once.

He raises his eyebrows.

He disappeared a half-dozen made men in one afternoon. I'm sure that's not the answer he's looking for, though.

"Brains?" I throw out, grabbing another grape. These men like to think they're clever. Really, it's just that they'll do what other people won't. It's the element of surprise. No one ever really expects evil in everyday life despite all the evidence of their eyes.

He ignores my answer. "Loyalty."

I bet Dominic Renelli would disagree.

"Do you know how I earned Nicky Biancolli's loyalty?"

I shake my head.

"Of course you do, Zita. You're a smart girl."

He reaches slowly for the grapes with long fingers and pops one off, snapping the stem. My throat tightens.

"Me," I say, hoarse.

"You." He places the grape in his mouth and chews, slowly, much longer than he should need to. "It was our little secret—Nicky and me. He's not totally fucked in the head. He realizes there's something wrong with him, but—" Lucca tosses a shoulder. "The heart wants what the heart wants."

I don't want to hear this. Not when it still hurts to sit on this hard chair.

Lucca leans forward. "Do you know that when he was a senior in high school, he killed a man so that I'd get Tony Junior to let him into your bedroom when you were sleeping over at your girlfriend's?"

His eyes light up. "Do you know how many bodies he's laid at my feet to earn you? How many of my enemies he's erased? How many bullets he's taken?"

The corners of his mouth twist. "How much money he made for us doing jobs for the Russians? He's fucking notorious over there. You know what they call him?"

I jerk my head.

"The Driver." Lucca waves his hand. "Only in Russian, right? Not in English. Obviously."

"He's a machine. He's *my* machine." The smile falls from his face like a stage curtain. "Do you know what that means?"

Icy hands squeeze my lungs. I clutch my thighs under the table and jerk my head again.

"It means that *you* work for *me*. I'm your pimp, Zita, and you've got one trick. One job. Keep Nicky the driver happy. If he wants his cock sucked, you get on your knees. If he wants ass-to-mouth, hold your nose and open up, baby." He lowers his voice. "You don't ever let another man touch you. Not your arm. Nothing."

He takes another fat grape and swirls it between his thumb and forefinger.

"If Nicky wants you to wear a white dress and say you'll love him forever, you will. Want to know why?"

I swallow.

"Do you?"

I nod. I have to.

"Because your daddy's head went like this when I shot him—" He pinches his fingers and purple juice splats onto the table. "I wanted to see his expression when he realized he was done, but—" Lucca shrugs and shakes skin and seeds off his fingers. "He didn't really have a face left."

Lucca cocks his head. "Mattie looks a lot like his old man. I could always recreate the moment. Couldn't I?"

"Don't—" The word is ripped from my mouth.

Lucca settles back in his chair again, takes a white handkerchief out of his breast pocket and wipes his hands. "You're in control, Zita. Do your job, and we all go home happy at the end of the day."

"Leave Mattie alone." My voice is thin, distant.

Lucca ignores it easily. "You're a good woman, right Zita? Like your mother. You understand how things are. I'm sure Nicky won't make it too hard on you." He folds his handkerchief and tucks it away. "Right, Zita?"

I'm about to say yes. Of course I am. There are footsteps in the hall, though, and this time the door opens. It doesn't quite fly, but I still startle as Nicky storms in, Dario and Tomas on his heels.

Nicky's shirt is untucked, and one of the buttons on his jacket is missing.

Tomas has a black eye, a scraped cheek, and a busted lip. Dario's nose is fucked up, and there's a splatter of blood down the front of his crisp white dress shirt.

All three are breathing hard.

Lucca smirks, taking them in. "I guess I don't have to ask who won."

Tomas heads to the fridge. Dario flips the bird and heads down the hall toward the guest bathroom. Nicky stalks across the room to stand behind me, resting his hands on the knobs on my chair back. His knuckles are swollen and red.

"That wasn't very subtle, my friend." Lucca pops another grape into his mouth, perfectly cool, perfectly casual.

Other men might not see it, but I've been hiding my fear under a façade of perfection for my entire life.

Lucca's too arrogant to be afraid, but he's wary.

"My bad," Nicky says over my head. He doesn't sound the least bit chastised.

"Zita and I were just having a pleasant conversation. Enjoying some fruit."

"Yeah."

"I'm sure Ray has smoothed everything over."

"Yeah."

"Zita assures me that everything is fine."

"Yeah."

There's something going on between them, and I can only see half of the exchange. Lucca's smug smile fades, and his eyes go icier. Nicky stands stock still behind me, his monosyllabic replies revealing nothing.

There's a long moment when Lucca says nothing and stares over my head, measuring. Finally, he lifts a shoulder and says, "I'm sure it won't happen again." He glances down and flashes his shark smile. "Right, Zita?"

Before I can answer, Nicky moves his hands to grip my shoulders. "It's done," he says. It's a final word.

Lucca takes his time getting up, brushing off his pants, and grabbing a paper towel to wipe the squished grape off the tabletop. Dario rejoins us, blotting at his shirt with a guest towel. I register Tomas leaning against a kitchen counter, icing his face.

The vibe is nothing like when my dad was with Renelli and his capos. They were formal with each other. Scrupulously polite when they weren't being vulgar as hell.

None of these men are obsequious. None of them are dick swingers. I can't read the room—I can't tell which direction the danger is most likely to come from—and it scares me almost as much as Lucca's threats.

I stay in my seat and hug my arms to my chest.

Nicky walks the men to the door. They speak quietly amongst each other for a minute, and then they leave. Lucca waves on his way out and winks at me.

I don't move.

Nicky bolts the door behind them and kicks off his shoes. He shakes out his jacket and hangs it on the back of the chair where Lucca was sitting. He opens the fridge, doesn't seem to find what he's looking for, and shuts it again.

"You didn't get milk?" he asks.

It takes a second, but when the words finally filter into my reeling brain and slap me in my numb face, I jump to my feet, instantly breathless.

"What the *fuck* did you just say?"

He pivots slowly to face me. There's ten feet between us, a table, and the corner of a breakfast bar, but I think I could vault them, leap them in a single bound, to punch him in his pretty, unconcerned face.

He's smart enough not to answer me. He exhales and crosses into the living room. Now there's nothing but empty space between us. I shiver and cling to my anger so hard my tired muscles ache.

"He threatened to kill Mattie," I hiss.

"No one will touch Mattie."

"If he hurts Mattie, I'll kill him. I'll kill you."

"No one will hurt Mattie."

"You can't say that."

He doesn't answer. He stares into my eyes, and I don't know if he's looking for something, or if he's trying to pin me in place, make me bow my head, make me give into the fear and cry, fall to my knees, beg him.

I grit my teeth and spit, "He said if you want ass-to-mouth, I should hold my nose and open up."

His gaze drops, and a mean little flare of victory sparks in my chest.

I lift my chin. "He said you killed a man to get into my bedroom."

He raises his eyes again, because this—*this*—I guess doesn't embarrass him in the least.

"Who did you kill, Nicky?"

I don't expect him to answer, and for several seconds, he doesn't, but then his fingers twitch at the end of the arms resting at his side, very intentionally loose, unignorably inches from the gun in its holster.

"A guy who tried to force Lucca out of the organization. He was a drug dealer. A pimp."

"Did I know him?"

Nicky shrugs.

"How did you kill him?"

"I shot him."

"You were in high school?"

He jerks a slight nod and shifts from one foot to the other.

"How many men have you killed for Lucca?"

He shrugs again.

I don't know why I have the balls to ask him, and I have no idea why he's answering me at all. Women don't ask. They don't *see*. And men don't have to tell.

We're alone, though, in this empty apartment with nothing between us, and I keep going. "Would you kill me if he told you to?"

"No."

"Would you kill Mattie?"

"No."

"Why not?"

"You wouldn't forgive me."

"Why do you care?"

Another shrug.

"What did you do in my bedroom?"

His forehead furrows. It takes him a second to follow the change of subject. "It was a long time ago."

"Was it just the once?"

"Yeah."

"I don't believe you."

He doesn't even bother to shrug.

"What did you do?"

He stares me straight in the eye while he says, "I looked through your stuff. Laid in your bed. Took a nap."

"You took a nap?"

"Yeah."

My mind is racing back to my bedroom when I was in high school. My underwear drawer with the period-stained panties shoved in the back. The vape hidden in a jewelry box. The tub of dolls in my closet that wasn't on a high shelf, but on the floor in the front. Had the lid been open the day he was there?

Oh God.

"Did you look in my dresser drawers?"

He nods.

"All the drawers?"

He nods again.

"The bottom drawer?"

He doesn't nod. He meets my eyes, steady, shameless. What is that like?

Heat floods my chest, burns my face, while my blood surges in my veins, roaring in my ears.

Why does shame feel like terror?

"I'm not afraid of you," I say, the words slipping from my mouth while my brain flashes back a decade, remembering the bottom drawer with the bulky sweatshirts that I never wore, and under them, boxes of fancy cakes, oatmeal crème pies, caramel cookie bars, chocolate-covered marshmallow puffs...

The wad of wrappers waiting for me to get desperate enough to hide them in my backpack, sneak into a bathroom at Saint Celestine's, and shove them into the metal bin for pads and tampons so no one would see me disposing of the evidence.

I'm out of questions now.

Out of bravado.

I want to get on my bike. I want to ride away into the sky like ET. I want to pedal so hard my legs fly off, and my arms and head follow, floating up into outer space in all different directions so no one can ever put me together again, can never make me be here in this shitty fucking world where they make you into this sad, pathetic thing, and then make you hide it, and stand there not blinking an eye when you fall apart.

"I hate you."

I do, with every ounce of my being, so why is it that I'm tearing myself up and not him? Why am I broken, not furious?

Nicky coughs, his face darkening, jaw tightening, brow furrowing. His gaze flits from me to the hall to the floor to the bare wall. An unbearably long minute passes, both of us stuck in place.

Finally, he shakes himself and starts toward the door. I startle. He takes his jacket from the chair, slips it on, and grabs his keys from the counter.

"Come on," he says.

I don't argue or ask where. I let him lead me to the elevator and through the garage. He opens the car door, and I sit obediently, hands in my lap, a cold sweat making me shiver in the evening chill.

He turns on the heat as we pull onto River Street and head west. I don't care where we're going. I don't care if he takes me to some warehouse somewhere and puts a bullet in my brain.

I think the thought, but I know, even as I do, that he wouldn't.

I am broken, but I'm not afraid.

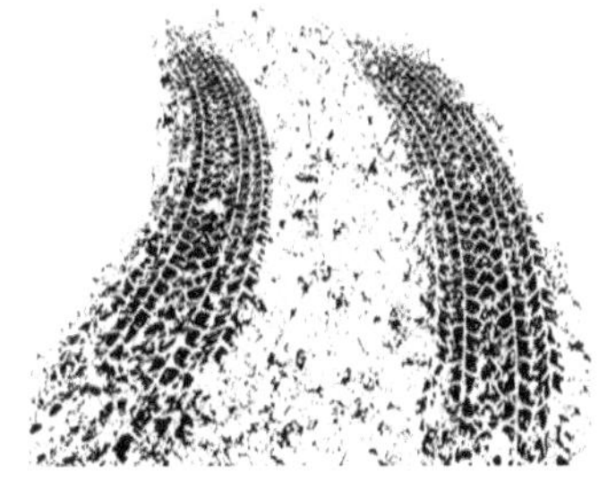

CHAPTER 6

Nicky

Z ITA'S UPSET.

She's slumped in the passenger seat, hugging herself like she's cold even though I've got the heat all the way
up.

I know her better than I know myself, but I often don't
understand her. Lucca threatened her—that'd roll off her.
She'd be scared, but not freaked. He threatened Mattie,

too. That would throw her, but she goes into protective mode when it comes to him. She doesn't shut down.

This has to do with me in her bedroom. Her bottom dresser drawer. Those fucking snacks.

Back in school, I used to think she had a sweet tooth. I thought about buying her chocolates and leaving them in her locker. That kind of dumb kid shit.

But my mother, before she ODed, kept her kit in a shoebox in the back of her top dresser drawer. Doesn't take a genius to realize that this is close to that. Zita's not fat, probably because she's always killing herself on that bike. She might puke, too. I've never seen evidence—like she doesn't go to the bathroom right after she eats—but she's good at hiding, and I don't see everything all the time.

I searched it on the internet. If she's puking or taking laxatives and shit, it could kill her. Ruin her heart, her kidneys. It also makes her fucking miserable, and that's reason enough to do something about it.

But what, right?

Dad would lock Mom in the basement to sober her up, and as soon as he let her out, she'd be down the street sucking dick for a dime bag. This isn't that kind of problem, and besides, that wasn't exactly a solution—unless Dad meant to make Mom desperate and reckless, which is what he did. When a hot shot took her out, she knew there was a bad batch floating around, but she was fresh out of the basement and didn't care.

I ease my foot off the gas. I don't like to go more than twelve miles per hour above the limit. That's the threshold for the speed cameras. There aren't any in the part of town where we're heading, but still—you've gotta keep yourself in the habit.

Criminals who get busted almost always have a story—pulled over for speeding, dropped something at the scene, something dumb. Like their subconscious is trying to get them caught. I'm not going out like that. I've got a reason to get away clean.

I glance over. Zita has her head turned, sullenly staring out the side window. It's hard to believe that last night, I was balls deep in her hot, wet pussy.

My dick hardens like it has a dozen times today when I let my mind wander. She was hesitant at first, wary, stuck in her head, but then she let go, closed her eyes and clung to me, nuzzling her nose against my pecs, tasting my skin with the tip of her little pink tongue, raising her hips so I could sink deeper, letting me make her feel good.

She is everything I knew she'd be.

Soft.

Hungry.

She takes me perfectly, clenching my hips with her sweet, strong thighs, holding my body as tight as I've held her all these years.

It was just like I knew it'd be, but also, more—

Between rounds, when she was satisfied and sleepy, she got bossy. She dragged my arm until she tucked it exactly where she wanted it, pried at my calves until I let her slip her cold feet between them. When I fucked her out of her head, she treated me like what I am—hers.

Now we're back to stewing in silence, stealing glances at each other. Well, she steals. I take.

I don't know how to fix this shit with food. She probably needs to go to therapy, but how does that work? If you talk about your problems enough, they go away? Really?

This thing with Zita's not a problem, but I guess there's a comparison to be made. I never talk about her, but if I did, would I feel differently?

If you talk about something, does it make you want it less?

All the bullshit that people spew all day, every day, and you want to believe words have that kind of power?

Anyway, we don't talk, she and I. It's not how we were raised. So I gotta do something. Quid pro quo. I saw the shit she didn't want anyone to see, so I guess it's her turn.

I turn off Central onto Fawn Street. This part of the old neighborhood never needed to come back. Ever since I was a kid, they've kept the murals of gondolas and women in billowy white dresses stomping grapes freshly painted. There are wrought iron benches at the end of each block and overflowing hanging planters on hooks screwed to the brick rowhomes.

I make a right on Trinity and slow down so Zita can take in the fairy lights strung over the street. It's early evening, the sky is a dark indigo, and folks are clustered on the sidewalks in front of the restaurants that've been there since before I was born. L'Aquila. La Famiglia. Osteria de Sabatini.

In school, I'd walk this way when the bus let me off on Central. I'd cut through the alley at High Street—that's where I knocked Tino Graziano out when I was thirteen—down four blocks where the houses became two stories instead of three and the small, manicured front yards disappeared. There's a rusted pedestrian bridge over the railroad tracks down at Albemarle, but no one bothers with it. The rails shook well before the trains came through.

Past the tracks is the *old*, old neighborhood. The houses might've matched when they were built, but eighty years later, every one has a different enclosed porch, addition, or shed eating up the yard. Most blocks have a unit that caught fire and burned past repair, and a poor sucker on either side who can never sell.

Somehow, it's exactly the same as when I was a kid—gangs of skinny, shirtless kids speeding nowhere on bikes, old ladies squatting on their stoops, flicking the ash from their cigarettes disapprovingly, junkies shuffling ghost-like down the alleyways, surreptitiously trying back gates and car doors.

Zita straightens a little. It's not the worst neighborhood, but it sure as shit doesn't have a community association like where she grew up. This slice of Pyle is holding on, but barely. The developers gobbling up homes from the old folks haven't set their sights on this side of the tracks yet.

I make a few turns, and I find a spot right outside Dad's. The lights are on, not that I thought he'd be out. He doesn't leave much anymore.

The house was my grandfather's. The curtains in the front windows are the ones my grandmother hung back in the '80s. They were white at the time, but they're nearly brown at this point.

The steps are missing chunks of concrete and weeds grow a half foot high in the cracks in the front walk.

I don't want to take Zita inside.

I don't want her body to touch anything in this place or her lungs breathing the air, but I button my jacket, buck up, get out, and open her door.

She gives me a questioning look. I offer her my hand. She doesn't take it, but she gets out. I twist my watch so the face is centered, set my jaw, and lead the way to the door. After a pause, I hear her follow.

The TV blares through the windowpanes. My Dad is braying, per usual, arguing with a woman who's confident enough to answer him back. She must be bringing money in. He wouldn't tolerate it otherwise. I listen a moment to make sure he's not working himself into a rage, but it's only his usual belligerence.

I bang with my fist, loud like the cops. Immediately, there's silence. The curtain sways. The woman says something low, and my dad barks, "That's my asshole son. Let him in."

I give my jacket another sharp tug. The door creaks open a few inches, and an older woman with matted blonde hair and blown pupils sticks her chin through.

"You're his kid?"

I jerk my chin. Her eyes narrow and then refocus behind me, probably on the Mercedes. "What are you, rich?"

I press my palm to the door, pushing it open, but slowly, so she can scramble back when she realizes she can't stop me with the shoulder she's using as a brace.

"Jimmy—" she whines. She must be bringing in a lot if Dad lets her act like this is her place.

He waves her off, not bothering to get off the couch. He's in a dingy undershirt, but at least he's wearing sweatpants. There are crumbs on the crotch, but they're clean enough. Or dark enough not to show stains.

"I said let him in, didn't I?" he says. "Go get us some beers."

She sniffs and grudgingly disappears into my grandmother's kitchen. From here, I can make out her porcelain rooster and decorative cookie jars covered in a thick layer of dust above the cabinets, half of which are missing their doors.

"This is Zita," I say, gesturing behind me. I don't turn to look at her. I don't want to see her face.

"Bringing the girlfriend to meet the old man?" My dad cackles. It ends in a phlegmy hack.

"Fiancée."

Dad raises his thinning eyebrows. "Well, have a seat, Zita. Make yourself at home."

He flashes a yellow smile. He's down a few teeth since last I saw him, maybe two or three years ago.

Zita hesitates at my side. Dad's sitting in the middle of the couch. There's another woman passed out in the seat to his left, leaning over the arm like she just tilted over. A fifth of gin sits on the rust orange carpet by her scuffed, kicked off heels, her tit almost hanging out of her halter top. She's my dad's age—at least fifty.

At least the women don't get younger as he gets older. Might be the only good thing I can say about him.

Anyway, there's another seat, an armchair stacked with free Sunday papers still in plastic bags. Guess Zita doesn't want to sit next to Dad. Maybe she doesn't want to come any further into the house. The ammonia smell is powerfully strong. I don't see any of the cats, but obviously, he still has them.

He always said they were my mom's, but when she died, he didn't get rid of them. He didn't start cleaning up after them himself either.

I cross the room to toss the newspapers into a pile on the floor and try to brush the cat hair off the upholstery. Then I take the seat next to Dad.

When I get home, this suit will go in the trash. Zita's shirt and pants, too.

I try not to let my back touch the couch, rest my hands on my thighs. Zita perches on the edge of the chair, and it tilts forward with a creak. She reaches out to steady herself, snatching her hands back as soon as they touch the matted, grimy fabric. My grandmother used crocheted armrest covers she made herself, but they were long gone before I left for good at sixteen.

"So how'd you meet this fucking ingrate?" Dad asks Zita.

"We went to school together," I answer for her. She's busy taking it all in, trying and failing to cover the fact that she's disgusted. She's trying to breathe through her mouth. I don't. Long ago, I decided I'd rather have cat piss in my nose than on my tongue.

Dad wrinkles his forehead. "The elementary?"

"Saint Celestine's."

He guffaws. "Your Aunt Gina was something, wasn't she? Wouldn't step foot in this house, not even when your mother was alive. She sure as shit wouldn't take you, not even for a weekend, but she paid for that school, didn't she? Dried-up Catholic bitch. She should've gone and become a nun like she was always saying."

He's wrong. Aunt Gina used to come by to visit Mom sometimes during the day when Dad was out. The last time was a few weeks before Mom died. I had a split lip, and my aunt wanted to know about it. She and Mom had a huge fight. Gina drove off angry, screaming at Mom that you can't save someone who won't save herself.

Then Mom died, and at the funeral, Gina told me she'd pay for Saint Celestine's if I kept up my grades and didn't make trouble.

I was pretty sure Zita went there with the other rich Italian kids from the other side of the river. I swore to her I'd make honor roll.

So I was happy that day we buried my mother. It was maybe the last time I prayed in church. I didn't have the words, so I repeated "thank you, thank you," over and over in my head, even though I knew there was no one who could hear or who'd cared if they could.

"How is Aunt Gina?" I ask.

"How the fuck would I know?" Dad scratches his crotch, gaze flicking to the TV. He hasn't bothered turning it down. It's one of those competitive cooking shows.

We watch together in silence until his girlfriend returns with four beers. She gives Dad his first. She has to nudge Zita to take hers. Zita's busy staring at the faded outlines on the wallpaper where the cross, the clock, the painting of the Sacred Heart of Jesus, and the family pictures used to be. I didn't know the frames were worth anything. Maybe they weren't, and Dad tossed them instead of carrying them back from the pawn shop.

Zita curls both hands around her beer bottle, but she doesn't drink. I take mine with a nod. The girlfriend huffs when she sees there's nowhere left for her to sit and wriggles her ass in between Dad and the passed-out woman.

I know that Zita feels ashamed when her food thing comes up. She's weird about food in general. She acts like it's a bomb.

Crammed onto the reeking old couch with my drunk father and his whores, maybe I should feel ashamed.

When I was younger, I would have been. I would have died before I let Zita in here.

But Zita is the reason I got out of here.

She's the reason why I could walk out now, never look back, and it wouldn't haunt me, not for a second. It hasn't haunted me in years.

None of it.

Not the woman who ran into my bedroom to hide from Dad behind my window curtain, blood streaming from her broken nose, sobbing so loud I knew he'd find her, even though I tried to tell her she had to be quiet. He found her, threw her down the stairs toward his room where his buddies had gone, and told her, "Get in there, and don't come out until you've earned fifty, or I'm gonna do your left arm next."

Not a woman, now that I'm remembering. She was probably only three or four years older than me at the time.

My mother doesn't haunt me. My own broken nose and arm. The doors I opened—the rooms I walked into—and ran from as quickly as I could. The images I can't scrub from my mind.

None of it touches me.

Later, the things I did to get out of this place, none of that can touch me either.

Some men have hearts. Souls. Walls.

I have Zita Graziano.

I'm not ashamed. I look at her, and something inside me chants "thank you" into the void like a hallelujah. I'm weightless. Superhuman.

Just a few more minutes, then I'll take her home and never come back. Maybe I'll burn it down, or maybe I'll just walk away and never think about it ever again.

"You haven't been keeping up with the family, eh?" I turn to my dad, distracting him. He'd gone back to watching his cooking show. "Just pimping whores and losing money at the track?"

He bristles even though all of us on this filthy couch know I'm right. "Who invited you anyway?"

"It's my house." My grandfather left it to me even though I was still a kid at the time. He knew his son was a piece of shit. Nonno hoped I'd go to work for Renelli like he had, go further than he did, become a made man, get the sharkskin suit and shiny car.

In his day, the organization was all running the numbers, loansharking, and protection rackets, but it had already changed before he kicked the bucket. If I wanted to rise under Renelli, I'd need to deal, at the very least mule. Traffic in the same shit that killed my mother.

Lucca Corso is insane, but he offered me a better job. And he gave me Zita.

He also thinks he can threaten her, make her worry about Mattie. That's not gonna work.

"You here to collect rent?" Dad snorts. "Why don't you take it off what you owe me for raising your ungrateful ass."

The school fed me. My mother clothed me by working on her back. There's no money in that account.

"Just dropped by for a visit."

"Well, since you're here, you got twenty for your old man? I could use it." He sniffs and wipes at his red nose.

I shrug and reach for my wallet. I give him a fifty.

"Big man, eh?" he says and settles back, shoves his hand in his waistband, and goes back to watching his show, laughing when the hosts joke and the contestants fuck up. The passed-out woman begins to snore. He jams his elbow into her side. She sputters and keeps snoring.

When the credits roll, I stand, brush my pants, spread the cat hair around. Zita immediately gets to her feet, too.

"Leaving?" Dad says, eyes glued to the TV.

"Yeah."

His girlfriend doesn't look up from her phone. The snoring woman doesn't move.

I gesture for Zita to head toward the door. She doesn't need prompting.

As soon as I step outside, the fresh air almost rushes into my lungs. I suck it down, hating the ammonia stink that clings to my clothes, my hair, my skin.

I unlock the car with a beep and open Zita's door. I'll have to call the mobile detailer to come tomorrow.

I drive home with both windows rolled down. Zita's silent. She's not being obvious about ignoring me now, but she isn't casting me glances either. She's deep in thought. I can imagine.

I've always known about her world. When I was a kid, my grandfather used to take me with him when he delivered those zippered, leather envelopes of cash to the big houses in Zita's neighborhood. He liked to stop at the strip club on the way home, the one out on highway eighty-four where no one knew him.

He'd leave me in the car to play the PSP he bought me at the flea market, and when he was too wasted to drive home, he'd have me cruise out toward Stonecut County on the back roads until he sobered up.

Where would Zita have learned about my world?

If I had my way, she never would, but she's strong. She's tough as nails when it comes to other people's shit.

"We're square now, right?" I ask as I ease to a stop at a red light.

She blinks. "What do you mean?"

"I was in your bedroom. You saw my house."

Her lips curve down, dimpling her chin. "No, we're not even. You broke into my private space."

"Your brother Tony let me in. Lucca made him."

"He had no right." She lets her head drop back to the rest. "*You* had *no right*. But men like you don't care about that."

"Men like me—" I let the sentence hang. When the light turns green and I accelerate, the wind coming through the open windows clears it, unfinished.

She stares out the windshield, her brown eyes dull. "Men who take what they want. Who don't give a shit about other people."

My fingers wrap around the steering wheel. I face straight ahead when I answer her. "I give a shit about you."

She scoffs softly, and she's silent for a few miles. I figure she's sinking back into her head, so I'm surprised when she clears her throat and says, "That's why you took me there? So we'd be even?"

My brain immediately offers up the easy dodges—

Are we?

What do you think?

But she has her lips clamped together like she's trying to stop the bottom from trembling or the words she really wants to say from escaping. She's so vulnerable. I want to build her a suit of armor. I want to arm her to the teeth.

"If I saw what you're hiding, I figured you should see that."

Her lip wobbles. My gut hurts.

"You don't know what you think you know." Her pupils are shining now as a passing car's headlights hit them.

"I do know," I say, keeping my eyes on the road. I feel every muscle in her body tense.

"It's no big deal. I'm fine."

She can lie to me if she wants. I'll listen. I'm not gonna believe her, though.

"I mean look at me—" Her voice cracks. "I look fine."

More than fine. She's beautiful. Her smile fucks my heartbeat up. Her body haunts my dreams. I know she doesn't see it that way, though.

"What about *you*?" she says. "You're not okay."

But I am. I pull down the ramp to the garage and a weight rises off my chest. I turn off the engine, engage the emergency brake, and for a minute, I sit in the stuffy silence and fumes.

"Maybe not," I say. "But I could be. *We* could be. You make me okay. I make you okay."

"Quid pro quo?" she says.

My lips curve. "That's what I was thinking." I reach over and smooth the hair already tucked neatly behind her ear.

She doesn't jerk away. Almost imperceptibly, in a move so slight it could be mistaken for the wind riffling her hair, except we're in an airless garage, she inclines her head into my touch.

A vise grips my lungs. I am so very careful as I lower my arm, unbuckle, walk to her side, and open her door. I don't offer my hand. I give her space.

I let her lead the way to the elevator. On the way to the apartment, I drop my jacket in the trash chute. I kick off my shoes in the hallway as I unlock the door.

"You take the shower in the bedroom. I'll take the other one," I tell her.

She doesn't argue. I grab a plastic bag to shove my clothes in, and as I strip carefully so they don't touch the bath mat or towels, I heat the water as hot as it'll get. Before I hop in, I duck into the bedroom, grab Zita's clothes from where she left them folded on top of the hamper and jog naked to the chute.

The building belongs to Lucca. The folks who live here all owe him in some way or another, and they enjoy the rent control. Even if they saw my bare ass, they wouldn't let on as a matter of principle.

When I return to the bathroom, it's thick with steam. I scrub my skin until it burns, shampoo my hair three times, scratch my scalp until my eyes water.

I can still smell cat piss, but it's hard to say if it's real or in my head. I scrub and shampoo again anyway.

After, I shave and splash on cologne even though it's time for bed. Even if it's a phantom smell, it helps. I do thirty minutes on the rowing machine until I'm sweating in sheets, and then I do a few sets, work my arms and back until the tension becomes a burn. Then I jump in the shower again.

When I dress and wander into the living room, I don't feel clean, but my body's tired, and that'll do. I check the fridge even though I know there's no milk. Force of habit.

The door to the bedroom is closed. I can't hear anything. Zita must have hit the sack.

I sink into my sofa, stretch my arms along the back, rest my bare soles on the cold, immaculate floor, and flip the channels until I find sports. I've got the volume so loud that I almost don't hear her small feet padding into the room, but I smell her. Lavender and vanilla.

She lingers behind the sofa for a while. I don't move.

She wanders around the arm, perching on it for a few minutes before she lowers herself to sit cross-legged on the cushion furthest from me. I extend my legs and crack my neck. She draws her knees to her chest, her pale pink sleep shorts creeping up her thigh.

She doesn't look my way, but she knows I'm watching her. She must.

She yawns, her eyes scrunching shut, her small hand covering her mouth, a quiet sigh escaping her lips.

My cock tents my joggers. I don't hide it, and I don't let on that I see her sneaking peeks. When the program goes to commercial, I flip to the home improvement channel she likes. She settles back. My muscles relax.

On the TV, a guy in a collared shirt uses a sledgehammer to demo a wall like he's swinging a golf club, and then he disappears while a bunch of dudes walk around in the background, working, as a lady in a hardhat and lipstick talks to the camera.

We watch, and a few minutes in, out of nowhere she says, "I like houses like that."

I'm startled, but I don't let on. "Craftsman?"

"Is that what they're called?"

"Yeah." I don't know why I know this. From TV, I guess.

"We don't have them much around here," she says.

"They have a lot out west." Again, I'm not sure where I picked this up, but I'm happy that I did.

"They look like what you draw when you're a kid, and they say draw a house."

"Yeah." They do.

She's quiet for a moment before she says, "That place was fucking awful."

She's talking about my dad's.

"Yeah."

"You grew up there?"

"Uh-huh."

"It was like that?"

"Pretty much. After my grandparents died. More people around, but yeah."

She keeps her eyes on the screen. A man is installing a cast iron farmhouse sink while the woman with the lipstick gets in the way, talking about how the apron requires a special countertop cut.

"What were your grandparents like?" she asks.

I recognize it's a normal question, but people don't ask me shit like this. I have to think for a second. Zita extends her small, pink painted toes and curls them back into the leather.

"My grandma was a good cook."

"Yeah?"

She was your typical Italian-American grandma, a feed-er. No one went hungry in her house. Eleven at night, five in the morning, didn't matter. Would it freak Zita out to say that? Because of her food thing?

She saves me from deciding, asking, "What about your grandfather?"

She must not remember him. Why would she? She was a kid, and for all I know, she only saw him the once.

"He worked for Renelli."

She perks up. "Yeah?"

"Hardly a soldier. More like an associate."

"But your dad's not—?"

"No." No one like Renelli would trust him with shit.

"Is that why you got in? 'Cause of your grandfather?"

I got in because Lucca Corso dangled her like bait, and I'm sure he said as much when he laid down the law earlier, but I guess it hasn't sunk all the way in yet.

If I tell her, will she clam up?

I want her to keep talking to me like this, like she's not afraid, and I'm not scary. We can be two normal people on a sofa having a conversation.

"I got in because it was the only way to get what I want-ed."

"How do you know? That it was the only way?"

My lungs tense. Does she understand what I'm saying? Are we talking about the same thing? We can't be.

Right?

"If there was another way, I couldn't see it." It's true. I'm not dodging her questions. Not anymore.

"Yeah," she says and focuses back on the TV, her mouth turned down in a slight frown. The show goes on, and whatever darkened her mind fades, and she resettles, a little contented sigh escaping her mouth, almost sotto voce.

She glances at me.

I pretend to watch intently as the owners are brought blindfolded into the house.

Her gaze darts to my dick. It's still hard. No hiding it, so I don't try. I watch the damn show.

She turns back to the screen. Seconds later, she checks out my biceps stretched along the back of the couch. I can't help but flex a little when she does. I feel stupid, but she lets her gaze linger, and more blood rushes to my cock.

At the end of the episode, the house looks perfect, but then again, all they show are the accent walls, shelving, and mosaic backsplash. I wanna know what the furnace and the roof look like.

The credits roll. Zita's gaze flicks to my dick again. She squirms in her seat. Licks her dry lips. Curves her shoulders so I can't see if her nipples are hard.

I bet they are.

I flip back to basketball. I can't take another reno. I like the houses, but the people—the way they talk.

Bob needs a workshop, and I have to have space for a home office and lots of storage. Like that's how life works. You act like you *have* to have shit, and you just get it.

I mean, it *is* how it goes, but it's annoying when you don't see all the shit Bob did so his wife could make fucking demands.

Zita hasn't figured out yet that she can ask for whatever she wants. Maybe she never will. Maybe she won't ever realize that there's no such thing as "men like me." There are men like her father. Renelli. Lucca.

I'm not the same.

She creeps her small, bare feet further over the edge of the sofa until only her heels are on the leather.

There aren't men like me, but there are people like us. Like Zita and me. Born in a minefield. A jungle.

I think she knows it now. Senses it. How we're connected.

Her breath quickens, her slender shoulders rising and falling like a kitten's ribcage, as terrifyingly delicate as that.

There are people like my mother, people who drown. Others, like Lucca Corso, who save themselves by climbing up other men's drowning bodies.

Zita's eyelashes flutter against her smooth cheeks.

She and I aren't drowning, though. Every day, we're working on our escape, and she doesn't know it, but I'm not leaving her behind. She's my strength. If I hadn't found her, my lungs would've taken on water years ago, but she saved me.

I reach out to stroke my fingers down her silky soft arm. She shivers under my touch, her eyelashes fluttering.

She doesn't pull away.

She slides me a look out of the side of her eyes. Confused. Assessing. Vulnerable.

I stand, slowly, carefully, scoop her up like a bride, hold her tight to my chest, and she doesn't fight me. Tentatively, she reaches up to wind her arms around my neck.

"I shouldn't let you do this," she murmurs, her lips brushing the stubbled underside of my jaw.

If it makes it easier for her to believe she's doing this against her better sense, that's fine. When she comes on my face, her scream's not gonna sound the least bit conflicted to the neighbors on the other side of the wall.

I carry her to our room and lay her down in the middle of the bed like a present. She stays where I put her, elbows bent, hands resting over her head like a centerfold, watching me with those big, solemn brown eyes. Her nipples are hard, poking through her shimmery pink cami. Her pulse throbs at the base of her delicate neck.

I did this. I got her this far. In my bed. Ready for me.

Absently, I rub my side where a bullet grazed my rib as I used my body to shield Posy Santoro from a hail of gunfire in that warehouse where Lucca and Dario put the old guard down.

When I *earned* Zita Graziano.

Even if she won't come with me the rest of the way, I have her now.

"You're perfect." I can't help but say it, even though I know her eyes will flicker, and she'll shift, nervous fingers fluttering to rearrange her pajamas to cover her perfect thighs, her perfect middle, her perfect breasts.

Her cheeks darken.

I remind myself to breathe.

I kneel at the foot of the bed. She squirms, props up a knee, clenches her thighs together, posing for me, consciously or not, teasing me by hiding what I want. And she watches me.

I peel my shirt off, toss it, and track her eyes as they count the beads of my tattoo, catch on the cross at the crease where my abs meet. Her lips part.

I will my hands not to shake as I prowl forward and draw the elastic waistband of her silk shorts down, slowly so I can trace the pale lines decorating the swell of her hips and the hard ridge of her hipbone. She lifts her ass to help me ease them off.

"I'll make you feel good," I tell her. I'll drive all the demons out of her mind. I'll break her free, and I'll build her a new life. I'm gonna see her laugh out loud. The little crease on the bridge of her nose is going to disappear forever.

She blinks her big, round eyes and worries her bottom lip with her teeth.

I grab her thighs and urge them apart. Brownish pink inner folds peek out of her rosy, juice-slick lips. I run a rough fingertip along them, teasing, and her breath catches. Before she can tense, I spread her open, pushing her knees back until her pink slit gapes.

She whimpers.

"So pretty," I say, letting a thigh go long enough to slap her pussy, once, twice, three times, hard enough so she cries out, legs and abs tensing, and it blushes pinker, her hard little bead poking all the way out of its hood.

"That's right. Don't try to hide from me." I slap it again. Zita moans, her hips raising to meet my hand at the same time her thigh muscles instinctually clench to protect her tender, abused flesh. I use my knee to brace her open. Panting, she does a curl so she can see what I'm doing.

I'm clearing her mind. Focusing her on me.

I lay a series of stinging smacks to her swollen lips, her pouty clit, the slick, taut patch of skin between her slit and her asshole.

She whines and drops back to the bed. I don't have to keep her spread anymore. She holds herself open for me.

My chest warms. I lower my head, run my nose down the soft skin of her belly, smile as the muscles under her padding tense.

Her breath catches, and she taps the back of my head. "Nicky?" she pants.

I splay her with my index finger and thumb. She smells faintly like her body wash, but also like musky, tangy woman.

My woman.

My cock throbs. I grind it into the mattress.

"Nicky." She thumps the back of my head again.

"Um?" I hum into her folds.

"You don't have to do this."

Her slit is glistening, leaking pussy juice. I lap it up.

She gasps. Her thighs quiver.

"*Nicky*." She clutches at my hair.

I hum again and swirl my tongue around her proud little nub. She lets out a sound halfway between a yelp and a scream, smothering it before I can tell if it's a happy sound or not.

"Nicky, you really don't have to," she manages between pants.

What the fuck is she talking about? I try to focus, but her scent is in my nose, her cream coating my chin, and I just want more. I want her to fuck my face, let go, let this happen.

She wriggles her butt away. Oh, hell no.

I nip the fold closest to my teeth and lift my head, lay down a few more slaps, increasing the force as her cries grow more raw, more desperate. I pin her waist down with a forearm.

"You like this." I dive back in, licking, spearing, feasting. She sobs.

Somewhere in the back of my mind, it occurs to me that she might not have done this before. Times may have changed, but still, eating pussy isn't something men around here will admit to, and plenty straight up refuse to do it.

Shit. Is my mouth her first?

My balls swell and ache, and that want that's always inside me surges, razor sharp and unbearable.

"Has anyone else tasted you, baby?" I slide two fingers inside her, crook them forward and suck on her pearl, lash it with the flat of my tongue.

She moans.

"Has anyone made you feel like this?" Her channel pulses faintly. She's close.

I lift my chin, but I keep working her with my fingers, harder, quicker. "Have they?"

"No," she cries, her hips working, trying to find my mouth.

"What do you want, baby?" I drop a kiss to the gentle swell above her spit-slick mound.

She drives her fingers into my hair again, hikes her hips, and shoves me into her salty, drenched folds. A starburst explodes in my chest. I suck and lick while she rides my face, and when she comes, screaming, legs seizing, I shuck my pants and fuck her until she comes again and the sheets are messy with her juices, my spit, and our mingled cum.

She's limp when I roll her away from the wet spot and tuck her against my side. She yawns and cuddles closer, throwing a leg over my thigh. A sense of well-being like I've never known floods me. It's terrifying.

Where's my gun?

It's in the nightstand.

Is it loaded?

Yes. Of course, it's loaded.

There's a fixed blade tucked in between the mattress and the frame at hand level. I can get in the safe in under thirty seconds, and there are five weapons in there loaded with a total of—

Quick math—

Fifty-one rounds.

I readjust us so my body is between her and the door. She wriggles backward, her ass pressing into my cock. It's too soon. I need a minute before I'm ready again.

I brush her damp hair aside and press a kiss to the soft skin behind her ear. She grumbles.

"Just because you make me come, doesn't mean I want to marry you," she mutters sleepily, making no move to escape my arms.

I tilt her face and kiss her stubborn chin.

"You can't blackmail people into happily ever after," she says.

I brush a kiss across her sweet lips.

"You need therapy," she says against my mouth. "*I* need therapy." She sighs.

I kiss her again.

"You're so weird." She's drifting off, but I'm hard again now. I kiss her while I hike her leg higher over my hip and slip into her from behind.

And when she comes, she's kissing me back.

CHAPTER 7

Zita

A ROUND TWO IN THE morning, Nicky's phone wakes me up. I'm jerked out of a deep sleep, and I miss what he says while I try to remember where I am. He's strapping his gun to his back before I have the wherewithal to ask questions.

"Where are you going?"

"Don't worry about it," he says.

"What do you mean, don't worry about it?" It's the middle of the night.

He slides on a black baseball cap, and irritated, he disappears into the closet. He comes out with a small, nickel-plated pistol. He shows me the butt.

"The safety is on. It's loaded. Seven rounds. One in the chamber. You understand?"

Kind of? I've been around guns all my life, but I've never held one.

Why's he giving me a gun?

He sets it on the nightstand where he keeps his piece.

"Don't worry," he says again. "You're fine. I'll be back as soon as I can."

I wasn't worried about myself. Should I be?

"Where are you going?" I ask again.

He hesitates on the threshold. "I have to take care of something. It's okay. You don't have to worry."

That is not how I work.

When the front door snicks shut, I scramble out of bed, pull on spandex shorts and a sports bra, and spend the next hour on the bike, standing because I can't bear the pressure of the hard seat on my sore pussy.

Given, I don't have much in terms of comparison, but Nicky fucks like a wild man.

Early on, Paul wanted to try everything, but over the years, he settled into his preferences. He liked reverse cowgirl so he didn't have to work and could just enjoy the view, he liked me bent over the bathroom sink so he could watch himself in the mirror. He was always begging for anal, complaining about how he'd had a rough week, a tough exam, whatever.

Nicky fucks like he's lost his mind, and he's trying to find it between my legs.

He fucks like I'm hiding something that he's desperate for.

Like I'm the holy grail, and he's an infidel, so he doesn't want to worship me, he wants to convert me, despoil me until I belong to him.

My brain tries to puzzle together the pieces—that disgusting house, that foul man, the boy I can hardly picture now because when I think back, I can only remember his dark, bleak eyes, and they haven't changed in all these years, except for when he's inside me, and they blaze like fire.

The man in the impeccable suit, fearless in the company of Lucca Corso, losing his shit when a stranger touches my arm.

He gave me a gun. I think because he figures it'll make me feel safer.

He's wanted me since junior high. He's done unimaginable things to get me.

Me.

I increase the incline and pedal harder.

It's not like it's a great compliment to be the obsession of a cold-blooded killer, but it sure as shit is mind-blowing.

What happens when he decides he wants someone else?

Why did I leave the gun in the bedroom? I should keep it on me.

Sweat dribbles down my forehead, stinging my eyes.

What if, though—

What if Nicky can't get over me? What if *nothing* can shake him out of this?

Lucca values Nicky. That's obvious. Maybe he even needs him to stay in power. Furio can't be the only one who resented the abrupt change in leadership. The rumors about Lucca and Tomas can't help either.

I picture the scars, the ugly gash along Nicky's right rib, the other, older silver ones. Nicky is dangerous. Not like a man. Like a *weapon*.

And according to Lucca, he'll do anything for me. Will he, though?

Anything?

The idea is heady. I quit at eight hundred calories. That's not much of a cushion, but for a change, I don't want to turn my brain off. I need to think.

I take a long, hot shower, and as the sun rises over the Luckahannock, I heat water in a pot to make tea—there's no kettle.

I sink into my side of the sofa and watch the joggers and dog walkers appear on the promenade. It's a beautiful morning, cloudless sky, clear air.

My body feels good. Wrung out, but not beat up. I changed into a pair of white cropped yoga pants and a scoop-necked pink top. The outfit works hard for me, covering my padded bits while showing off my collarbone, the swell of my breasts, my tanned legs, and my toned calves.

I took the time to style my hair, and I've arranged—and rearranged—the soft waves over my shoulders.

I'm pretty.

But am I brave?

Can I do the thing that's spinning into a plan in my mind?

And where the hell is Nicky?

When Dad went out in the middle of the night, there'd always be hushed voices when he came home, and Mom would end up running the washing machine at three in the morning, and for the next few days, she'd jump out of her skin whenever the phone rang.

The anxiety can't get its teeth into me, though. I have no problem staying out of the kitchen. I'm too fascinated by the idea—

What if Nicky Biancolli really would do anything for me?

Nicky gets home at eight. No blood, no new bruises. His clothes are clean. His eyes find me, and he crosses the room in three strides, barely stopping to kick off his shoes.

Gently, he takes the teacup from my hand, sets it carefully on the floor, and he picks me up and folds me over the arm of the sofa, the meat of his palm on the base of my spine as he drags down my pants and sinks to his knees.

He holds me open and eats me, nose in my ass crack and tongue lashing my clit, as I struggle and shriek and flush hot red. He's relentless, stronger than me, single-minded, and at some point, the switch inside me—the one that says you can't stop this, so you don't have to fight—flips, and I sidle my legs wider and cant my hips.

He hauls me up to kneel on the arm rest and fucks me hard and fast, his forearm like a seat belt across my chest, fingertips digging into the crook of my neck, holding me to him like a vise. I come in minutes.

Then he sets me back on the cushion—naked and brain-numb—hands me back my tea, kisses the top of my head, and struts down the hall for a shower.

I leak cum on the leather, stare out the window at the rush hour traffic on River Street, and wonder—

If he won't let me go, would he break me out? Me and Mattie?

Or would that be jumping out of the frying pan and into the fire?

If I ask him, is that when he locks me in a room, and this becomes something else? Something so ugly I can't ignore exactly what it is?

Nicky comes out dressed in a gray suit, straightening his tie. I quickly stand to face him, nerves jumping as if he can read my mind, which he can't, but of course now I look guilty as hell.

He raises an eyebrow but takes it in stride. "There's money on the bedside table."

"What for?"

He shrugs. "Whatever you need." He tucks his phone in his breast pocket. "You could get some milk."

He sits on a dining room chair and begins to put on his dress shoes. "I put the gun back in the safe."

Shit. Why didn't I keep it on me? Why did I make it easy for him to take it back?

I cross my arms.

He looks up from tying his laces. "What?"

He waits, black eyes boring into me from under impossibly thick, dark lashes, and he's so intense, so beautiful, it muddles me, and something deep inside me, a survival instinct, an audacity I never knew I had, makes me say, "I want it back."

He slowly straightens, those smoldering eyes narrowing. "You want the gun?"

I hug my arms tight against my chest. "Yeah."

A second passes that feels like an hour. Then he sniffs, stands, goes to the bedroom, and comes back with the nickel-plated pistol. He shows me the butt again. "Safety's on. It's loaded. Seven rounds plus one in the chamber. Okay?'"

I nod. He sets it on the marble-topped kitchen island.

On his way out the door, he stops and says over his shoulder, "I drink two percent. The organic shit."

When he leaves, the apartment is oppressively silent. I turn the TV on and the volume up, but it echoes and makes the space feel even emptier. I do an hour on the bike, shower, and take my time blow drying my hair into pristine fat curls, filing my nails into perfect ovals, buffing them smooth, and painting them a pale, pearlescent pink. I pluck my eyebrows and restrain myself from going overboard, carefully following the shape my girl makes when she waxes.

Eyebrows are hard. Beauty is pain, right? High heels. Chemical peels. Scalp burns when your girl mixes the color wrong. With brows, you start plucking, and it hurts, so you kind of instinctually figure you're on the right track, and then you look up, and you've plucked yourself patchy. I've done it before, but not today.

I'm in full control.

I put on a matching white lace bra and panties, white shorts, and a teal crocheted tank top that my mother hates. She says it looks like a doily from the '70s. I told her it's boho, and she said, yeah, it sure is bozo. The chunky knit "hides a multitude of sins," though, as she says, so I keep it in rotation.

I'm as put together as I can get by early afternoon, and I don't particularly feel like watching more TV. I throw in a load of laundry. There's really nothing else to clean. The apartment is pretty immaculate.

I don't feel like going on another walk, so I search 'buy milk near me' on my phone, and there's a corner store two blocks away. I go buy Nicky a gallon of two percent. They don't have organic.

I leave the gun on the counter. When I come back, the first thing I see is it laying there, and a frisson of fear skitters up my spine. At least, it feels like fear.

I put the milk away and linger in the kitchen. I haven't eaten yet today. I'm hungry. And jittery.

I idly check the fridge and the cabinets. For something to do, I give the tomatoes and basil another rinse and lay them to dry on a dish towel.

I open the cabinet with the snack cakes. If I wait long enough, I'll be so starving that I'll be able to shove the shame easily to the side. Nothing will be able stop me. I'll be able to do what I want.

No, not what I want. What I can no longer stop myself from doing.

The bananas are right there. Or I could make myself avocado toast, drizzle a little olive oil on it, maybe toss on a few walnuts. That's a good, healthy choice.

There's a gun on the counter.

I'm a prisoner.

I'm nothing but a body. A piece. Collateral.

I could take a box of chocolate cupcakes into the living room, shove them into my mouth until they stick in my throat, until the icing coats my teeth, and I make all my fear disappear and replace it with shame, which is so much more powerful.

Or.

There's a gun on the counter.

I'm armed.

I'm willpower. I can take a beating. I haven't given up yet.

I take the gun and put it in the front pouch of my red purse. Then, I go to the bedroom, grab one of Nicky's blue dress shirts from the closet, and put it on over my clothes, rolling the sleeves up to my elbows.

I haven't made Nonna's marinara in a while. Paul was paleo for the past few years, so pasta was out. It's a simple recipe, though. The key is using fresh tomatoes and letting it simmer.

I loved cooking with Nonna when I was little. She'd have me "help" by fetching things from the pantry and rinsing her measuring cups and spoons, and all the while, she'd tell stories about when she was a girl in Salerno and sneak me bites, licks, and tastes. Little balls of dough rolled in sugar. The tenderest slice of roast for me to "test" and let her know if I thought it was done.

Nonna's kitchen was warm and safe, and I was special there.

And then, at dinner, I was expected to eat in silence while the men talked, and Mom would smack my hand if I reached for seconds, hissing something like "supermodels always go to bed hungry." It's strange how they set us up—we're supposed to be beautiful, skinny, and silent, but the love we're given, it's always rich in butter, always sweet and forbidden.

I try to think of the kitchen, not the dining room, as I play music on my phone and blanch the tomatoes, peeling off their skins and crushing them by hand into a large glass bowl.

I heat the olive oil in a skillet that's never been used while I chop the garlic and oregano. Nicky doesn't have a garlic press, but they're a pain in the ass to clean anyway.

My stomach growls, so I rinse the strawberries and pop them in my mouth in between stirring the sauce. Like Nonna, I add an extra pinch of salt and sugar halfway through, and I taste frequently. Sauce splatters on Nicky's shirt, and I don't feel bad at all. I wipe the bigger drops off and lick my fingers, smearing red all over the slick fabric.

I'm kind of lost in it when a knock at the door startles me. My gaze flies to the empty counter before I calm myself down. Bad guys don't knock when they come to do bad things. I guess they drag you out of your bed.

When I check the peephole, it's blacked out.

"Mattie?" Covering the hole with his palm is one of his things.

"Let me in, Z."

I undo the chain, and he strides on in, carrying a crate of my binders, a stuffed duffel bag slung over his shoulder. He has a black eye.

"Jesus Christ, Mattie." I take the duffel, my fingers reaching to hover over the swollen socket. He ducks his head.

"Is he here?" Mattie searches the room for evidence of Nicky as he tries to shrug me off.

"No." I don't let him go. "What the hell happened?"

"Life," he says, dodging past me to set the crate on the table.

"Tell me." I grab and turn him, trying to make sure there's nothing else, but he's taller than me, and he's wearing his hair down, letting the beautiful, brown waves fall in his face. "Mattie, please."

I'll kill them.

"What else? Where else did they hurt you?" I explore down his arm, squeezing, testing, and he humors me, lets me reassure myself, and that's how I know that it was bad.

This isn't the first time.

"Oh, Mattie." I grab his chin, but gently. There's a faint line of sparkly blue shadow in the crease above his eye.

He sniffs the air. "You making spaghetti?"

"Marinara."

"Sweet." He tilts his head down and busses my cheek. "I could eat."

"You could eat, eh?" My eyes sting, and I can't stop smoothing his worn hoodie over his shoulders, tucking loose strands of hair behind his ear with the empty holes. "My Mattie."

He's the one who was born with natural grace. Delicate. Lovely. Always hiding himself away, so whenever he lets me catch a glimpse of the real him, my heart twists, because he's beautiful, and perfect, and I'm not strong enough to protect him.

"I'm going to get us out of here," I swear, squeezing his cool hands.

"I thought you were gonna feed me." He grins, wincing as his black eye crinkles.

"Oh, Mattie," I say.

"You should see the other guy."

I squeeze his hands once more before I drop them and move toward the kitchen. I pass the crate on the table. "You brought the binders?"

"Mom decided to clean your room out. The rest of your shoes are in the bag. There's more, but I caught a ride share, and dude drove a Smart Car."

"Seriously? Mom's cleaning out my room?"

"I think it's like her version of burning sage. She wants to exorcize the house."

"Oh." Paul. Now Mom. I guess I am easy to get over.

Mattie makes himself comfortable at the table, digs out the flower binder, and starts flipping through. I fill the stock pot and put it on a back burner. I forgot to buy salt, so I have to use packets from the plasticware drawer to flavor the water.

The kitchen begins to smell really good. Evening rush hour is starting, and honks float up from the street. With Mattie lounging at the table, the apartment almost doesn't feel lonely.

"Are you really gonna marry Nicky?" he asks.

"You say that like you know the guy." I lean against the counter, waiting for the water to boil. It'd heat quicker with the lid on, but Nonna'd roll over in her grave if I did it the lazy way.

"Are you gonna, like, elope to Vegas?"

"He wants to get married in church."

Mattie rounds the eye that isn't puffed shut. "That's top-tier delusion right there."

I guess. In my bedroom back home, the binders made me happy. They're pretty, cloth-covered with applique bouquets on the front. Here, in a plastic crate on a bare table, they look—well, delusional.

I shrug. "We all do what we gotta do, right?"

"You could still bail. He's not here right now."

"I wouldn't leave you. Never." I stare him down until he blushes. He's only eighteen. Just a kid. My love embarrasses him.

"We could run away together."

"In what car? With what money? We've been through this." What would we do when Lucca found us? Dario found Posy Santoro. It didn't even take him that long, and when she ran, she had a head start.

"We could kill him. Poison his spaghetti."

I roll my eyes. "I kind of feel like that'd create a whole new host of problems."

"I'd do it for you, big sister."

"You'd poison a man's spaghetti?"

"Hell, yeah." Mattie's mouth curves up in his trademark elfish smirk.

"Tell me who did that to your face, and I'll kill him."

Mattie drops his attention back to the flower binder, tracing the outline of arrangements I printed off Pinterest and stuck in a plastic sleeve. His nails are filed like mine. Perfect ovals.

"You do enough for me already, Z."

"What do I do for you these days?" It was true before I left for college, but I haven't been able to do much these past four years. I comforted myself that that would change when I married Paul.

Deluded myself.

"Well, you're making me spaghetti."

I want to make Mattie promise that he'll be careful. That he won't take risks. He won't go anywhere alone with anyone. I want to tell him the world is out to hurt him, and people are cruel, but he already knows, and that's not how our pact works.

So I rinse the pasta in a cheap wire colander and serve him a big plate smothered in sauce. He slurps the strands up just like he did when he was a kid and he'd only eat his noodles buttered.

I take the other seat and finish the carton of strawberries to keep him company, watching him, worrying, smiling as I flip through the flower binder and ramble about in-season blooms and color palettes.

God, how much I used to care about those things. Well, I used to think about them a lot so I didn't think about other stuff. And that wasn't years ago. It was last week.

Damn.

I should expect him, but when the door suddenly opens and Nicky stalks in, kicking off his shoes, I startle. Mattie drops his fork with a clatter.

Nicky takes in the scene and freezes for a moment before he drops his keys and shrugs off his jacket, snapping it once to get out the invisible wrinkles. He can't hang it on the back of his chair. Mattie is sitting there.

Even though Nicky doesn't step toward him, Mattie hops up, babbling about it getting late, homework, being full. He pats his nonexistent belly.

"It's okay," I tell him. "You're fine."

Nicky doesn't say anything. He crosses to the kitchen, opens the fridge, and there's a click as he unscrews the cap on the milk bottle, and a quiet glug, glug, glug as he swigs it down.

Mattie and I stand next to each other and stare.

Nicky recaps the milk, replaces it, and wipes his mouth with the back of his hand, sighing.

"I'll drive you home," he says to Mattie.

"Oh, no—"

"You don't have to." Mattie and I speak at once.

"I'll call him a ride share." I go for my phone.

"Yeah, it's no problem." Mattie's voice is painfully casual. "That's how I came."

"No. I'll take you." Nicky spears Mattie with his cold, black gaze, letting the mood grow more and more fraught until Mattie squirms. Then, Nicky lifts an eyebrow. "You've got no problem letting me help you out, do you?"

Mattie drops his gaze and shakes his head.

"Good." Nicky grabs his keys again and slides his shoes back on. "Come on." He claps Mattie on the shoulder and holds open the front door for him.

I reach for Mattie's forearm, but I'm too slow. Nicky's already escorted him out and down the hallway. The apartment is silent again except for the plink of water drops in the sink from the faucet I didn't turn off all the way.

I cover the pasta with plastic wrap, spoon the sauce into a bowl, store it on an empty fridge shelf, and then pick at my thumbnail skin for the next forty-five minutes until Nicky walks back through the door.

Shoes. Keys. Jacket.

I'm on my feet, my face draining. Nicky looks unruffled. That's good.

He scans the kitchen. "Did you put the food away?" He sounds markedly disappointed.

"Mattie" is all I can say.

"What about Mattie?" Nicky says.

"You took him home?"

"I said I would."

"But you did?" I don't know why panic is beating in my chest now. If he was going to do something, it's already done. And I let Mattie go with him. Why? Why am I panicking now that it's too late?

He exhales a short breath, and after a beat, he says, "Where's your phone?"

I gesture at the counter where it's charging.

He taps it a few times, it rings, and Mattie's voice comes through on speaker. "Z? You okay?"

"Tell her you're fine," Nicky says to him.

"Z? I'm fine," Mattie says. "Are you?"

"Yeah." My voice comes out strangled. "I'm sorry. I'll talk to you later. I love you."

"Okay, Z." He says it like I'm being crazy. Maybe I am. My natural instincts are fried. I've been fucking my stalker who's forcing me to marry him. I *am* crazy.

Nicky ends the call, and he eyes me from the other end of the table. "Can we eat?"

"What? Oh. Yeah." I move on numb feet to the kitchen, unwrap the pasta and sauce, and take out a clean plate. Nonna would be horrified, but I see no other way but to reheat the noodles in the microwave.

Nicky pours himself a glass of milk and seats himself at the head of the table, face unreadable, watching me ladle pasta and sauce, punch buttons, pluck a stray noodle from the counter and flick it off my fingers into the trash. There's a light in his dark eyes. Anticipation.

The microwave beeps.

"You're wearing my shirt," he says as I place his plate in front of him. I return to the kitchen for utensils. His gaze darts between me and his spaghetti.

"I got sauce on it." I plunk down a fork and knife.

"I see that." A small grin plays at the corner of his mouth. "Sit with me."

"I already ate." I make to leave, but his steel forearm hooks me around the waist, dragging me into his lap. He holds me there while he swirls spaghetti around his fork.

When it hits his mouth, he moans, and then it's like I don't exist. His hold on my middle doesn't loosen, but he's one hundred percent fixated on his meal. Like the other night, he conveys the food to his mouth in a way just shy of shoveling.

At one point, he mumbles *'s good* through a mouthful, but otherwise, he's all business.

He eats like he's not sure where his next meal's coming from.

Oh.

Yeah.

I get why he does.

I crane my neck back, trying to make out his expression, but I'm too close. I can only see his sharp jaw working, his hooded eyes closed to drowsy slits. He looks as blissed out as he does when he's inside me.

I reach up to graze his cheek with my fingertips—I'm not sure why. He grunts, grabs my hand, and tucks it back to my waist. I guess no one's getting between him and his microwaved spaghetti.

"You know, I can make pasta from scratch."

That catches his attention.

"My Nonna taught me." I use her Mercato Atlas. Well, I did. I haven't made it in years. Not since Paul cut carbs too. "It's easy. Semolina, eggs, olive oil, and salt."

He hums. Interested.

"The pasta maker is at my mom's." She let me take it to college, but when I moved back, I put it back where Nonna kept it. I wonder if it's in one of the boxes that Mattie hasn't brought over yet.

"She's getting rid of my stuff. That's why Mattie came over." I gesture at the crate. His gaze flickers up, but not for long. He's a man who likes to keep his eye on his plate.

"Good thing you've got all this room." I don't know why I'm telling him this, or why I sound sorry for myself. "She was helping me out anyway. I could have sucked it up and gone back to the barista thing. Gotten my own place until—you know."

Until Paul started med school, and we got married, and I rescued Mattie with the power of my pretty face, undemanding pussy, and unobjectionable personality.

I squirm. Nicky tightens his grasp, winding his fingers between mine, pressing our hands to the roll impervious to crunches that I can't suck in, not sitting like this.

"I went on interviews, you know. I got some call backs for second rounds." I have no idea why I'm defending myself.

He grunts. He doesn't lose focus on his food, but I can tell that he's listening. He always listens.

"It's not like I was super-excited about any of the jobs. Maybe that's why I didn't get them." I don't know; I'm pretty good at acting interested.

Nicky makes an "um" sound in the back of his throat. It's muffled by pasta, but it sounds pretty noncommittal.

"The job market is a lot more competitive than people think. They're only desperate for workers in shit jobs."

He makes another "um." This is ridiculous. I'm lecturing a hit man about the economy like I know anything about it, or like he gives a crap.

His hold isn't easing up though, so I relax into his chest. "I didn't mind the coffeeshop. I mean, I wouldn't want to do it forever, but until I figured stuff out, it was fine."

But I had figured stuff out, right? Paul was the plan. Marriage. Moving. A fresh start in a new place. What's wrong with wanting that?

"Why do you want to get married?" I ask.

Nicky takes his time swallowing the last bite of pasta. He shifts back in the seat, tilting me a little more against his chest.

"Is this what makes you happy?" I nudge his clean plate. "You want a housewife?"

He fiddles with the bottom button of the dress shirt I'm wearing, slipping the plastic through the hole and back again.

For a minute, I think he won't answer, but then he says, "Yeah, this makes me happy."

He leaves the button undone and starts playing with the next one. I shift so his erection isn't poking directly against my spine, draping my legs over his so my heels bump against his shins.

"Why?"

I feel his shoulders lift.

"Hot food. Hot woman." He pops the button, and impatiently goes up the line until the shirt's hanging open. "What the fuck is this?"

He fingers my crocheted top, crestfallen. I smother a smile. "My shirt."

"Why are you wearing a shirt under a shirt?"

"You mean like an *undershirt*?"

He pokes a finger through a gap in the stitches and wiggles it. I squeak and bow backward.

"Why are you wearing a sweater? It's eighty degrees."

"It's not a sweater. It doesn't have sleeves."

"No?" He slides the blue dress shirt off my shoulders to my elbows, revealing my bare arms. "I guess it doesn't." His lips brush my skin as he speaks, sending shivers down to the tips of my fingers and up to the nape of my neck.

His hand slides under my top, over the belly I'm holding in, to cup my breast. He strokes my lace covered nipple with his thumb, and I jerk, the sensation too much, but he doesn't let me go. He gently squeezes, molding me with his palm.

"You know what's going to make me happy?" he murmurs into my ear.

I tense, grabbing his outer thighs like they're the edge of a rollercoaster seat, excitement swirling in my stomach. My body is already conditioned to him.

"We're gonna get that thing inside of you out, and I'm gonna put a baby in here." He palms my pussy, hard, and then slides his hand to my lower belly, gently. "And you're gonna get fat with our child, and you're gonna be even more beautiful, and you'll know it."

Cold terror trickles through my chest like it always does when I think about my body swelling, not being able to stop it no matter how hard I work out, and the fear mingles with the heat Nicky's stoking in my heavy breasts and aching pussy as he kneads me and slips a finger past the gusset of my panties to stroke my wet folds.

I'm so fucked up.

"But that's the future," he goes on. "After."

"After what?" My voice is unsteady, almost strangled.

"After you have all the shit you want from those books." He nods toward the binders.

"I don't really want any of it," I say and realize it's true.

"What do you want, then?" He works my pussy with two wet fingers while his other hand plays with my breasts, hyper-focused, hungry. I grab my ankles and arch my back, toss my head back on his shoulder, shameless, short-circuited by everything that's wrong with me intersecting with everything my heart is desperate for, everything I want juxtaposed with everything I can never have.

"Tell me." He finger fucks me harder, nips my earlobe with his even teeth. "Come on, Zita."

It's a dare.

Tell him.

Trust him.

That would be insane.

"You tell me," I pant. "What do you want?"

"You." He doesn't hesitate.

"Why?"

"I'll tell you if you tell me." He's nailing the spot, the one I had no idea I had until he found it.

I'm whining, bearing down on his hand, wishing the cock thick and hard against my ass was inside me, wishing he'd shut up and stop looking at me, stop *seeing* me.

I drop my heels, raise up on shaking legs, and twist to fumble with his belt buckle. His dark eyes are hazy, his reflexes a touch slow, so I've got his zipper down and his cock out before he can lift me back onto his lap, and he's too late. Before he can recapture my hands, I've got my shorts and panties off, and we're skin to skin.

"Quit avoiding the question," he says, breathless, trying to grasp me by the hips and pin me in place.

I don't know what I really, really want. Right now? I want the thing he does to me, how he mutes the ugly shit in my head, takes it all away.

I wriggle, slip free from his grip, and while he's trying to tuck me back against his chest, I spread my legs over his lap, grab his cock through my straddled knees, and grip him at the base while I sit back and impale my pussy with his hot, thick length.

He groans. "Fuck, Zita."

Now, I let him grab my hips and help me rock up and back, balancing precariously on his thighs while I brace myself on the edge of the table, rattling the fork and knife laying across his empty plate.

He stretches me, fills me, and like he knows what I need, his raspy fingers find my clit and circle it, brushing the exquisitely, agonizingly sensitive nub just the slightest bit, just enough to drive me out of my mind.

I want more. I elongate my spine and fuck my pussy with his cock, digging my knees into his thigh muscles for leverage, scooting the chair across the floor with a creak.

He leans forward, holding me still with one arm while he sweeps the plate aside, and then he lays me down on my front, lifts my right knee onto the table, and fucks me, deeper, faster, until I'm so sweaty that my breasts slide along the wood.

He's not touching my clit anymore, and I'm stuck teetering on the edge, and it feels so good, and I'm so fucking frustrated, and I don't want it to end, don't ever want him to stop, but still I fight him, kick my legs, duck my hips, try to make room to touch myself, to make him remember what I need.

"Ask me," he growls, his voice vibrating against my shoulder blade.

"Touch me," I beg.

"Like this?"

I sob as his fingers find me again, and I pinwheel into outer space, mind blank, muscles melting.

"I'll always give you what you want," he says, breathless in my ear, his weight covering me. "Just ask. Always."

He stands, and before I can push myself up, he scoops me into his arms, shaking and jelly-boned, and carries me out of the kitchen, down the hall, and into our room, kicking the door shut with his heel.

He lays me on the bed, and I settle, languid, humming with what comes next, the hours as he makes me come until I pass out, as he magically turns my body into something I don't hate, something soft, but lovely, full and flushed, but content.

He doesn't follow me down. Not right away.

Instead, he stands at the foot of the bed, unbuttons his own shirt, tosses it onto the closed lid of the hamper, peels off his white undershirt, balls it up, pitches it after, looms there, muscles rising with the swell of his breath, black eyes burning—for me—and he swallows, his mouth opening once, twice, before he finds the words he wants to say.

"A house. A dog, if you want. A cat."

He pauses, scrubs his neck.

"A big yard. Pictures on the walls. One of those swings on the porch."

I struggle to my elbows. What is he saying?

"Whatever you want, Zita."

The words dance on the tip of my tongue. The room is so quiet. He waits, so patient, listening, so intently.

What do I want?

I want to be able to say no.

I want to be so strong that I never have to smile again, or look pretty, or worry that somehow, I'll drop the ball for a second—a split second—and somehow *let myself go.*

I want to be so strong that no one can ever hurt Mattie, nothing can ever destroy me from the inside.

Strong enough to control my brain.

So my brain never ends up in chunks in my brother's hair.

But yeah. I guess a dog would be nice.

He's waiting. Listening. Watching. Trying to read my thoughts.

I lower my back to the mattress. Close my eyes. Bend my knees. Spread my legs. Stick my middle finger in my mouth, suck it, swirl it against the insides of my cheeks, and then slide it in my pussy, sidling my feet further apart, making sure he can see everything.

I'm still slick with his cum, so it goes in easy. He groans my name through gritted teeth.

With my free hand, I cradle my tit, moaning, and that's all it takes. The bed frame creaks with his weight, he bats my hands aside, and he shoves his cock inside me, taking over.

It feels good. Eventually, the words dissolve, the impossible recedes, and I lose myself in his touch.

I win.

Can't trick me.

I haven't forgotten who the enemy is.

And in the back of my head, so faint, so hesitant that I almost—almost—don't hear it over the roar of mindlessness I'm hurtling towards, a voice whispers, "It's me, isn't it?"

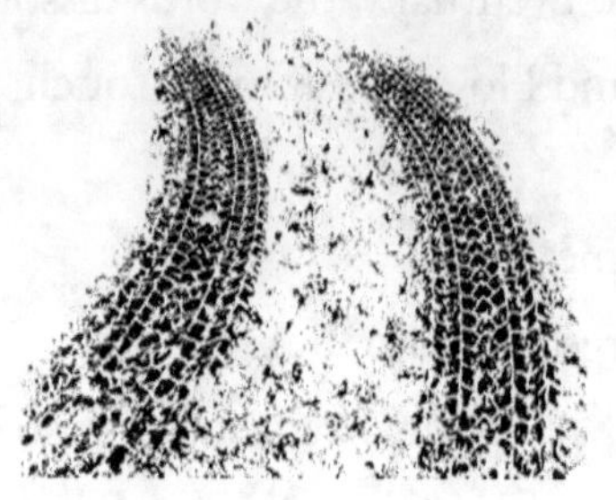

CHAPTER 8

Nicky

Zita's pretending to sleep again when I head out in the morning. She was restless last night. She kept trying to roll away, getting up to pee. Does she have a UTI?

We've been fucking a lot. My dad's girls would bitch about them all the time. I should pick up cranberry cocktail on the way home. And what was it she said? Semolina, eggs, olive oil, and salt.

I've got an errand to take care of first, though. Luckily, Lucca doesn't have anything on my schedule for the day. I drive him and Tomas to Dario's out in the 'burbs, and they're cool with Ray driving them back when they're done with whatever it is they do in that office.

Days like this, I usually hang with Ray or use the basement gym. Being a button man is a lot of hurry up and wait. If my envelopes are thick enough, it's fine by me. I prefer to be driving, but I'm not the type that needs to be busy.

I duck out in time to make the dismissal bell at Saint Celestine's. When Mattie sees my car, at least he doesn't try to bolt. That would be embarrassing for us both.

His shoulders drop, and he slows down. I pull over and push the passenger door open. He slinks in, kicking his backpack into the footwell. His face looks worse. That's how it tends to go—bruises look worse before they look better.

He sighs real loud so I know exactly how he feels.

"Put your seatbelt on," I tell him.

He does it, but grudgingly. It cracks me up how much he's like Zita was at his age. Same expressions, mannerisms, the way they don't say shit, but you can read their eyes perfectly.

He huffs, tossing back a thick lock of hair that's lost its gel during the day. It's almost too long to keep slicked back. He's going to be breaking dress code soon.

"You ready to tell me who did it?" I ask.

He glares straight ahead. I hide my smile.

"I'm gonna find out," I say.

When he called me, it was already over. He'd left the club, and he was hiding in the women's room at an all-night diner, scared to come out because he'd cried off his makeup.

"I didn't know him," he says.

"Bullshit."

Just like Zita, I know when he's hiding shit from me.

"I don't want you to kill anyone." He folds his arms, hiking his chin.

That's a difference between the two of them. Mattie has never had any doubt as to what I'd do for him.

"I won't kill him. Just fuck up his face."

Mattie presses his lips together so I don't see the wobble. "I thought we were done. You've got Zita. I'm out."

"Then why'd you call me?" I ask.

He blinks and turns to look out the passenger window. It's strange to see him like this. Tan slacks. A man's hoodie unzipped over his blue collared shirt with the Saint Celestine's emblem on the pocket. He looks washed out. Jumpy. Like a hostage.

Ironically enough, my deal with Mattie started because of that rosary. I was trying to open Zita's locker when everyone else was in class. I'd seen two of the three numbers, and I thought I might be able to luck into the third before I got busted.

It just so happened that Mattie was taking the long way back from a bathroom break, and he noticed me. To his credit, he started out by trying to kick my ass, but when I got his arms pinned in like three seconds, he decided to negotiate. The last number for twenty bucks.

At ten years old, he already knew to start high. I talked him down to ten.

I figured it was a once off until a few weeks later, he came up to me in the hallway and demanded another ten to keep his mouth shut about the locker. I convinced him to take five for telling me what brand of shampoo Zita used. I fucking loved that smell, and it wasn't any of the bottles at the pharmacy.

From then on, every so often, we'd make a deal. He had a line he wouldn't cross. He never told her secrets, not that I asked. I'd always hang out for a while after dismissal, leaning against the red brick wall behind the statue of Mary standing on top of the world, her foot crushing a snake. Sometimes Mattie would find me there.

Sometimes, he'd tell me some shit that a kid said to him. I sorted that out. Or sometimes it was a teacher or the bitch who worked in the office at the front desk. That I couldn't help him with.

Sometimes he asked me if I wanted to see a picture on his phone, candid shots of Zita goofing around the house, or the two of them with their faces done up the same. Other times, he asked me for cash.

Once, he asked me how I knew what I was. I didn't know how to answer him.

After I graduated, we mostly texted, except when he needed a ride. Mixed with the memes, and the occasional plea to Venmo him twenty, and the pics of him and Zita at the pumpkin patch, the summer carnival, the promenade, there were selfies. When he was younger, goofy faces with animated stickers of deer in sunglasses and shit like that. Then, when he got older, filtered pics with his hair brushed out and curled. His eyebrows plucked. His eyes done.

But he's never told me his secrets, and I don't ask.

When he started sending full length selfies where he's dressed for the club, I bought him a compact .45 and took him out to the old dump on 98 where my grandfather taught me to shoot.

A man is going to do what he's going to do. I guess a woman is, too.

"You can tell me, you know." I'm careful to keep my eye on the road. I'm taking the long way.

Mattie snorts. "You couldn't handle it."

I'd meant that he could tell me who hit him. I *will* find out. I bet what I need to know is on his phone. But I guess he took me to mean something else.

I cough. "I can handle it."

He laughs, bitter, but also so much like Zita. "Right. Sure."

I glance over. His arms are crossed so tightly, his hands clasping his elbows so hard that his fingers blanch. It's a cool day. Overcast. I turn the heat on.

"Better?" I ask.

He sighs and relaxes a little into the seat. "You are so fucking weird."

It's true.

"Want to do the drive-through?" I ask. He likes strawberry shakes. Or he used to. He's changed a lot this past year.

He rolls his eyes. "The machine's always broken."

"Want to go anyway?"

"Well, yeah." His lips curve, and there he is. My partner in crime.

I do a U-turn, and Mattie begins to fiddle with the radio until he finds the most garbage Top 40 station. I exhale, loud, and that makes him smile so his teeth show.

"If Zita doesn't want your crazy, stalker ass, can we still have this?" he asks.

"Yeah."

"Big brother?" he says.

"Yeah." He first called me that when I picked him up soaking wet and wasted at a convenience store all the way in Shady Gap.

"You can call me Maddie-lynn. Maddie for short," he says, looking out his window. "Maddie with a 'd' instead of a 't.'"

I know I have to be careful now. No sudden moves. "Maddie-lynn," I repeat.

"Maddie sounds exactly the same, doesn't it?"

"Yeah."

"But it's not."

"Yeah."

"Just when we're alone. For now."

"Okay." I clear my throat. "What about, uh— Do I say 'she' now?"

He licks his lips exactly like Zita does when she's buying time. "Yeah. When we're alone."

"Okay."

Mattie—Maddie-lynn—reaches for the dial and flips it back to my station. "Better, square?"

I grunt. "Much."

We're silent until we pull in the line at the drive-through. Maddie-lynn waits until we're almost to the speaker. "You don't have to worry about the asshole who hit me. I fucked him up."

The car in front of us moves. The truck behind us honks.

"What happened?" He—she—wouldn't tell me last night.

"The guy was just a creep. He got handsy. I guess he figured I wasn't down to scrap."

"But you won?" I inch forward in line.

"Oh yeah, I won." He—she—smiles.

A crackling voice asks what we want. I order the extra-large.

And she leans back in her seat, folds one leg over the other, and says, "Fries, too, please."

I order the fries, and after we get our order and we're pulling away from the window, I ask, "Did I do that right?"

"Well, you didn't totally fuck it up," she says, smiling.

"First time for everything," I say.

And she laughs with her mouth full of fries.

CHAPTER 9

Zita

Nɪᴄᴋʏ ᴅᴏᴇsɴ'ᴛ sᴇᴇᴍ ᴛᴏ have days off. He has put on a suit and left every morning since I got here, so when a random Thursday rolls around, and for the first time, I wake up before he does, I'm uneasy.

I roll onto my side and watch him for a change. He sleeps like the dead, flat on his back, eyelids twitching but otherwise still. Paul looks younger in his sleep—a lot of people do—but not Nicky. Nicky looks like a cyborg put in stasis to recharge.

I can't decide if that's what he is, some kind of psychopath who doesn't have human feelings, or if he's figured out how to hide his true self completely. Either way, I'm jealous.

When he wakes up, he blinks, but his expression doesn't change. He sits straight up. No stretching, no yawning.

"What time is it?" he asks.

"Ten."

He nods. "We'll have plenty of time," he says, getting up in one smooth movement and heading to the bathroom.

"For what?" I ask his retreating back.

"Date," he says.

"What?" I heard him, but even though I woke up a half hour ago, my brain is still sluggish.

"Picnic."

I hear him start to pee. He's left the door open. I flop back on the bed and stare at the ceiling. "Shut the door," I call to him.

The toilet flushes, and he comes back to lean against the door frame. "You see my cock all the time."

Like he summoned it, blood surges to my pussy, making me aware of how sensitive and raw I am between my legs. He's insatiable, and I—I don't say no. Sometimes I pass out after I come, and he's still inside me, but I don't turn him down.

Right now, out of the corner of my eye, I see that he's stroking himself, considering me on the bed. I squeeze my thighs together and tug my nightgown down. He sighs. "I'll shower across the hall. You can have this one."

I'm surprised when he just leaves, but I seize the reprieve, scurrying into the bathroom and twisting the lock. I take my sweet time exfoliating and moisturizing and soaking the ache out of my muscles. By the time I finish with my hair, it's almost noon. Nicky is in the living room, patiently watching ESPN.

It takes me a second to realize why he looks so different. He's wearing jeans and an honest-to-God faded T-shirt. It's tight around the biceps and pecs, but it's not the kind that's cut to fit that way. It's just old and shrunken. The logo is a circle made of rainbow stripes with the outline of a palm tree and waves. Underneath, it reads *Seaside Park, New Jersey.*

He hears me, turns off the TV, and grabs a brown grocery bag and his keys from the kitchen counter.

"Where'd you get the T-shirt?" I ask.

He points to *Seaside Park, New Jersey.*

"Palm trees don't grow in New Jersey," I say as he opens the front door for me. I don't know why I'm being a bitch.

Lord knows I puked in a potted palm tree outside a bar in Seaside Heights the summer after senior year.

"Ain't my fault," he says, the corners of his lips twitching. He doesn't mind when I'm grumpy. I think he's just happy I'm talking to him.

The uneasy feeling grows, swirling around my stomach.

"We're going on a picnic?"

He grunts in the affirmative and calls the elevator.

"Where's the basket?"

He raises the brown grocery bag.

"So romantic."

He winks at me. My belly flutters. I fold my arms over my chest. Perhaps unwisely, I'm wearing a cream minidress with black dots and three-quarter bell sleeves. I did think to bring my wide-brimmed straw hat, but I hope we don't have to hike anywhere because my sandals aren't getting me far.

"You're dressed fine," Nicky says as we descend to the garage.

Sometimes it feels like he can read my mind.

Sometimes it feels like he's politely refraining from doing it.

The hairs on my bare forearms prickle.

He opens my car door, I settle in, and we're silent for the drive. As soon as we leave Pyle, I recognize where we're heading. The Wade Arboretum. It's a half hour outside the city on several acres of land donated by the Wade family in order to grease the wheels of some development deal a century ago. It's my favorite place.

As Nicky mentioned during Pre-Cana.

Did he follow me here? How many times?

I should be freaked out by that thought, right?

The day is so close to perfect, though. It's full-blown spring. The blue sky looks like paint, and busyness is in the air—buds busting open whenever you blink, birds rustling in treetops, the sun gently warming your winter-weathered skin.

There aren't many cars in the parking lot. Nicky gets a wool blanket from the trunk before he opens my door and helps me out.

I don't know whether it's the faint scent of honeysuckle on the breeze, my floppy hat, my big sunglasses, or Nicky at my elbow carrying our things, but I feel pretty. Light.

We follow the path along the hillside planted with azaleas in bloom, past the koi pond, through the grove of bur oak that folks have had planted in memory of loved ones. There's an old Victorian mansion by the gates that they've transformed into a museum with a greenhouse and gardens attached, but we head away from where the crowds are wandering—if you can call them that. It's the middle of a workday, so there are only a few retirees.

I love it here. Despite the pollen, I can breathe better.

Eventually, we get to the long lawn that slopes gently down to the Luckahannock where folks sunbathe and hangout. At the top of the hill are the huge Corinthian columns that used to decorate the front of the courthouse in Pyle before the building burned.

The columns are situated around a fountain with spiral paths for meditation winding between them. I've never walked it, but it's nice, made from all different kinds of stones smoothed into the same shape.

Nicky stakes out a spot midway down the lawn, as far as he can get from a couple doing tai chi and a guy reading in a beach chair. He lays out the blanket, and I kick off my sandals. He sits so his feet are on the grass, I guess because he doesn't want to take his shoes off. It makes sense. I've seen him sleep, but I've never seen him relaxed.

He doesn't move to take out whatever's in the bag, and I'm happy to leave dealing with that for later. The sun is sweet on my skin, stirring that tickly feeling in my stomach. I take my hat off and lie on my back, bending my knees. I can't see Nicky or the river, only the wide blue sky, and if I tilt my head backwards, the columns at the top of the hill.

For a while, we're quiet, and I'm lulled into a dopey laziness by the flow of the current. The river's wide, deep, and slow here.

When Nicky breaks the silence, I'm so chill, I don't even startle. "Why do you like it here so much?" he asks.

It has to be obvious, right?

But then again, I don't know—is it?

It's beautiful, but that's not why I like it. "I've never run into someone from the families here. I can't imagine I ever would. It's a different place."

He seems satisfied with the answer. He's quiet again for a while. I'm surprised when he says, "I like how everyone leaves it alone."

I push up on my elbows so I can see him.

"Everything's done nice, and no one messes with it."

My gaze slides past him to the lush green lawn, the grass mowed in immaculate stripes. I think about the walk to the house he grew up in, the cracks, the clumps of brown weeds.

He's resting his forearms on his knees, staring at the river, his crooked jaw tight.

"You followed me here."

His chin dips, a slight jerk.

"How many times?"

"When I could. When I knew you were coming."

How did he ever know I was coming? I never planned on it. I'd have a few free hours, the weather would be nice, and I'd bring my books and tell myself I'd study when I knew all I'd do was tan and daydream.

"How did you know?"

He coughs and takes a breath before he answers. "If I was around, and you came here, I came, too."

"Around?"

He doesn't answer. His temple tics. He thinks I'm going to get mad, and I should, right? Absolutely. No doubt. I'm a broken mess, but I'm not stupid.

I shouldn't just be livid, I should be terrified. He's a stalker.

He's *my* stalker.

He's Nicky.

"Where were you?" I ask, glancing around. There aren't many places to hide. Of course, he wouldn't have had to. I thought I'd gotten away from the life clean for a few hours. I wasn't searching my surroundings.

He glances over his shoulder, to the columns at the top of the hill.

"You hid behind a pillar?"

"I didn't hide. Just sat up there. You never looked back."

No, I liked watching the river current, rushing like it has somewhere to go, and thinking dumb stuff like how it's like breathing, always the same, but never the exact same twice.

"You just watched me?"

"I brought a book."

"What book?"

"Whatever you were reading."

"I never actually read the books I brought."

"I know." His lips curve in a faint, wry smile. Mine soften.

"Why didn't you come talk to me?" It didn't happen a lot, but on occasion, a man would interrupt me, loom overhead and block my sun. I always said I was waiting for my boyfriend, and arboretum dudes were not the persistent type.

"You were happy. Peaceful. I didn't want to fuck that up."

I was.

"Did you actually read *The Sound and the Fury*?" I carried that book around the whole semester it was assigned, and I could never do it. I ended up taking a zero on that essay and squeaking by the course with a curved C.

"Yeah."

"What was it about?"

"Bad men doing bad shit. Women left to clean it up."

"I didn't miss anything then?"

"No." For a moment, he seems like the guys my age I met at college, confident and self-contained on first glance, but a little bashful, a little nervous under the cool. Words dance on the tip of my tongue. Take us away. Let's run. No more bad men. No more bad shit.

But then there's the poorly concealed, gun-shaped lump under his T-shirt at the small of his back.

He's not a dude who comes to the arboretum to read books.

His eyes darken as if he notices the shift in my mood. I bet he did track it. He knows my tells. If I wasn't so practiced at hiding my real self, he'd actually know me.

He tilts his head slightly, inviting me to say whatever it was he figures I swallowed.

"You sat up there when you watched me?" I nod at the columns.

"Yeah."

"Show me where exactly."

His brows draw together. I firm my jaw. He exhales, and unhurried, rises to his feet, slapping the thighs of his jeans even though they didn't touch the grass. He strolls up the hill, and when he gets to the top, he sits on the edge of the fountain, back straight, shoulders squared. Like he's braced for a fight.

He looks lonely.

He's looking down at me. I had been leaning on my hip to watch him climb the hill. I shift to my knees and rest my butt on my heels. He's several yards away. The shadow of a column falls across his face, so I can't make out the exact shade of his dark eyes, whether they're blazing like they do when he wants me or blanked like when he's holding his cards close.

He's repainting my memories. Now, I was never alone here. He was up there. Not coming closer because I was happy. Peaceful.

Sometimes I feel like he's a robot. An alien. And these days, sometimes, I feel like I could read his mind. Or that I'm restraining myself from doing it.

Because what if I look inside, and he's not a monster. What if he's not so different than me?

What does that make me?

The twirling, frenetic feeling in my chest—like panic, like being cracked open—sweeps away my train of thought, and I act on instinct. I push my sunglasses up, arch my back, and I let my butt sink to the ground, inching my knees further apart.

As his eyes track my every movement, I splay my fingers above the hem of my dress and curl them slowly, inching the fabric higher, not much, a quarter inch at most. No one could possibly see anything, not with the chub I can't work off my inner thighs.

Still, Nicky rises instantly to his feet and strides down the hill. Like I called him.

Which I did, didn't I?

The wild beating in my rib cage quiets, mellows, the closer he gets, the clearer I can make out his expression, the quirked corner of his mouth, his blown pupils.

He stops at the edge of the blanket, and instead of reaching for me, doing the things I can read in his eyes, he crouches and rummages in the brown paper bag. He takes out a carton of strawberries and a bottle of red.

"No champagne?" I ask.

"You like merlot," he says, pouring me a drink in one of those unbreakable stemless glasses made from space age plastic.

I do. If I'm wasting the calories, merlot gets the job done quickest.

He passes me the wine, plucks the stem from a strawberry, and hands me that, too. Then he pours himself a glass and settles beside me on his back, resting his head on his folded arms. He makes no move to touch me.

It takes me a minute to resettle myself, too. I nestle my wine in the grass, stretch my legs, and exhale. Nicky fumbles with something in his pocket, and then he lays an earbud on the blanket beside my head.

I turn to look at him.

"It's new," he says. "I haven't used these yet."

"Did you make a playlist for the picnic?"

He stares up at the cloudless sky. I tuck the earbud in my ear.

If the first song wasn't "Chiquitita," I might never have put it together, but that's mine and Mattie's song. I don't even remember where I heard it, but I loved it, and when he was little, I'd sing it to him as a lullaby or when he'd skin a knee. Later, I'd belt it out when we were alone, and he was in one of his moods. It was guaranteed to piss him off and get him off the sofa, at least to run away from me.

I twist my neck so I can see Nicky's profile. "What's the next song?"

Nicky blinks a few times like he's trying to remember before he says, "I don't remember."

"I bet I'm going to love it."

His jaw tightens. He knows I'm on to him.

"Did Mattie pick the songs?"

He jerks a nod.

My heart judders. "What did you hold over him?"

He snorts. "You mean, what did she hold over me? That playlist cost me a hundred bucks."

I'm halfway upright, hands fisted, blood pounding, when the word registers. *She*. I deflate flat on the blanket.

Abba harmonizes in my right ear.

My eyes prickle. "She told you?"

"Yeah."

"She never told me."

"She will." His voice is gruff.

My mind reels. "That's how you know about my hair products. The wine. Everything. *Mattie*."

"Don't be pissed. She's a kid. She would never tell me anything personal."

I don't have the bandwidth to be pissed. My brain's too busy clicking puzzle pieces into place.

"That Mancini asshole when he—she—was in seventh grade. That little shit who wouldn't leave Mattie alone, even after I talked to him, and then one day—poof. The kid wouldn't even make eye contact. That was you. You did that."

Nicky grunts. He's staring at the sky again.

"Mattie told you," I repeat under my breath. I don't know if it hurts, or if this feeling is gratitude, or if it's a mash-up of all the things I carry for Mattie—fear and pride and hope and desperation.

"Yeah. She wants to be called Maddie-lynn. Maddie for short."

"She asked you to call her that?"

"Don't be mad," he says. "She loves you."

I'm not mad. I'm past all emotions that are easy to define. All I can do is lie here next to this man—this stranger who isn't, not at all—and let the sun warm my skin until my muscles relax and my pulse slows.

I listen to a playlist of what turns out to be Mattie's—Maddie's—favorite songs while in the background, the river rushes, and every so often, I idly take a strawberry from the carton, pluck off its stem, and without thinking too much, nibble it bite by bite. And every other berry or so, after I get rid of the stem, I pass it to Nicky, and he pops it in his mouth whole.

I PLUNK A STEAMING plate of stuffed shells in front of Nicky, and before I set my own plate down, he's got a whole shell in his mouth. The ricotta is super-hot, so he kind of gasps for air to cool it, but it doesn't slow him down.

I've been feeding him.

For the past two weeks. Lasagna. Chicken piccata. Chicken marsala. Meatballs. Arancini. I made branzino, and never again. They kept looking at me. I get enough of that from Nicky.

A few days ago, I started getting up when he leaves the bed and making breakfast. Eggs and toast mostly. I cut up fruit and make parfaits with Greek yogurt.

I don't know this person.

I was usually responsible for feeding Maddie, but that was sandwiches and cereal. Occasionally, I'd cook for Paul at his place, recipes I found on the internet like zucchini pizza crust and sweet potato hash. I don't cook for myself. I assemble meals. Salads. Wraps. Smoothies.

When I'm good.

But I guess I remember more from helping Nonna than I would have figured. It comes back. Flattening rice in my cupped hand, not too thin, not too thick. Oiling my hands and balling the meat quick and gentle so it doesn't turn out rubbery.

I don't *touch* food. I don't spend time—hours—with it. I don't get the smell in my hair.

But if food is my kryptonite, it's Nicky's too.

When he's eating, forget about it, but afterwards, when he leans back in his chair or wanders to the living room to watch TV—

He's a different man. He doesn't watch me so closely. He'll glance at me once in a while, lazily, but he loses his intensity. He never quite relaxes; I never get the sense that he'd be slow on the draw if shit were to go down. And except for when he's sleeping or in the shower, he's always got his gun tucked in the small of his back.

So he's never not dangerous, but when he's flirting with a food coma, he's as close to disarmed as he gets.

I take advantage.

It's his fault.

He asked me what I want, and now it's clear as crystal in my mind.

Maddie's bruise is fading, and she seems no worse for wear—she's actually dropped by a few times conveniently around dinner time. She's not the least bit intimidated by Nicky. The other night, she speared the last meatball while Nicky was going for it, and Nicky muttered, "Watch your back, kid," and Maddie grinned, making a big show of chewing very slowly.

I want Maddie to grin all the time. I want her to live in her body in a way I never could. However she wants. In a place where no one says shit about it. And I don't know if that place exists, but it sure as hell isn't here.

We have to escape, so Nicky has to break us out.

This isn't new to me, using my body in service to the masterplan. Nicky's a different proposition than Paul—hell, he's a different species—but the basic tactics are the same. Give him what he wants. Make him believe I am what he thinks I am.

Paul was easier. With him, I never had to face what I was. There was a polite fiction. The high school girlfriend who followed him to college. The girl from back home. The one he was always going to marry.

When Nicky's on his last shell, I slide him one of mine. Even with double the spinach and only a dollop of ricotta—the way I made mine—they're at least two hundred calories a piece, round up to three hundred to be safe. I'm only going to eat one.

Nicky casts my plate a disgruntled look, but he doesn't turn the shell down.

With Nicky, there's no polite way to put it. I'm fucking and feeding my captor until he likes me enough to bust me loose. I think I'm supposed to feel ashamed. After all, a whore is the worst thing a woman can be, right?

But I don't. I feel like Mata Hari. The orgasms might have something to do with it. And the fact that even though Nicky has the gun and the muscle and the mob behind him, I can make him do things.

By asking.

I drop my napkin on my plate. "I don't feel like going to Pre-Cana tonight."

It's the third session. Last week's was boring as hell. Ava and Maddox didn't show—no surprise—and there were no games and no cookies. Deacon Dan was struggling with his allergies, so us ladies had to take turns reading aloud from the packet to help him out.

It's not a big deal. I could suck it up and go. But I want to see—

Nicky casts a regretful look at the empty casserole dish sitting on the stove. "We gotta go."

"I don't want to."

"They won't let you schedule the church until you get it signed off on."

"You can get Deacon Dan to sign off." I'm not suggesting that Nicky threaten the man or anything; he wouldn't have to. Deacon Dan's been around long enough. If he doesn't know exactly who Nicky is, he knows his type.

He sighs. "Zita."

He gazes at me, and I can read his dark, carb-dopey eyes. He knows I'm being a brat on purpose. He knows why, at least partially. He knows what I'll do to get him to fold. It excites him. I bet he's hard under the dinner table.

A thrum flutters to life under my breastbone.

He's still wearing his day clothes. A navy dress shirt with bright white buttons. Dark gray pants. He took his tie off with his jacket, tucking it in a pocket. The jacket hangs from his chair.

A pulse begins to throb between my legs.

"I don't want to go," I say.

His eyes glint.

"You can't make me." It's a dare, and he knows it.

His lip twitches.

"I don't like lying to them." It's true, as far as it goes.

Nicky's jaw tightens. He stands, his seat scraping the concrete. My heart pounds faster.

"No?" he asks, but it's not really a question. He's not waiting for an answer. He drags my chair away from the table and steps in front of me, one hand going to his belt, the other winding in my hair, forcing me to look up.

Arousal stokes a gush between my legs, soaking my panties. I squeeze my knees together. I'm wearing another sundress, thin, pale-yellow cotton, not thick enough to stop me from getting the wood wet.

"No." I don't blink.

There's a clunk—his gun on the table—and then I hear his pants drop, the buckle hit the floor. I clutch the skirt of my dress with clammy hands, my breath quickening.

I have no idea what I'm going to do.

"Open your mouth," he says, voice gravelly. I gaze up at his face, and slowly, I bite my bottom lip.

His lungs catch.

Softer, he says again, "Open your mouth." With his thumb, he strokes the indent that my teeth made.

I do.

His thumb slips between my teeth, swipes my tongue, drags my bottom lip down as he pulls it out, pushing my chin down, opening my jaw wider.

I let him, closing my eyes.

I taste him first, salty and warm. I have to tuck my tongue back to make enough room for him. He groans.

"Suck me," he says, his hand cradling my jaw, his thumb caressing the hinge that aches.

I do, taking him deeper, but not so much that I gag. He doesn't try to go that deep.

He takes one of my hands and wraps it around the base of his cock, his hand lingering on top, applying pressure, but not so much it crushes my fingers.

His other hand is still wound in my hair, tight, prickling my scalp, but he's not pushing me down.

I've given plenty of blowjobs before, when I had my period, or I didn't feel like having sex. I know how to stop my throat from closing up and what to do with my hands to get it over with sooner.

This is different. It's so quiet in the apartment, Nicky's ragged breath echoes.

I peek up. His head is tossed back, his Adam's apple prominent, his neck muscles straining. At some point he got rid of his shirt. His shoulders rise and fall along with the rosary beads and the crucifix, the angry scar along his right rib, the fainter marks marring his olive skin.

Behind him, his gun sits next to my plate.

The air smells like tomato sauce, and my mouth is filled with the musky taste of him, his hardness stretching my lips.

It'd be so easy for him to hurt me. Take too much.

My heart thumps double-time.

I let go of my damp dress and dig my nails into his bare thigh, pushing him away with all my strength, wrenching my head backwards. He almost, *almost* lets go quick enough, but not quite. My scalp twinges as I lose a few strands.

He stumbles back a step, chest heaving, face darkening.

"I don't want to do that anymore," I say, something inside me taking flight, wild and giddy and reckless.

He runs a hand through his thick, glossy hair.

He's not going to get mad. He's not going to force me or pout. I don't know how I know, but I'm utterly sure, and I can't wait to see what he does do.

He scowls at the brown hairs in his hand before shaking them onto the floor. Then, for a few seconds, he just considers me, naked, his cock bobbing against his abs, red and slick with my spit.

I'm tingling, inside, as the moment stretches, stretches—

In a dramatic swoop, he hauls me up and tosses me over his shoulder. I shriek. He claps a heavy hand on my ass and strolls down the hallway. My mostly empty stomach sloshes as I try to sort up from down. I've achieved nothing, my head still reeling, when he drops me to my feet, drags my dress over my head, and rips my panties apart, leaving me with nothing but a band of elastic and torn lace around my waist.

And then he moves so quickly, with such certainty, that I have no time to tell my own arms and legs what to do. He sits on the edge of the bed. Lifts me to straddle his lap. Lays back. Hauls me up his chest, lifts me, and settles me over his face, his hands gripping my hips in a punishing grasp.

I squeeze my knees together, scramble to back up off him, and he lets go of my waist long enough to spank my ass, hard, over and over as I grapple for his swinging arm, missing again and again.

"Quit being difficult," he says, gasping—we're both gasping—and he drags me onto his face again, this time not hesitating, diving into my slit with his chin, his nose, his tongue.

I slap at his hands.

He nips my clit with his teeth. But gently.

All my blood rushes between my legs. I whimper.

He lets go with one hand to grab a pillow and shove it under his head. He's saying something, God knows what, his voice is muffled, but the tone is coaxing. Demanding.

I inch my knees wider, wobbling. He steadies me, tilting his head back for air.

"You're okay," he says, his breath hot on my mound. "Come lower. Ride my face."

He licks my outer lips, nibbles their fat, swollen folds, and swipes his tongue along the inner lips that peek out.

"I'm going to smother you." I squirm.

"You hate me, remember?" he says. "Do your best." And he pries my thighs further apart, and I lose balance, sink down, my pussy splaying for his hungry, relentless mouth.

His hands glide to cup my ass, urging me on, to rock, grind, get myself off on his beautiful face.

I do. Oh, God. I chase the high, shove my clit between his lips, bearing down, riding his mouth like I don't care if he lives or dies. I come with a scream, thighs shaking, head tossed back, back arched—like a queen.

I'm grinning when he flips me onto my back, throws my legs over his shoulders, and drives his cock into my still spasming pussy, his faintly stubbled cheeks wet with my juices. I come again, soaring and then floating down like a feather, as he finishes inside me, grunting, jacking his cock so hard it bangs my cervix, and I wince. He grunts an apology and flops on his back at my side.

He didn't turn the overhead lights on, and the room's getting dark.

"Too late to go now," I mumble, stretching and pointing my toes.

He laughs. Not much. A few deep chuckles.

I roll so I can see his face. His eyes are closed as he catches his breath. He's less intimidating like this, in the dimness, his hair mussed, no suit, no polished shoes. Just a body. A strong one that's been through some shit, yeah, but a body like mine, like anyone's.

I reach over and trace the ugly pucker along his right rib. "Is this a bullet wound?"

His eyes blink open, but otherwise, he doesn't move. "Yeah."

"How'd you get it?"

He moves now, punching the pillow back into shape, propping an arm behind his head. Buying himself time. Probably deciding whether he's going to tell me the truth. And how much.

"The deal was that I protect Posy. I put myself in front of her. When shit went down."

"When Lucca took out Renelli?"

Nicky jerks his chin. When they killed my father and Frankie Bianco and Joey Zito.

"Did you shoot my father?" I ask.

"No."

"Who did?"

"I don't know."

"What was the deal? Posy for what?" I know, but I want to hear him say it. I want to see his face as he confesses.

"If Posy lived, I got you."

I rest my fingertips on the scar. I can feel his heart beat against my palm. His face is somber. Wary. For a split second, before he forces them to relax, his hands clench at his sides.

I spread my fingers so they cover more of his chest. I curl them, let my nails prick his tan skin. His pecs jump, his abs tensing into sharp ridges.

"You didn't make a deal with me," I say.

"Do you want to?" His voice rumbles.

"Maybe." This is when I ask—save us. Take Maddie and me so far away that they can never find us, keep us safe, help us make a whole new life, nothing like this one, better than anything we're even able to imagine.

I'll give you—

What?

What do I have that I haven't already given up?

My eyes burn, and my nose itches. I fall to my back and exhale.

"Change your mind?" he says.

I don't answer.

We lie side by side as the room grows dark, wide awake, not strangers, not lovers, not enemies.

Not brave enough, but not such cowards that we turn our backs to each other. We fall asleep inches apart, the sound of our breath breaking the silence, the heat of our bodies keeping the chill away.

DEACON DAN AGREES TO sign our Pre-Cana papers, but he strongarms us—well, Nicky—into coming by the Saint Celestine's Spring Carnival. When I was in school, the carnival was a huge deal. It was always the third weekend in May, and the drama stirred up there usually lasted the rest of the year.

I haven't been since I graduated. My last carnival, I was assigned to work the "kissing booth" with the rest of the prom court. It was a variation of a spinning prize wheel where winners won chocolate kisses instead of the cash laid down—'cause that would be gambling.

It was basically an excuse for every skeevy dude in the diocese to make inappropriate comments to the girls working the booth while bitching about losing their hard-earned money.

Usually, the whole community shows up, the dads high-tailing it to the beer garden while the women wrangle the kids, and the teenagers try to sneak off behind the old rectory.

I liked it when I was younger. Maddie would get so excited, and Mom and Dad would be too busy acting upstanding for the neighbors to cramp our style. I'd stuff him—her—full of cotton candy and caramel apples and boiled hot dogs and let her ride the scrambler as many times as she wanted.

I never minded watching Maddie. Never resented it. Taking care of Maddie filled up a part of me, blunted the bad shit—there wasn't time to worry about myself if Maddie needed a bath, a haircut, a bedtime story.

I called Maddie yesterday and asked her if she was coming this year. She said she'd be goddamned before she came willingly to Saint C's on a weekend. I suppose that's fair.

Mom will be here. Apparently, she's coming with Alonso Silvestri. We used to call him Uncle Al when he came over for dinner. He's not a real uncle, but he was one of Dad's good friends. As much as any of these men are friends to each other, I guess.

It's fine. Mom's taking care of herself. That's good. I can't worry about her, too.

Nicky wanted me to wear a dress, and I wasn't in the mood to mess with him, so I did. It's a blue paisley maxi dress with white espadrilles. It's close enough to Memorial Day if that's still even a rule.

I've almost asked Nicky to take us away a half dozen times. After I've fed him, after we've fucked. When he brought a bouquet of sunflowers home and then went out again to buy a vase since he didn't have one.

I always chicken out.

If—when—he says no, it's all over. I don't have another plan. I lose.

The weather is perfect today. Cloudless, bright blue sky, high seventies, a light, occasional breeze. We wander around, keeping an eye out for Deacon Dan. We play Skee-Ball, watch the high school Battle of the Bands competition for a while, check out the basket raffles.

Everyone's at least vaguely familiar. My dad's friends nod at Nicky while we pass. My mom's friends squeal and hug me, tapping their phones with their long nails to show me pictures of their daughters with their husbands and their new grandbabies.

Old classmates say hi to me, look at me to introduce them to Nicky. No one remembers him. Not even the nuns who've been teaching at Saint C's forever.

Thank God Paul isn't here. Nicky parked at the back of the field, so we walked past all the rows on our way in, and I didn't see his car. The DeStefanos always have a booth to sell pizza by the slice, but that'll be easy enough to avoid. They always put folks in the same spot.

There's an outside possibility that Paul didn't want to drive his precious baby through a muddy field, and he found street parking and walked, but I doubt it. Revisiting high school isn't his scene. He's always been about the next bigger, better thing.

Nicky and I don't go to the beer garden, so I don't run into Mom. Nicky's content to let me lead. He wants to buy me a candied apple, but when I say no, he doesn't push it.

I'm in a strange mood. It's a strange place, popping up every year, exactly the same, a literal walk down memory lane. The dart game where Maddie won the big prize, and she wanted the stuffed mermaid with sequin scales so bad that she cried until her snot ran—and she never cried—and to make people stop staring, I let her have it.

Dad found her playing with it on the back patio a few days later, smoothing the scales one direction and then the other, pink then purple, and Dad tried to take it. Maddie wouldn't let go. Dad dragged her across the bricks, calling her the ugliest names, but Maddie held on, and she didn't cry then, not until later when I dabbed peroxide on the scrapes.

I hid the mermaid in my room until I could throw it away. Maddie asked for it, and I told her I didn't know where it went.

The memory hits different now that I'm thinking of Maddie as "her." Even uglier. Even more brutal.

I don't know if she'd forgive me if I told her now what I'd done. She'd understand though. Violence haunted that house. You did what you had to do.

But would she forgive me for not being brave enough to let her take the risk? For choosing her safety over her happiness?

"Zita."

I'm so lost in the past that it takes a few seconds for my stomach to drop to the ground. Vaguely, I register Nicky's hand moving to rest on the small of my back.

"Hey, how are you?" It's Paul. With a funnel cake. And a woman. I've met her. She's in his study group. Becca. Skinny Becca who doesn't wear makeup.

She has a funnel cake, too. She has a mouthful. She's chewing. There's powdered sugar on her chin.

Paul puts his hand on the small of her back, too, and urges her forward. "You remember Becca Szymanski?"

Somehow, Nicky and I are face to face with them, do-si-do, spin-your-partner close.

Did I just blindly walk into this? I blink up at Nicky. His face is blank.

Paul's smiling expectantly at him, no recognition in his eyes. When neither of us say anything, Paul awkwardly transfers his white paper plate and sticks out his freed right hand.

"Paul DeStefano," he says.

Nicky shakes his hand. "Nick Biancolli."

The name doesn't seem to ring a bell with Paul either.

"Hi, Zita. Good to see you again," Becca says after she finally swallows. She dabs at her face with a thin napkin, laughing, self-deprecating. She turns to Paul. "Did I get it all?"

"Almost." He swipes her chin with his thumb.

Asshole.

Paul watches me closely, making sure I see how it is, his forehead furrowed like he genuinely cares how this news hits.

I twist Nicky's ring on my finger, my palms gone clammy, and suddenly, the sunshine's too bright. It hurts my eyes.

"Have you guys tried the funnel cake?" Becca says to fill the silence. "It's so bad, but so good, you know?" She offers me her plate. "Try some."

I can't even begin to guess how many calories are in that. A thousand at least. I've never had one. I would never put that in my mouth, eat something the size of a whole plate, get the sugar all over me. Not in public.

"No," I say. "Thanks."

Paul's brow furrows deeper, his obvious concern about my delicate feelings perfectly performed. Nicky glares at him, mouth drawn in a straight line, eyes dark and unreadable.

"I didn't see your car," I say. It sounds like a complaint, and I guess it is. I thought I was home free.

Paul's face and neck redden. "It was stolen. Can you believe it? Right off the street. Punks didn't even strip it. The cops found it in some lot down by the river, burned out."

The pain in Paul's eyes is real. Beside me, Nicky barks a short cough. For a second, the oppressive awfulness of the moment lifts, allowing my lungs to inflate and oxygen to flood my brain.

Nicky stole Paul's car and lit it on fire. That second night when I was so scared of him, and he came home smelling like smoke and gasoline. I wish I'd been there. I wish I'd lit the match.

Then, maybe because she sees a spark of life flare in my eyes, Becca steps forward and winds her arm through Paul's, staking her claim. Like she's the one who's come to this carnival with him every year since junior high, like they'd cut the opening ribbon together senior year, like she's always belonged exactly where she is—a brilliant medical student just like him, physically fit without trying like him, happy, with the kind of easy confidence that comes when you've never known real fear.

The awfulness crushes my lungs again, twice as heavy.

"How have you been doing, Zita?" Paul asks as he snuggles Becca closer to his side, balancing his paper plate in his free hand, so serious, so sincere. "I've been thinking about you."

I want to slap his funnel cake into the matted grass. Shove his face in it.

I ignore his question and ask one of my own. "How long were you fucking her before we split?"

It's funny. There's a good two or three seconds before what I said registers, when we're all looking at each other to the background noise of the grinding Ferris wheel, shrieking kids, and the bingo caller droning over a distant, crackling speaker.

Then, Becca grits her teeth. Paul draws in a deep breath. Beside me, the corner of Nicky's mouth twitches.

And a jolly voice rings out, "Biancollis!"

Suddenly, Deacon Dan is clapping Nicky on the back, beaming at Paul and Becca. "Oh, my, funnel cake. I haven't gotten mine yet. The wife has me limited to one. But what she doesn't know can't hurt me, right?"

He laughs. Paul and Becca chuckle politely. Nicky's face is inscrutable again.

"And how are you doing this fine afternoon, soon-to-be Mrs. Biancolli?"

Paul's smile fades. He looks at my hand where I'm still twisting the sweat-slick ring. His eyebrows rise to his hairline.

He never did like to be one-upped. I never did it, of course, but if one of his buddies did better on an exam or got some kind of accolade he was angling for—he'd always have to talk about how they had some kind of advantage, and good for them, he was happy for them, truly, really, just— Rinse. Repeat.

Did I even like him?

I did, right? Or I wouldn't be so angry now. So hurt. I liked his ambition. How things seemed to unfold exactly the way he planned them. How he ate to live, he didn't live to eat, and if he said that incessantly, and I wanted to vomit every time, that was on me, not him.

I loved him. He made my heart race, in the beginning, and we were partners, too, for such a long time. But we haven't been partners for a long time, too. When did it change?

How long was I using him and not the slightest bit sorry for it?

Who am I really angry at?

My brain is buzzing, and Deacon Dan is going on and on, turning his high spirits on Paul when I don't answer and Nicky only grunts. When Deacon Dan learns that Paul's parents own Italiano's Pizza Grille, it's on. He's a fan. I figure we'll be here for a while.

But then Becca, out of nowhere, lays a hand on Deacon Dan's forearm. "Now you've got me craving a slice of pepperoni. Want to come with me? I've got the hook up. Free pizza."

She's met Paul's parents. They know her.

My stomach sours.

She turns her wide smile on Nicky. "Let's go get slices for these guys. Give them a minute alone to talk."

She oozes understanding and compassion, straight up *secretes* it.

Nicky shows no sign of budging. Deacon Dan is stoked to go, oblivious to the tension. Is the only way to get rid of him to send him for pizza?

I grit my teeth, and then I say to Nicky, "Can you get me a slice of cheese?"

He blinks, his lips tightening, a wrinkle creasing the skin above the bridge of his nose.

"Please," I say quietly, aware that everyone's watching us, that Nicky doesn't do what he doesn't want to do, that he's taking way too long to say sure.

Finally—finally—he asks, "Root beer?"

"Yeah," I answer quickly. "Yes. Please."

And without a backwards glance, he strides off toward the food concessioners, Becca and Deacon Dan hurrying in his wake, leaving Paul and me alone, surrounded by folks milling from ride to ride, licking ice creams, kids riding their parents' shoulders, stuffed animals stuck under the dads' arms.

Paul watches them go, and then he turns to me, puts his hands on his hips and slants them forward like he does when he's about to pose a question to you which he is prepared to answer himself, at length, ad nauseum.

"What are you doing, Zita?"

"Getting married." I stick up my ring finger.

"Who is that guy?" He doesn't wait for an answer. "You can't just rush from one relationship to another—thinking that's going to solve all your problems—without taking the time to work on yourself."

"How long have you and Becca been a thing?"

He sighs, exasperated. "That's different."

Please, please, I don't want to know how she's so fucking different than me. "Whatever. It's not your business."

"Zita, please." He grabs my hand, and for some reason, I leave it limp in his grip. "I care about you. I'll always care about you, no matter what."

He believes it. He's a good guy. Of course, he cares about me.

And for some reason, a memory pops into my head. Junior year. We'd just started having sex, and we were obsessed. A few hours here and there weren't enough. We wanted to sleep with each other, wake up in each other's arms. I told my parents I was sleeping at Jen Amato's. Paul snuck me into his basement, and we slept on the leather sofa in the freezing cold clubroom.

Somehow—I forget now—I got busted. When I got home, my father beat my ass while my mother cried over the sink, washing the same dish over and over. He said I'd better hope the pissant would marry me because no real man wanted used goods.

The beating wasn't too bad. I'd had worse. Dad left my face alone, and Maddie was somewhere else, maybe at one of my aunts'.

But that's not what sticks in my head now. It was the next day. After school. When we were clinging to each other in Paul's car, and I hissed. He insisted on looking. My side was black and blue from my father's shoe.

And Paul cared. A lot. He cried. He got himself all twisted up about what he should do. He *is* a good guy. It was so hard to convince him to leave it alone, he'd only make it worse, he didn't know who he was dealing with, and one day, we'd leave together, and it'd all be behind us. Nothing but a bad memory. It took a while before Paul stopped bringing it up, but he never said shit to my father.

Nicky would have killed him.

There's not a doubt in my mind.

And it has nothing to do with feelings, with love or obsession or whatever you want to call it. It's who they are. Paul is a good man, but I think Lucca Corso is right—Nicky is a weapon.

Paul's waiting for me to speak, his eyes brimming with emotion. He needs me to believe him. Absolve him.

He needs me to be the one who's hurt. The tragic mafia princess with the secret eating disorder. The proof that he's good and brave. Even now, this late in the game.

If we used each other, does that make it better?

Does it matter?

I'm searching for words when I see Nicky striding back to me, a flimsy paper plate in both hands. Deacon Dan and Becca are nowhere to be seen. I realize that Paul's still holding my limp hand, and I tug it loose.

The knot in my throat loosens. "Nicky went to school with us. You don't remember him?"

The concern in Paul's eyes turns to vague confusion.

Nicky returns to my side. I take a slice of pizza, fold it, and bite off the hot, cheesy tip. Twenty-five calories. Better double it for the grease I didn't dab off. Still, worth it to see the expression on Paul's face.

"Delicious." I take another bite. Beside me, Nicky inhales his slice. When he's done, I hand him the rest of mine. Nicky takes it with a grunt and polishes it off, staring Paul down, his expression hard. Menacing. Paul won't meet his eye.

"Ready to go?" Nicky asks me when he finishes the last bite of crust.

"Yeah. Bye, Paul." I don't wait for whatever he's working himself up to say, the resolution that he wants to nail down. If we could really be honest with each other, if we could really say what's in our hearts, I'd tell him that neither of us is good, and neither of us is bad.

We are how we were made, walking the path we've been given.

Trying to be brave when we're outnumbered, out-gunned, and fighting uphill.

All of us.

Including me.

I take the high road for a total of five feet before I catch sight of Becca waving to Paul as she makes her way back. She's unwrapping a candy apple.

I stop mid-step and turn back around. Paul quickly masks whatever he was feeling and puts on his "I'm listening" face. I look him straight in the eye, and for the first time in a long time, I don't bother putting on any particular expression at all for his benefit.

"I'm sorry about your car," I say. "What with the timing, I bet you thought I'd gotten one of my 'connections' to steal it and blow it up." I force a laugh.

He fakes a chuckle, but I can read his face like a book. The thought most certainly crossed his mind.

I wait—one second, two, three, four—and when I see the flicker in his eye, the realization that even if I'm telling the truth, there's not a damn thing he has the balls to do about it, I wink.

And then, I walk away.

CHAPTER 10

Zita

Nicky is agitated on the ride home. He keeps cracking the windows and fiddling with the rear and side views.

I'm restless, too. I tighten and re-tie the dress straps behind my neck, surreptitiously watching Nicky track my movements with his pitch-black eyes.

I'm not wearing a bra. My nipples pucker and chafe against the fabric. He's got the air conditioning going.

I'm unsettled. It feels like my perspective has irrevocably shifted, except it hasn't, or I came to some kind of conclusion, but I didn't. What's different now except that I know Paul's been boning his study buddy, and Nicky blew up his car? Neither of these are outside the realm of normal for men in my world.

I should be more pissed about Becca than I am, but she keeps floating into my mind and drifting out again when Nicky catches my attention.

His fingers move to undo another button on his collared shirt, and I get a peek of the black hair that's lightly smattered across his chest, which makes me think of running my fingers over his pecs, how soft the hair is, how taut the muscles are, how warm.

Which makes me think of him covering me, pushed up on his sculpted arms, staring down, his burning gaze darting from my eyes to my lips to my breasts, as if he can't bear to stop looking at me, and at the same time, he can hardly hold himself back from filling me with his cock.

The thought doesn't just turn me on because he's hot or because he wants me. It's deeper than that. I understand exactly what he's feeling when he looks at me like that. Not because I feel that way about him. Not yet. But because his craving speaks to something inside me. Not the ugliness that tries to drag me under but the longing that keeps me going, keeps me fighting, maybe down but never out.

I look at Nicky, and I think maybe, one day, he could understand me. I could *let him*. And the thought intoxicates me. It turns me on.

I part my lips slightly so Nicky can't hear that I'm breathing harder. I recross my legs, and my pussy lips slide together, making me squirm, so I uncross them and drum my freshly done acrylic nails on the door handle.

Nicky casts my drumming fingers a black look. Guess he's capable of being annoyed. I turn my head to stare out the passenger window.

Really, it's only natural that I should be falling for him. Nicky's amazing in bed. Sometimes I wonder how he got so good, but I don't want to know. There can't be a happy answer, no first love, no friend with benefits. Not from what I know of his life.

I shiver. For once, Nicky doesn't notice. At least he doesn't turn down the AC.

When we get to the garage, I'm so buzzing with this strange feeling that I hop out before he can reach my door. He's obviously not pleased that I don't wait for him, but he falls in step behind me as I make my way toward the elevator. I let him push the button, lead us down the hall, and unlock the apartment.

I get him before he gets his second shoe off, grabbing the front of his shirt and throwing him against the wall. Of course, I couldn't budge him if he didn't let me, but he does, eyes widening in surprise. I rip his shirt hem from his pants, smooth my palm up his chiseled, tensing abs, feel the slight tackiness of his skin from the afternoon heat.

With my other hand, I cup his neck, urge him down, rise on the toes of my espadrilles to find his mouth, kiss him, plunge my tongue past his teeth. For a second, his muscles stiffen, but then with a groan, his tongue twines with mine.

I let him go to untie my straps, let my dress fall in a puddle, shove his shirt up until he finishes it for me, tossing it on the floor. He goes for his buckle, but I beat him to it, chip a fingernail on the brass, ignore it as I jerk the leather through the loops.

My vision's hazy, my lungs tight, my blood rushing in my ears. I yank down his zipper, pull down his boxers with his pants, and when I have him naked, I grab his biceps and pull him away from the wall, down to the floor, and he goes where I put him like I made him out of clay. He watches me, even when our tongues are twining together, always watching me.

I lay him flat and drag his arms over his head.

"Don't move them," I pant, straddling him, hooking my panties aside with a finger while I seize his hot, hard cock in my fist, holding him up so I can sink down, moaning from the back of my throat. I ride him hard, my eyes screwed shut, until I come, shuddering, with a guttural scream, shameless, knees bruised by the brushed concrete.

He slams me down a few more times by my hips before he follows me over the edge, but he comes quietly, with a grunt.

When my eyes flutter open, he's glaring at me, hard, the black burning. He props himself up on an elbow.

I slip his cock out of my pussy and our combined fluids gush onto the taut skin between his hips.

"What was that?" His voice is cold but contained.

"Sex." I struggle to my feet, bending for my crumpled dress.

His sits up, wraps his muscular arms around his bent knees, and watches me readjust my panties and step into the dress, tying the straps yet again, hissing when I catch a strand of hair in the bow.

"Were you pretending I was him?" he asks.

"What?" I say, backing away, my voice too loud. "Of course not."

He rises to his feet in one smooth motion, and I'm reminded for the hundredth time how strong he is, how sure and stealthily he moves, how I'd be an absolute fool to let his seeming devotion convince me that he isn't a killer, that his obsession won't turn off like a switch at any moment, tonight, tomorrow, now.

I back further away, putting the kitchen island between us.

"You don't initiate," he says. It's an accusation.

I shrug a shoulder.

"What the fuck was that, Zita?" he asks again, stalking forward, biceps tensing, fists balling.

I back into the counter by the sink, hiding my trembling hands in the folds of my dress.

"If you didn't want it, you could have said no." My shaky voice doesn't match the words at all.

He braces his hands on the island, but at least he doesn't come around. I think he's staying away on purpose. He's angry. Like with the man on the street, his eyes flash, drilling into me like he's narrowing his aim. Like any second, he'll blow.

I can hardly breathe. The counter cuts into the base of my spine.

"You were holding his hand." He glares at my right hand like he'd happily cut it off. I drop it behind my back.

"It didn't mean anything." My survival instincts flare, and my voice comes out high and soft, pleading and weak, and I hate it.

"Like this didn't mean anything?" His voice is different. Cutting. Cruel. "Are you jealous? Is that it?"

"Why would I be jealous?"

"Because your boy Paul's fucking someone else. Because he replaced you like—" He snaps, and he's watching me so closely, like always, that he can't possibly miss how the words land. If I weren't used to cruel, cutting men, I'd flinch, but my skin is so thick, I can't feel it. I can only feel a wild rage worm up through my knee-jerk fear.

"No. Not at all. I want him to be happy. Because I *love* him." I watch my words fall, too, and if I hadn't spent these past weeks tuned into every twitch of Nicky's finger and shift of his eye, I would never have been able to tell the blow landed, square and hard.

"He was fucking her before I made you get rid of him."

"I figured that out." I don't even give him a second to be self-satisfied, thinking he got a hit in. I'll always be crueler to myself than anyone else could ever be.

His hands tighten on the edge of the island. "So you finally decided to use me like you used him." He lifts a shoulder. "I guess that's what I've been asking for. Be careful what you wish for, right?" He smiles wryly, and he so rarely smiles. It's crooked like his jaw.

It feels like a jagged claw slicing me open, neck to belly, right through my breastbone. I don't let my face react. I don't move an inch. I make my lungs work, in and out, and I keep my gaze leveled in his direction while I let my mind disappear like the tiny dot when my Nonna turned off her old black and white television.

What I was thinking earlier in the car? That's my delusion. Nicky Biancolli is nothing to me but my jailer. I'm nothing but a hostage.

He knows I'm gone, and his teeth clench, his muscles vibrating with frustrated rage. He stalks to the crate with my binders, dumps them onto the table, and begins to flip through clippings of wedding dresses, sneering at them, at me.

"How are you better than me, Zita?" he asks, flipping, flipping. "How are we different?"

I never said I was better. Not once in my life to anyone, never even thought it in my head. I'm not special. That's *his* delusion.

And I guess all it took to make him see the cold, hard truth was to want him back.

For the first time, I hate him. Really hate him.

"Does it even matter to you who you're fucking?" he asks, flipping back to a picture of a woman in a ballgown with yards of tulle. In the background, there's a blurred man in a tuxedo. He taps him, and then he flips to another picture of a smiling bride in a mermaid dress lounging on a chaise, the groom behind her, the image cut off at his neck.

My eyes grow hot.

"How are we different, Zita? Explain it to me." He shuts the binder and flings it across the table with disgust.

I can't. I can't form thoughts, let alone sentences, not when I'm holding the split sides of my chest together, keeping my guts from spilling out onto the floor.

"I guess you saw Plan A is well and truly fucked, so you decided to nail down Plan B." His temple tics. "I did ask for it." He draws in a breath. "And it's not as if I didn't know exactly what you were like."

He exhales, and with slow steps, he circles the island. I brace myself. When he comes toe-to-toe with me, he grips the back of my neck and steers me away from the counter, walking me toward the bedroom.

"It's getting late," he says. "You need a shower."

I don't fight. I haven't got any left. He leaves me in the doorway. I expect to hear the shower, but instead, I hear the clink of weights and then the whir of the treadmill. For a while, I huddle on the edge of the bed, shivering as the air conditioning kicks on, but I don't cry.

Not one single tear.

Eventually, I wander to the bathroom, wad up my dress and soiled panties, shove them into the trash, and climb into the tub, scalding my skin until it's pink and raw. I use the brush with the nylon bristles that scratch my scalp, pluck my eyebrows, and search my hairline for rogues.

Nothing's changed. Not really.

As I lie on the bed, curled on my side to stare at the wall, I feel a rush of gratitude that I wasn't stupid enough to ask Nicky to take Maddie and I away, and then, quick on its heels, a rush of bitter disappointment floods my aching, empty insides.

My pussy is sore, and my mouth is sour. I can't tell if it's my imagination or if the pizza from earlier is still sitting in my gut like a greasy rock.

I lie perfectly still, knees tucked to my chest, as the room turns from mellow gold to gray to darkness. The shower across the hall turns on and cuts off and the TV goes on. I drowse. There's a knock at the front door, and the smell of Chinese wafts into the room.

I jerk from a light sleep when the mattress dips. My phone on the nightstand reads midnight. Nicky doesn't say anything. I don't turn to look at him. I hug my knees tighter to my chest.

After a long while, he sighs. "I'm sorry," he says.

Squeezing my eyes shut, I wish I could stop myself from smelling his soap and feeling his warmth on my back.

I want to eat.

The cabinet is so close.

Rainbow sprinkle cupcakes. Chocolate peanut butter wafers. Jelly-filled crumpets.

In my head, I rip the cellophane apart, tear the seam, lick the plastic. I cram cake into my mouth. Shove it down. Suffocate all the shit, all the noise. Stuff my belly until it's impossibly full like how they say Renelli filled Uncle Arturo's guts with stones before he threw him in the river.

The kitchen is so close.

Just down the hall.

My heart pounds, and my palms sweat.

I stay very still until, almost an hour later, Nicky's breathing finally deepens. Carefully, I unfold my stiff legs and ease them over the side of the bed.

He shifts. I freeze, my pulse racing. I wait one minute. Two. Three.

I lower my bare feet to the floor, and as quietly, as slowly as I can, I tiptoe for the door. He left it open. I speed faster when I get to the hallway. I don't turn the lights on.

The streetlamps along the promenade shine just enough through the windows so that I can see what I'm doing.

I force myself to breathe shallow as I ease the cabinet open and take out the chocolate donut bites, using my chipped thumb nail to unseal the box. I rip the bag open. There's no being quiet with the wrappers, best to get it over with quickly.

I stuff two donuts into my mouth. The chocolate tastes like wax, and the cake is dry. It lodges in my throat. I reach blindly into the fridge for the milk, fumble with the cap, and chug so I can swallow and make room for more.

The sugar hits like a drug. Or maybe it's the act, the secret, the masochism.

Whatever, I lose control, let my agency blithely slip through my fingers, don't even try to stop myself. As I shove donuts into my face, I fumble with a box of coffee cakes. Crumbs are hard—impossible—to hide, but that's a worry for after the crushing, grinding shame, when the terror of discovery takes over, fueling my pumping legs.

I don't hear him before I see him, and when I do, my heart screeches to a halt, leaping into my crammed throat. My cheeks bulge. I'm clutching a gallon of milk by the cold handle with one hand. The other's stained with cheap chocolate.

My shoulders bow.

He's standing by the washing machine closet in a white undershirt and gray sweatpants. Watching.

"Fuck off." Crumbs fly from my lips. I shove my fist into my mouth, staring at the counter, the scattered wrappers, the empty box, a scream stuck in my chest.

"Fuck," he mutters low but so damn loud in the barren apartment.

I stare at my mess, at what I've done, and I force my esophagus to suck it down. I swipe my teeth with my tongue, swallowing spit a few more times while every inch of my skin burns.

If there was a clock, it would tick, but there isn't, so the silence just gets thicker and thicker until I break.

"Will you fucking *go away*?" I slam my hand on the marble, sucking in a hiss as a sharp pain shoots up my wrist. I cradle it against my distended belly. "Go away," I whisper down at all the wrappers I licked clean.

He won't.

He grabs the trash, scoops up all of it easily with his two large hands, and drops it in the can. He screws the cap back on the milk and returns it to the fridge. He puts the coffee cakes back, shuts the cabinet, and stands behind me, his chest not touching my back, but close.

He reaches around me and gently takes the hand that throbs. Carefully, he tests the bone in each finger, the center of my palm, the mound of my thumb. I whimper.

"It's probably just bruised," he says.

"Go away." It's a sob, a moan.

For a moment, I think he won't. He'll do something insane like wrap his arms around me and hold me together.

For a moment, as his breath feathers my ear, I think he considers it, but then he straightens, steps back, and awkwardly clears his throat.

"Come back to bed," he says, and then after a yawning pause, I hear his footsteps retreat.

I don't do what he says. I ball my fists, tight, tighter, so the pain in whatever bone I bruised is sharp, like I deserve.

I stiffen my spine and stalk to the gym. I'm wearing silk sleep shorts and a cami, which isn't ideal, but it'll do. I'm not stopping for anything, anyhow. I'm a wind-up soldier, an automaton.

A penitent who doesn't deserve mercy, not an inch, not any, not ever.

I climb on the bike. It's instinct. I immediately up the incline and the resistance, standing as I pump as hard and as fast as I can. My stomach churns, a clammy sweat breaking out before I've even broken five minutes. I pant through the urge to puke and ignore a calf cramp, forcing my spasming leg to pedal like it's an inanimate attachment, and its pain means nothing to me.

The box of mini donuts had twelve packs of six each. Three hundred and sixty calories a bag. Four thousand three hundred and twenty calories.

How much milk did I drink? To be safe, call it three cups. Four hundred fifty calories. Round up to five hundred.

And I ate some of the coffee cakes before Nicky—

No. Focus. How many coffee cakes?

Two or three. Let's call it five. One hundred seventy times five is eight hundred fifty. Round up to nine hundred.

Nine hundred plus five hundred plus four thousand five hundred—round up to six thousand calories.

If I go hard, I burn an average of five hundred an hour on the bike. That's twelve hours.

My heart falls, panic bursting from my chest, but I don't let myself lose speed. I did this to myself. It's my fault. Because I'm weak. Stupid. Disgusting.

Worthless.

If I can't even keep myself pretty, I'm nothing at all. If I'm nothing, I can disappear, and no one will even say my name again.

Sweat burns my eyes, soaking the back and butt of my pajamas. My brain won't stop. It spins, careens, pinballs.

You can't just rush from one relationship to another—thinking that's going to solve all your problems—without taking the time to work on yourself.

Does it even matter to you who you're fucking?

I'm your pimp, Zita, and you've got one trick. One job.

Go easy on yourself for once.

My foot slides off the pedal, hard, my shin scraping the metal teeth. Blood beads on the skin.

In the doorway, Nicky sucks in a breath.

My entire body tightens, every burning muscle, but I don't stop. I go harder. Sweat mixes with blood and dribbles down to my ankle.

"You've been going for an hour," Nicky says to my back.

I have? I check the screen. Yeah. Seventy-three minutes. Six hundred and nineteen calories burned. Not even close to enough.

Nicky walks into the room with slow, careful steps. "Your leg is bleeding."

No shit. I'm a mess. "It's not as if you didn't know exactly what I was like," I say between jagged breaths.

I'm not looking at his face, so I don't know if he recognizes his own words. In my experience, when men lose their shit, their brains erase everything they do and say as soon as they calm down.

Nicky exhales as he sits on the end of the lifting bench parallel to the bike. I glance over. He's still in the white undershirt and sweats. I refocus on the screen. Six hundred and twenty-three calories.

He lays back as if he's going to lift and folds his hands over his flat stomach. For a minute, he stares at the ceiling.

"You don't remember when we first met, do you?" he asks, breaking the silence.

"Saint Celestine's." Answering is somehow easier than refusing. What he says doesn't matter anyway. Not any-more. My eyes prickle from the sweat.

"It was before that. We were kids. Eight."

We're the exact same age? I guess so, since we were in the same class in school. I can't think of him as twenty-four, though. He seems older.

"You remember that my grandfather worked for Renel-li?" he goes on. "This was back when your dad was still a capo. My grandpa had turned in an envelope that turned out light. By five hundred bucks."

My shoulder blades tighten. I know how this kind of story ends.

"I don't know if he took it, if someone else ripped him off, whatever. Doesn't really matter. It was on him. As soon as he got the five hundred, he went to take it to your dad. People were already out looking for him."

Nicky pauses. I glance over. His lips are curved in a bitter smile. "My grandpa was either wasted or insane. He took me with him to your house. I guess he figured if he showed up like a man, with a kid in tow, your dad wouldn't kill him, and somehow, he'd smooth it over. Just two family men, right? Just business."

My father wasn't a family man. He wasn't a businessman either. He was a vicious bastard who'd found a win-win career. If he didn't get rich, he'd get to beat on people.

"Your mom opened the door. She let us wait in that big foyer with the pink chandelier."

It's still there. Dad hated it, but Mom somehow convinced him it was peach, not pink, and it was classy because it cost three thousand dollars.

"We were standing there when this baby comes toddling in, grinning. Little guy. Maybe two."

That would've been Maddie.

"Then your dad shows up. Pissed. He hollers for your mother. When she doesn't answer, he calls for you. You show up so fast, you must've been looking for the baby already."

I would've been shitting myself. I was the one responsible for Maddie, and I'm the one who got the belt if the baby got hurt or dirty.

"You scooped that kid up, and you were so skinny, it was like you were hauling a bag of concrete." Nicky's lip quirks at the corner. "Your father told you if you let Maddie run off again, he'd beat your ass."

That sounds about right. I was good at watching her, but Maddie was just so fast, so excitable. As soon as you put her down, she was like a racehorse out of the gate.

"So, my grandfather gets to the point, and you can tell he miscalculated coming to your father's house. Big time. Your dad wasn't stoic like Renelli. You could see him get angrier."

True. Dad's face would flush red to purple, the veins on his forehead would pop, and his lips would draw back like a gorilla baring its teeth.

"My grandfather wouldn't shut up. He kept going on and on about how it was an honest mistake, and he came to your father's house like a man, with his grandson as witness, to make it right, and all the while I could see your father getting closer and closer to the point where he was gonna lose it."

I can picture it so vividly in my head that the old, cold fingers of paralyzing fear wrap around my ribcage, stealing more breath from my overworked lungs.

"I tried to tug at my grandpa's pants. He swatted me off." Nicky's still staring at the ceiling, but his eyes are far away. "It went down so quick. Your father told my grandpa to shut his mouth and swung on him, and at the exact same second, the baby came running around the corner, straight for us. You were hot on her heels, but too far back to get her before she was gonna bust onto the scene."

I still don't remember this day. For a good year or two, all I did was chase Maddie, catch her from falling, and snatch her before she could climb too high on the furniture.

"I saw your father's face. I figured my grandpa wasn't getting out of this, and there was nothing I could do about that. But you—"

His eyelids drift shut and his lips curve.

"You were so pretty. Your hair was curled in pig tails with these big loopy pink bows, and your fingernails and your toes matched. Just so damn pretty."

His eyes blink open, and he turns to face me, still with that vague, small smile. "I couldn't do anything for my grandpa, but I could protect you. I drew back, far as I could, and I punched your father in the gut. Maddie was right behind him. Inches away. And you got her, hoisted her up, her little arms and legs windmilling, and you bolted like you were on fire."

He tucks an arm behind his head. I let the pedals slow to a stop. His gaze sweeps down my body, and his smile grows sadder.

"Your father backhanded me into a wall, broke my jaw, but you got away clean."

"I don't remember," I say softly, but it could have been any one of a dozen, a hundred close calls.

He turns back to stare at the ceiling. "Your father had one of his people drive me home. I never saw my grandpa again."

"I'm sorry."

"Don't be," he says. "Before that, I was a weak, scared kid who was gonna end up on the needle like his mother, or in and out of jail like his dad. You made me strong. Nothing could take me down after that. I had a reason to fight, you know?"

"I could've been anyone."

"But you weren't. You were Zita Graziano. Before I was brave, you were. And so fucking fierce. I had nothing in me except rage, but you—you had so much love, and you've never let anything touch it. You had a reason to fight, too."

Maddie.

I blink, my eyes wet and burning from the sweat. I scrub them hard.

"I'm sorry about earlier," he says. "I was jealous, and I was an asshole. I don't know how to do this, Zita."

I look at the counter blinking on the console—six hundred fifty-two calories.

I don't know either.

I don't know how to get off the bike. To tell Nicky that I had started to trust him, not a whole lot, just a little, but still more than anyone ever except Maddie. That he broke that trust, and I hate him because I shouldn't have ever let him have even a small sliver of myself. And I need him. Not only to rescue Maddie and me, but to—

To make that story true.

To make me worth fighting for.

Make me believe I'm worth fighting for.

But the thing in me doesn't just hold up its hands and surrender. Only six hundred fifty-two. It doesn't ever shut up. It gets louder.

"Talk to me, Zita," he says. "Please."

I can't. Everything I feel is stuck in my throat. I can't even look at him. I keep my eyes on the calorie counter and start pedaling again.

And he just stands there, watching me spin out of control, like he has the right. A sudden, blinding fury—at myself, at my life, at him—rises, surging upward until it streams out of my mouth.

"None of that fucking matters, you know? You don't own me. You can keep me here, but that does not mean I belong to you."

The words drop like weights. For a long minute, Nicky is silent. I pump the wheels as fast as I humanly can.

Then, when I don't think I can bare his eyes on me one more second, he finally sighs and says, "Okay, Zita," and he gets up and walks out.

Two hours later, when the front door shuts as he leaves for the day, I'm slumped on the bench, chugging water, waiting for my legs to recover enough to get back on the bike.

Two thousand and thirty calories.

Not enough.

Not nearly enough.

Nicky doesn't say another word to me before he leaves. He doesn't tell me there's cash on the nightstand. He doesn't ask for dinner. He doesn't poke his head into the gym.

Because there's nothing he can say or do. This is impossible. And we both know it.

H E USUALLY COMES HOME by six thirty. Rarely, he walks in closer to seven, but if he's that late, he texts. The first time he did it, I snorted. The captor letting his captive know he was held up in traffic.

Then I got used to it.

Seven comes and goes, and there's no sign of him.

I had to give up at two thousand and seven hundred calories. My leg muscles were seizing up, and even with stretching and breaking down and eating a banana for the potassium, they wouldn't cooperate. I soaked in the tub, but it didn't help much, so I hobbled down to the trash chute and threw out all the contents of the bad food cabinet and collapsed on the sofa to watch TV.

Around seven thirty, I start watching my phone. I idly scroll through our text history. He's a man of few words and no emojis. *Brb. Here. Yes. Get milk. Please.*

He's a hard man to know, and if I'd thought about it yesterday, I'd still say he was pretty much a stranger to me. But here, now, after I've beaten my body worse than my father ever did, after last night, I don't have the energy to lie to myself.

I know him.

I have no idea what makes him capable of what he does. I'm sure it has something to do with his fucked-up childhood, same as me, but other than that, I couldn't say.

But I know how badly he wants the things he wants.

I know what it's like to cling to the one good thing in your life so you can force down all the shit you have to eat.

I'm not mad anymore. Not at him or myself. Sometime during the early morning hours, I exorcised the anger along with the calories.

I check my phone. Seven forty-two.

I wish he'd fucking come home. I don't know how I'll look him in the eye, and I'm not sure if I want to give him the cold shoulder or sweep everything under the rug or what, but the apartment's too quiet, and when he's around—

I'm stronger. Even when I'm falling apart.

I huff and stretch my cramping legs. After the bath, I struggled into a pair of navy polka dot capris and a white, sleeveless shirt that buttons. Very Sunday brunch at the yacht club. I felt better once I was dressed, my hair was done, and I'd filed the chipped nail.

I didn't cook dinner. I'm still pissed. Well, not exactly, but we haven't made peace, and I'm not going to sweep everything under the rug like my mother.

I shift, crossing my legs at the ankle. There's no way I can lift one over the other. Despite my bruised body, though, I've got a strange energy. I feel like I'm on the verge of something, and even though I know it can only be disaster, my heart thumps with excitement, not dread.

A new show comes on the TV at eight, Nicky's still not home, and there's no text. I'm not going to text him first.

I could, though.

I could tip this thing over. Admit what's happened. Hold my hand out to him like he's held his to me. Leave my soft underbelly exposed. Make it really easy for him to knock me down and take me out.

I stand and wander to the window. There's the remnant of sunset behind the bluffs, but the sky overhead is dark. No stars tonight. I lean my cheek against the cold glass and watch a couple stroll along the lamplit promenade with their dog.

I've drifted off into daydreams when a loud knock startles me into a gasp. It's followed by three more sharp raps. I hurry to the door, my gut sinking. It's dread pumping my heart now.

I look through the peephole, and Lucca Corso smiles back. "Open the door, Zita."

My mouth goes dry, and my fingers shake, but I don't hesitate to undo the chain and unlock the deadbolt. Lucca shoves the door open himself. I jump back, out of the way.

He stalks forward, raising his finger, his freakishly pretty face twisted in a joker's smile. "You had one job, Zita. Didn't we agree on that? Just one."

My back hits the kitchen island. Lucca's breath reeks of whiskey. His golden, highlighted hair falls in his face as he studies me. My throat squeezes shut.

He cocks his head. "Nothing to say for yourself?"

His hands move so quickly, I have no chance to duck or throw my own up. He slaps me and grabs my hair, jerking my head back and forth until I taste blood, my ears ring, and my eyes water. It's not my first time. My nose stings, but it's not broken. Neither is my jaw, and none of my teeth are loose.

My hands fly of their own accord to clutch his wrist, ease the horrible tearing at my scalp.

My mind focuses. He's stopped. I can get out of this. The pistol Nicky gave me is in my purse. My purse is hanging from my chair at the dining room table. Ten feet away.

"What did I do?" I pant.

He laughs. "How the fuck should I know? I'm just the one who gets the call that my best button man is down at Sugarbits, looking like his dog died, getting wasted and starting shit with civilians." He shakes me by the hair. "One fucking job, Zita."

"I'll fix it."

"Damn straight you will. Do you think I have the kind of time to be trotting my happy ass down here to remind a whore to do her *one fucking job*?"

"N-no."

He shakes me again. I make my limbs as loose as I can so it hurts less as he slams my side into the counter.

"Do I need to find that little brother of yours, get him to explain it to you?"

"N-no. Please."

He shakes me a few more times before he throws my head toward the counter. I catch myself with my hands.

"If I don't get a call within the hour that Nicky is happily back home, I'm sending a man for Mattie. Capisce?"

I nod, keeping my head lowered, my shoulders hunched to my ears.

He slaps my ass. "Go to work," he says as he turns to leave. "One hour."

I'm sprinting to the bedroom for my shoes before the door clicks shut behind him. I grab my purse, dash down the hall for the elevator, and wait two seconds before I give up and take the stairs. I'm in the garage when it hits me that I don't have my car.

Shit. *Shit.*

I fumble with my phone, order a ride share, and while I wait in front of the building, I try Nicky over and over. My calls go straight to voicemail.

Luckily, the car comes quickly, and it's only a half hour across town to Sugarbits. I have fifteen minutes left when the bouncer waves me in. I've never been inside, but the guy has been over to the house before with Tony Junior. He recognizes me, and he doesn't seem surprised that I'm here.

I guess everyone knows that I'm Nicky's whore, here to fetch him home. My cheeks flame, my brain whirling.

An hour ago, I was thinking—

I was *deluding* myself that we were something to each other. I don't know what, but something not quite ugly. Not all ugly.

Doesn't life always do this, though? Grab you by the hair and smash you against reality until you focus.

I have to get Nicky out of here. Keep Maddie safe. Nothing else matters.

As I pass through a narrow hall into a large room, painted black with neon signs on the walls, I search for Nicky. The light from the glowing pink silhouette of a naked woman and the *Girls, Girls, Girls* sign doesn't do much to help me see.

The place is set up like an amphitheater with tall-backed booths in the back and a sunken lounge area with dark, modern sofas in front of the stage. A woman is idly twirling around the pole, strutting aimlessly between the two customers bellied up on bar stools.

There aren't many people. A bartender at the bar. Two girls working the room, their pasty, sparkly skin and neon wigs bright in the darkness. Maybe a dozen men scattered at the tables. The DJ didn't adjust the volume to account for the small crowd, so the music blares, harsh and echoing.

Even though he works all nights that the club is open, I don't see Tony Junior, but I spot Nicky. He's on a sofa in a conversation pit close to the stage, Tomas sprawled next to him, arm flung along the cushion behind Nicky's back, ostensibly casual, but obviously hovering and tense, as if he's expecting action.

Nicky sits straight-spined, a glass of whiskey in one hand, the other clenched and resting on his thigh. His knuckles are swollen and scraped. His jacket's missing. The cuff on his left sleeve is undone. The button must've popped.

A dancer struts in front of him, not quite between his knees, but close. Inches away. There's not an ounce of fat on her body. You can count her ribs when she raises her arms above her head, but her bare ass cheeks are round, and her tits are full and high.

I realize that at some point, I must have started across the room toward him, but I've stopped between the tables, stupid and out of place in my mom-capris, collared top, and white Keds.

The dancer draws her pristine painted nails along his crooked jaw, and he lets her. He just sits there and watches her as she effortlessly smiles and offers up her perfect tits, writhing, showing off, like there's no doubt in her mind that she's beautiful and desirable and in control.

Inside my chest, something splinters and crashes like a pane of glass.

That's mine. His eyes belong on me.

Suddenly, I'm uncertain on my feet. I'm standing in the surf, and the waves are rushing out. I've dropped something, and I'm reaching, but it's slipping through my fingers. And I'm scared in a way I've never been before, not *of* something, but that if I don't act—*right now*—I'll lose something I'll never be able to find again.

The dancer laughs at something Tomas says and bends over, sticking her ass out as she rests her hands on Nicky's knees and tosses her wavy pink wig. She asks Nicky something. He doesn't answer.

Hold up.

He's watching her, but he's not paying attention. I know what he looks like when he's focused, when he can't look away. My heart still hurts like it's been cracked open like an egg, but a little sliver of courage zips up my spine.

His expression is blank, but I *know* him. Nicky's miserable. Lost. Hopeless. But when he notices me, his face is going to change. His eyes are going to come alive. His world is going to narrow until there's only me. There is not a single doubt in my mind. It plays in my head like a movie.

What happens to my face when I see him? My eyes? Do they come alive like my insides?

I bet they do.

I bet, if I call his name, he'll come. If I reach out my hand, he'll take it. Without hesitation.

My pulse thuds harder and faster. A song ends, and after a roaring second of silence, another starts.

I bet if I hold out my hand, he'll come and take it. But what of it? You can't love someone just because they love you.

You love someone because you admire them—their ambition, their discipline, their goodness. Because they're better than you. Because they're what you strive to be.

Nicky is no better than I am. Well, he's stronger. But he says I'm the one that made him strong. The idea of me—that I'm full of love and not rage.

He's so fucking wrong. On a daily basis, I'm almost bursting with hate and despair and desperation and fear.

But love, too, right?

All I have to do is picture Maddie—her beautiful face, the smile that not a damn thing on this earth can stop, no matter how hard it tries—and yes, I think love, too.

Big, huge, fierce, fearless love. That's inside me, too. When Nicky looks at me, that's what he sees. I want to see myself like he does, to be as good as he thinks I am. And how is that not love?

My nose burns, and I blink fast. It's hard enough to see in the dim light. I don't need to cry in the middle of a fucking strip club. Besides, I never cry. Not since I got old enough to realize it only makes shit worse.

And then, at that moment, while I'm trying to suck tears down like air, Nicky sees me.

I was right.

His eyes light on fire. My heart leaps. For a split second, he leans toward me, but then his uneven jaw tightens, and he forces himself to sit back. His free hand balls into a fist as he tosses back the rest of his drink. He drags his gaze back to the dancer. My heart falls.

But his eyes flicker back to me. Once. Again. My breath shallows.

Tomas finally notices me. He mouths something in Nicky's ear. Nicky ignores him.

My heart beats like it never has before, raw, thick, loud. Nicky should be able to hear it across the club.

The dancer turns, touches the ground and twerks, smiling over her shoulder at him. My own hands fist. His gaze drops to my sides. He notices.

He's mad. Hurt. Jealous. My stomach aches with the same feelings.

His wonky jaw twitches. He's miserable. He should come to me.

I want him here. Away from her. Where he belongs.

Even if it's crazy. Even if *I'm* crazy.

I fiddle with the top button on my blouse. Like a magnet, Nicky follows my fingers. I pop the button open. His head tilts ever so slightly. No one else would be able to tell. Only me. I'm the only one who knows him to the centimeter.

I pop the second button. He leans forward, his whole body tensing. I pop the third. He soars to his feet. Startled, the dancer hops aside.

Heat rushes into the emptiness in my chest.

I pop the fourth. All you can see is the pink rosette at the center of my white lace bra, but he takes a few urgent steps forward until something—pride maybe—stops him in his tracks.

We stare at each other, the connection so strong I feel like I could reach out and curl my fingers around it, reel him back to me, and I want to with everything I am, not because Lucca Corso threatened me, but because Nicky the driver isn't his.

Not the smallest bit of him belongs to anyone but me.

Every messed up, stubborn, prideful part. His crooked jaw, his loyalty, the fear I know must have made him into what he is—as mine made me what I am—all of it belongs to me.

I lift my chin, popping another button to reveal the bare skin under the band of my bra. His teeth grit, his throat works, and even though I can't hear it, I know it's a growl. I begin to ease my shirt down over my shoulder. His black eyes flash a warning.

For a breathless moment, we're playing chicken, except the conclusion is foregone. I win. I'm the queen. He's my knight. I fiddle with the last button, the one that'd let my shirt fall open, and every visible muscle in his body strains, his neck, his forearms.

And then, the second before he loses it, I turn on my heel. With my shoulders thrust back, I stride, calm and unhurried, between the empty tables and down the narrow hallway, out the front door, across the gravel parking lot that crunches under my soles. As I walk, I do up my buttons, like it's nothing, like I'm not leading the most dangerous man in this city out of this club like the Pied Piper.

Sugarbits is under an overpass in a down-at-the-heel part of town where the steel mill used to be. They've redeveloped the land for warehouses and distribution centers, but the industrial chemical funk somehow still hangs in the air and mingles with the smog from the highway overhead.

It's a lonely place, all the windowless box-like buildings dark at this time of night except for a gas station two blocks away. I head for it. I walk with a light tread, soundless under the rumble of passing traffic.

I can't hear Nicky's steps either, but I know he's there. Following me. Watching.

I feel him.

My stride grows surer, my spine straighter. When I hit a streetlight with an unbroken bulb, I stop. Turn. Slowly. Because I want the moment to stretch in my memory, to be long enough to pin so that I can keep it forever. Proof.

Evidence. Once upon a time, for a brief, shiny moment, I was the strongest woman I know.

I turn, inch by inch, and he's there, maybe fifteen feet away, cuff undone, knuckles busted, face unreadable, black eyes blazing.

He draws in a breath, his chest rising, but he doesn't come closer.

I have to do it now.

With my eyes wide open, I leap. "We have to get the fuck out of here," I say, holding his gaze, firm and sure, the way he's always held my hand. "You, me, and Maddie."

Nicky doesn't miss a beat. "Where do you want to go?"

"Far away."

"Okay," he says.

"Okay?"

The tension in his frame dissolves. His crooked smile transforms his face, softening my own mouth, banishing the ache in my tight shoulders. I did it. I trusted myself. I leapt, and he was there.

"You know I'd do anything for you," he says.

I don't think he expects an answer, but still, I say, "Yeah."

I go to him, close the distance between us, coming to a halt inches from his shiny black shoes. I raise up on my toes and tilt my head back. Tentatively, carefully, he cradles the nape of my neck and lowers his mouth to mine.

He kisses me.

Or maybe I kiss him.

No, we kiss each other.

The late spring night air is humid and cool, but his body's warm, the arms folding me to his chest are strong and certain. The hazy moon is low in the sky, and he tastes like whiskey and reeks of some other woman's vanilla body spray.

I fist his shirt, holding him close while I angle my head away, turning up my nose. "You smell like stripper."

He tightens his arms around me. "I'll shower."

"I hate it."

"I won't do it again."

"You're an asshole for doing it tonight." I glare at him.

"You made me pay for it," he says.

"You didn't like it when you thought I was going to show those other men my tits?"

"It was killing me," he says. He's not the least bit embarrassed by the admission. I consider him. He stares at my lips, hungry, shameless.

Yeah, he's not going to do it again.

I lower my eyes, glaring at the cracked concrete sidewalk, as I say, "That shit. Before. I can't talk about it." I squeeze my eyes shut. "I can't control it. Once I start, I can't stop."

He tucks me to his chest. "I know."

I exhale, and for a while, we stand there, wrapped in each other, his hand stroking down my back, mine reaching up to smooth along his crooked jaw, erase that woman's touch.

"Where do you want to go?" he asks me finally.

"Somewhere Maddie will be safe. Where she can be—herself." It's going to take me a little time to get used to this new reality, but it also *fits*. Like when I was a kid, and I learned that our neighbor Mrs. Klinedinst's first name was Citrine, and it felt strange, but also, I could see a little better who she was.

"Okay," he says again, and for the first time I get the sense that yeah, it might be.

He takes my hand, and I hold his back, and we walk to his car at the rear of the lot. He opens my door, and I get in my seat. He waits until I'm buckled to shut me in and walk to his side. And as I tell him about Lucca's visit, what Lucca said, and what he did—and even though the veins in Nicky's neck strain and his eyes burn black—he drives at exactly twelve miles above the posted limit, indicates his turns well ahead of time, and leaves at least three seconds between us and the car ahead.

He does it for me. Because I am precious to him. Even though he knows all my secrets.

Maybe *because* he knows them.

The idea is so big, so incomprehensible, that I can't think it. I can only hold it in silence as we drive toward whatever happens next.

WHEN WE GET BACK to the apartment, everything moves in triple time. Nicky has me call Maddie to tell her to pack and be ready to meet us outside of my mom's house in an hour. Maddie doesn't ask any questions, she just says to make sure we leave enough trunk space for her.

Then Nicky throws a big black duffel on the bed and tells me to fill it with whatever I want to take and enough clothes to last him a couple days. Nicky disappears into the closet, and then busies himself stuffing a smaller duffel with guns and cash. Stacks and stacks of it.

I ask, "How much is there?"

He says, "Enough."

I'm still cramming bottles of hair product into the pockets on the sides of the bag when he gets on his phone, his fingers flying.

I lean over to look at the screen. "What are you doing?"

"Buying plane tickets. Do you have a passport?"

"It's at my mom's."

"Call Maddie and tell her to get both of yours. Tell her don't let your mom know." He looks up from his phone. "Tell her if your mom asks any questions, she needs to barricade her in the downstairs guest bathroom without her phone."

"Maddie's not gonna be able to barricade someone in a bathroom." She's not like my dad or Tony Junior.

"Maddie can handle herself," Nicky says as he lifts a foot onto the bed and straps on an ankle holster.

Do I even want to know how he knows that? I open my mouth to ask, but the question flies out of my mind as Nicky releases the cylinder of a silver revolver, loads the cartridges in rapid succession, thumbs the cylinder closed, tucks it away, and smooths his pant leg straight. His movements are so practiced. So economical. Cold trickles down my spine.

The veil is gone. I'm seeing things as they are, no delusion or willful blindness, no way not to stare down the fact that the man I've finally asked to rescue us is a killer for hire, and a good one based on the stacks of cash. Even Dad didn't have that much in his safe.

A smart woman, a sane woman, would use Nicky to get out of town and then ditch him. She'd give herself a fresh start. She'd recognize that none of these feelings star-bursting in her chest could possibly be real. It's a trauma response. Stockholm syndrome.

I can't worry about it now. Nicky took me to mean "right the fuck now" when I said we needed to get out of here, and I'm not going to give him time for second thoughts.

Sooner than I thought possible, we're ready to leave. Nicky has the duffels slung over his shoulders, and I'm clutching my red purse. I moved my pocket pistol to the outside pouch so I could fill the bag with the rest of my skin products.

Despite his load, Nicky opens the door for me. Heart thudding, I lead the way down the hall. Lucca could very well be in the building. He was earlier. I've never run into him in the common areas, but tonight feels different. Nicky's not nervous, but he's hyper-alert. For once, his eyes aren't on me. They sweep our path and dart over his shoulder.

I hold my breath when I call the elevator, letting it out in a rush as the doors shush open to an empty car. Only a few floors down and then a few yards and we'll be at the Mercedes. A minute after, we'll be home free. I've never seen Nicky drive like his ass is on fire, but I have no doubt that he can.

When we hit the basement and the elevator doors slide open, the stagnant, gasoline-tainted air burns my nose. Nicky's car isn't too far. I can see it from here, and I don't see any people or hear any engines. It's a crowded space with a low ceiling, crammed tightly with as many vehicles as can fit between the concrete pillars of the foundation.

I force myself to suck in a shallow, steadying breath. Almost there.

Nicky braces the elevator door open with his forearm and gestures me through. I scurry ahead of him down a dim aisle, clutching my purse to my chest. When the car lock chirps, I nearly jump through my skin.

For once, he doesn't open my door first. He pops the trunk, setting the bag with the cash and guns down at his feet while he stows the larger duffel with our clothes.

A man clears his throat. A safety clicks.

A wave of sheer, paralyzing fear crashes through me. A scream ricochets in my brain, but I can't make a sound.

Nicky freezes.

They came from nowhere. No, they were hidden behind two pillars, and they stepped out like ghosts. Lucca and Tomas. Guns leveled at us. No. At Nicky.

Slowly, Nicky turns to face them. His gaze doesn't flicker to me. Not for a second. Panic squeezes my throat shut.

"You followed us at the club," Nicky says.

Tomas nods.

"I didn't see you." Nicky's voice is somehow as blank as his face.

Tomas shrugs. "You were distracted."

By me. My gaze darts from man to man. Lucca's five feet or so closer to us than Tomas, but they're both much too close to miss a shot. Nicky has at least one gun holstered at his back and another at his ankle, but he'll never be able to reach them before they shoot.

My little nickel pistol is so close, less than an inch below where my forearm hugs my purse to my breasts. Seven rounds. Safety's on. Could I get to it before they could get a shot off? No way, not even though they're aiming at Nicky.

Lucca lowers his gun to his side and smiles. Ice trickles through my veins. "No such thing as loyalty in this wicked world, eh?" he says to Nicky.

Nicky lifts a shoulder.

Lucca tosses a stray lock of silky gold hair out of his face. He really does look like an old movie star from the '90s, when actors looked like grown men with indestructible jaws. In contrast, Tomas looks like the stunt man playing a thug who gets thrown through a window in the first scene. Complete opposites, but they operate in total synchronicity. It doesn't matter that Lucca lowered his weapon. If Lucca thinks "shoot," Tomas will fire.

Nicky and I are not getting out of this. They'll force us to another location, and we'll disappear like my dad and Renelli and all the others. Maddie will have no one.

Another wave of panic tears through me. I can't leave Maddie alone. I have no choice. I have to go for my gun. I have to try.

As if he hears my thought, Lucca shifts his cold blue gaze to me. "Finally summoned up the courage to make a move, eh, Zita?" He shakes his head. "You really don't play chess, do you? A big thinker would have asked Nicky here to kill me."

My gaze darts to Nicky's face. It's unreadable, but even without confirmation, I know—he would. He'd do Tomas, too, if I asked. He'd do anyone.

Lucca's right. He's a gun. My gun.

It's as if the volume on my terror is muted. It's still there—I can see its lips moving—but it's not screaming in my head. My vision clears. The cars beyond Lucca and Tomas sharpen into vivid shapes and colors. The barrel of Tomas's gun is too long. It's got a silencer.

They can shoot us here and throw us in the trunk. Lucca owns the building. They had an hour head start on us. The cameras overhead aren't recording. I bet the doors to the garage are locked and someone's stopped the elevators. We're not walking out of here.

I shift closer to Nicky, instinctively seeking safety. He doesn't react. All of him is motionless, body and face.

Lucca flashes me another smile, jarringly bright in this dingy space. "But this is your lucky day, Zita. You get to walk out of here. You get to go home. Get your little brother. Go somewhere far away. Make a fresh start."

My brain sputters, trying to comprehend what he's saying.

"Go ahead and take the bag with the cash. There's a bag of cash, right?" Lucca nods at the duffel by Nicky's feet.

"Take the car and go. We won't stop you." He raises his palms, his gun pointing at the concrete beams overhead. "You have my word. We won't come looking for you."

He shifts his focus to Nicky, his smile widening and somehow turning almost bitter. "You almost had it all, didn't you? But men like us are always the architects of our own destruction, aren't we? Wanting what we can never have."

Nicky's face betrays nothing, but when he glances over at me, his eyes soften, and they speak. Go. Run. "Keys are in my pocket," he says.

"Take them out," Lucca orders. "Slowly."

Nicky does, making no move toward the gun tucked in the small of his back. He's letting me go.

Lucca won't, no matter what he says. He'll come after me, and he won't ever stop. You don't walk away from the organization. He'll do Nicky, and by the time I pull up at the house, he'll have men there. Maybe Tony Junior.

But I'll have time. I can call Maddie to sneak out, and we'll have a head start. Lucca thinks I'm stupid, but I'm not. I've daydreamed my escape a billion times, and I can drive fast. And with a duffel bag of cash—we could disappear.

I realize my hand is hovering in the air.

"Zita," Nicky says softly and glances at the keys he's holding out to me.

Take them, a part of my brain shouts. Speed away. Escape. Wind in your hair. Free.

The cuff with the broken button is hanging loose, exposing Nicky's tanned forearm. Although he holds the keys lightly, his muscles are taut. Veins like tributaries run from his wrist, disappearing into the dangling sleeve.

I know the pattern by heart. I could draw them from memory. I've traced them while we've lain in bed in silence, me lying between his legs, my back to his chest, his heavy arm resting across my middle, our minds as incomprehensible as black holes to each other, each of his breaths lifting me, lowering me, until my lungs begin to work on his time.

I've traced the scar on his right rib and the ink beads circling his neck, laying across his heart. I've cradled his crooked jaw while I kissed him like I loved him.

Is this how you feel about a body that belongs to you? That every imperfection is a story, a tribute, a victory—

That every drop of blood in its veins is precious.

Nicky's eyes shine, and in slow motion, his lips curve, and he gives the keys a slight shake.

Slight.

But enough.

Lucca and Tomas's eyes dart to the motion.

I draw my pistol from my purse and let it fall to the concrete as I release the safety and fire. Lucca's shoulder jerks, and he tips backward, stumbles, topples. My shots go wild, my vision tunnelling until all I see is the red bloom on his white shirt.

Vaguely, as gunfire rings in my ears, I watch events unfold as if I'm suspended in the thick air.

Nicky throws me behind him as he draws his gun. Then, he fires while he wrestles open the back door of the Mercedes with his other hand.

Tomas fires back as he tries to drag Lucca out of the aisle while covering him with his own body.

Nicky heaves me into the car.

Lucca struggles, grappling for his own gun, and knocks Tomas's weapon to the ground.

Nicky slides into the driver's seat, slams into reverse, and peels backward. Tomas throws himself on Lucca, barely rolling him out of the way of the screeching tires.

"Buckle your fucking seatbelt, Zita," Nicky says as he shifts, and we careen around a corner, fly up a ramp, and rocket down River Street.

I sink back against the seat. "The money," I pant.

"I've got more," he says. "Fucking *seatbelt*. Don't make me come back there."

Laughter bubbles up my throat, hysterical, maniacal in the silent car until a deep chuckle joins it from the front.

"You're laughing," I say, wiping tears from my eyes. "I've never heard you laugh."

"You shot Lucca Corso."

"I didn't kill him."

"You can't expect to hit a homer fresh out of the gate," he says, slowing to a steady fifty-seven miles per hour as he slips on the sunglasses from the case attached to the visor.

And that's how I fell in love with Nicky the driver, escaped the mob, and started a brand-new life.

Like a fucking madwoman.

Wild and brave, underestimated and unstoppable.

In the back seat of a Mercedes, laughing with the windows down and the wind in my hair.

Epilogue

Zita

"H E'S AGITATED," MARISSA SAYS. She doesn't glance in Nicky's direction, but we both know who she's talking about.

He's been pacing for the past ten minutes. He'll step into the pool to get his feet wet, wander to the bar to watch the game for a minute, go to the railing and watch the waves for a while, stalk back to the bar.

"We have ten more minutes." I close my eyes so I can feel the sunshine better and stretch my legs as long as they'll go. The wicker lounge chair is warm on my back.

"You could put him out of his misery." Sometimes I think Marissa loves Nicky more than she loves me. It's definitely close. I don't mind. I want her to have all the love in the world.

We have a good life here, but it's quiet. We have the beach. Our cottage. Occasional trips to the city. Sometimes, Nicky goes away for a few days, and when he comes back, I cry, and he worships me with his body until the voice in my head becomes background noise again.

I know that eventually, Marissa is going to want more. Night life. Boyfriends. Maybe hormones and surgery.

I eat the fear because it belongs to me, not her, and even if I can't protect her, I'm not going to give her anything but love and courage and the words no one ever gave me.

I turn to her where she's stretched in the lounger beside me. "You're beautiful, you know? Inside and out."

She sighs, squirms, and fiddles with the poor lock of hair that she's always smoothing and tucking behind her ear. "Don't get weird."

"And smart and brave and perfect."

"Today's about you, not me," she says. I can see her smile peeking out, though.

"I'm so grateful for you."

"I'll cannonball in this pool and splash your ass so that you have to do this thing looking like a drowned rat. I will."

"You'll ruin your hair," I point out. She has it up in space buns with perfect tendrils framing her face. There's no way she's wrecking all that work.

"I'd do it for you," she says.

"You'd screw up your 'do to stop me from telling you how amazing you are?"

"*And* my face. And don't pretend that this is some innocent love fest. You're about to sit down and talk to someone about yourself and your shit for a whole hour, and you're scared, and what does Zita do when she's scared?"

"Is this rhetorical?"

"*Anything* but feel her feelings." Marissa flounces back in her chaise, self-satisfied, and examines her long, powder blue nails. Her toes and her bikini top match. As a nod to Nicky's overprotectiveness, she's wearing a sarong. So am I.

We're unmistakably sisters. Marissa is taller and leaner, her legs are longer, and she's got a concave stomach even when she's not lying down, but our skin is the same olive, and our hair's the same sun-streaked brown. She likes a red lip, and I like a nude matte, but our lips are shaped the same, and we have the same clear, wide-open eyes that you see in Renaissance portraits.

When we first came here, she went by Maddie-lynn, but after a few months, she thought it was too close to Mattie, so she changed it to Marissa. She's Marissa in my head now, so I hope she decides to stick with it.

At first, we all kept our heads down. Nicky left a lot, doing jobs for the Russians, establishing a relationship with them of his own, sussing out what was going on back home. We stayed inside and wore baseball caps or hoodies when we went out.

Then, Nicky got us new passports and moved us down here. He says we're safe. He made a deal with the Russians for protection against the Renelli organization, and as long as we're reasonably cautious, we'll be okay.

That's when Marissa started to wear her hair down. She'd wear makeup sometimes around our little cottage on a hill above the beach. Then she started doing her face every morning, like me. We went shopping in the village up the coast.

One time, there was an incident with a clerk. We left, and Nicky hung back. The clerk doesn't work there anymore.

That's how Nicky is. He hangs in the background, quiet, but he's always there, protecting us.

Watching me.

Still.

That's what he's doing from over at the bar while he sips his whiskey neat, and he's not being subtle about it. He wants me to head back to our place. He's worried that the internet connection will go out, but it's not like if we set up early, it'll be guaranteed to work. The Wi-Fi around here is temperamental.

I watch him, too. He keeps his cards close to the vest, but he can't hide anything from me. Marissa's right, I'm scared, but Nicky's terrified.

He thought if he took me away, I'd leave the thing that's wrong with me behind, too. Then, as soon as we settled here and established a bank account in our new name, I had a bike delivered. He freaked, but I knew that's how it would go. It's like when you take the lid off a boiling pot, and it spills over.

He doesn't understand that even though I seem worse, I'm not. If I were worse, he'd never, ever know.

It was the night the bike arrived that he made me promise that I'd talk to someone. If I didn't agree, he swore he'd pitch the bike in the ocean. He wasn't dramatic about it or anything. He said, "I'm gonna find you one of those—" He snapped a few times while shoveling plantain in his mouth. "Those people. Who do the talking. And you're gonna listen to them. Or I'm throwing that fucking thing in the ocean."

It took him a few weeks to find a person and set up the intake appointment. He didn't complain to me, but from what I overheard when he talked to Marissa, paying cash actually complicated things. The lady he found is in Sydney, so there's a fifteen-hour time difference.

I don't know how it's going to go. I don't talk about it. Never. To no one. Only to Nicky, only the once.

Do I just sit there for an hour? Let her talk?

I can do that.

I wipe my sweaty palms on my sarong. Marissa eyes me. "I'm gonna hang here while you do your thing."

My first impulse is to say no, but I breathe through it. People here know us. They know Nicky. She's as safe as you can get in this dangerous world.

For a second, I remember her streaking through the house, maybe three years old, fresh from the bath and buck-ass naked, one of those hooded towels flapping behind her like a cape, shrieking with giddy happiness.

I remember sprinting after her, fear seizing my lungs, terrified that my father would see her, get annoyed at the interruption, swing a careless fist, break her small, delicate bones, steal the only love I had that loved me back.

I remember catching her, and how I wanted to yell and shake, but instead I swung her in a circle because I didn't want to break that smile, that laugh.

I want to say be careful. Don't venture too far. Keep your head down.

But I don't.

"Do you need some money for snacks?" I ask.

She holds out her palm as Nicky comes to the foot of my lounger. He digs out his wallet and gives her enough for a week of groceries.

"Ready?" he asks me.

"No."

He holds out his hand. I take it, and he draws me to my feet.

"Be sure to hold everything in," Marissa says as she turns over to sun her back. "I've heard they like that. Make 'em work for it."

"You've got your phone?" I ask.

Marissa waves at the straw bag on the ground beside her.

Nicky squeezes my hand. "You've kept me waiting long enough," he says low in my ear as he leads me out of the beach club to the stairs carved in the hillside that lead to the cottages.

"We could skip this. Get naked. I'll let you take my ass again."

He grips me even tighter. "After," he says.

When we get to the veranda, he opens the door for me. He has the laptop ready on the kitchen table, set up so that the therapist will be able to see the coral accent wall I've hung with framed molas of birds and fish and turtles.

I duck into the bedroom to change out of my swimsuit, and then I take my seat at the table, sinking into the cushion. "Where are you going to be?"

"I was gonna wait on the porch. Okay?"

"Okay." I reach for the mouse, but Nicky beats me. He clicks a few buttons, and the telehealth waiting screen pops up. "Are you gonna listen in?"

"Do you want me to?"

It's been super-weird, negotiating this part of being together. Nicky's habit of watching me is deeply ingrained, and a while back, I figured out it wasn't about control so much as fear. If I'm safe and at least not in active distress, he can function.

The other part of it is that he doesn't lie to me. And that's not about principle, it's about how he sees me. I'm the only good thing in his life—well, me and Marissa—so he's never going to disrespect that. If he doesn't want to tell me something, he keeps his mouth shut.

So it's kind of like dealing with a genie from a fairy tale. If I ask the right question, he'll answer, and if I phrase a request the right way—make it about me being happy—he'll do it.

"I won't be able to talk if you're listening."

He nods. Message received.

He drops a perfunctory kiss to the top of my head and lets himself out the front door as the screen flickers and an older woman in blue-framed glasses appears, smiling and squinting, too close to the camera.

"You must be Angela," she says. We all have new names here.

After the session, I check my face. The tip of my nose is a little red, but my eyes look fine. I run a brush through my hair. When we first got here, I had the idea to cut my hair into a page boy and dye it blonde like Marissa. Nicky said if I was going to do that, he'd just go back to Pyle and finish Lucca off, so I left it.

I rearrange the sleeves of my off-shoulder white lace dress, and when I figure Nicky has sweat enough, I go join him on the front veranda. The sun is a huge golden ball hovering above the horizon. The palm trees are black outlines, and the sky overhead is dark, but the Pacific glows, the waves shining as they lap the beach.

I go to cuddle next to Nicky, but he moves immediately to stand behind me, bracketing me in his arms, resting his hands next to mine on the white railing.

He nuzzles my neck. "Made me wait, eh?"

I smile. "It was fine."

"Good?"

"Fine."

He drops a soft kiss on the tender skin behind my ear, and despite the mellow heat, shivers race down my spine.

He doesn't push. He never does. Instead, he takes my left hand and slides off the three-stone ring. Butterflies flap in my belly. He tries this every so often.

The first time, I said that I'd take his proposal under consideration.

The next time, I cried. He left in a huff and came back with a grocery store bouquet of flowers, more sorry than I've ever seen any man.

The last time, he just held it up and raised an eyebrow. I snatched it back and went back to making dinner.

"Would it make a difference if I got down on one knee?" he asks, his voice low.

"I wouldn't know what to do if you did that."

He holds the ring up so it sparkles in the last rays of sunshine. "What if we went and you picked out your own ring?"

"I like this one."

"The ring, you like," he says. There's a grumble to it.

"Yeah."

"But not the man."

"The man's growing on me."

"Oh, yeah?" There's a smile in his voice as he kisses my bare shoulder. "So one day, you'll say yes?"

I make him wait. Below us, a lone sanderling wades through the surf, pecking every few steps, probably searching for crabs.

I lean back into his strong chest. "Yes," I say, and hold up my hand.

"Yes?" Hope makes his deep voice ragged.

"Yes," I say, and he slips the ring on my finger. It's only fair, I think, since he belongs to me, that I belong to him.

One of my good things in an ugly world.

The beginning of many more good things to come.

Three Years Later

Zita

“**O**H, HE’S BIG MAD.” Marissa slips her sunglasses down her nose and sips noisily from her iced mocha. I can’t lie—I’m delighted by this late ’90s version of Cher from *Clueless* phase Marissa’s going through. It’s pure playfulness, not a shadow in it.

I can't say the same for the man confronting me across the clinic parking lot. Even three years later, his corners are still a mystery to me. Shivers zip up my spine, and my fingers curl into the leather of the purse I'm clutching to my chest.

Nicky *is* big mad. He's standing in the aisle in front of his car like he's waiting to get jumped, biceps straining against the seam of his jacket, teeth grit so hard that the angle of his wonky jaw is cast in sharp relief. Blood rushes to my pussy.

Nicky doesn't get angry often, but when he does, it's like fireworks, bright and explosive, and ultimately, safe. He'd blow himself up before he'd hurt a hair on my head. Knowing that has long since gone to my head. I understand lion tamers now, why they'd put themselves in an animal's mouth.

I shift in my red ballet flats, and his eyes narrow. He can read my excitement, like he can somehow sense the tingle erupting between my legs, and like always, his instinct is to make me feel good, but he's furious, and he's not giving it up. My heart rate kicks up a notch. Maybe we're finally going to have a fight.

We haven't done that yet. Lisa the therapist says conflict avoidance is a normal reaction to childhood trauma. I say that when you've seen your father bounce your mother's face off a French door because he didn't appreciate her tone, you learn not to sweat the small stuff—and it's all small stuff.

I offer Nicky a wavery, conciliatory smile. His scowl doesn't budge. He's been gone five days. Usually when he comes back from a work trip, he scoops me up and carries me off, no matter where he finds me, but he's just standing across the parking lot, glowering at me, taut with some kind of intensity I don't recognize.

"You didn't tell him about the appointment, did you?" Marissa guesses.

"No."

"And he didn't know anyway?"

"I guess he didn't." I didn't know I was going to go through with it until I was actually on the table, so I didn't want to jinx anything by telling him. Also, I needed it to be my decision. And if I was going to wuss out, I didn't need the guilt.

"He's not gonna like it." Marissa's straw gurgles as she reaches the bottom of her drink.

That's the understatement of the year.

Marissa sighs. "You know, not to take sides, but you've been married for *a while* now. You're clearly as obsessed with him as he is with you, so when are you gonna, like, *let him in?*"

It's my turn to sigh. It's a good question. The thing with Nicky is that he's so tuned into everything I do, I don't have to let him in. He's already made himself at home.

I don't have to risk anything.

For a long time, that made me feel safe, but now, the stronger I get—I'm starting to feel like an asshole.

"Go to him," Marissa stage whispers as she snatches my keys from the hand lax at my side. "I'll drive the convertible home."

I reach for my keys a second too late. She's already across the lot, hopping into the car, wrapping a scarf around her hair like an old movie starlet. She trails her fingers in the air as she peels out, grinning ear to ear.

I'm not even a little mad. Happy, carefree Marissa is the greatest gift Nicky has given me.

Suddenly, I don't want him mad anymore. It doesn't feel like a thrill or a novelty. It feels rotten.

I walk to him, measured and contrite, and he doesn't move to meet me. I stop a few feet away, digging the toe of my flat into the loose dirt and gravel.

Lisa the therapist has told me about how self-focused attention is a requirement of adaptive self-regulation which means it's normal for me to have my head stuck up my ass while I'm trying to be less crazy, and I shouldn't beat myself up for that, too.

Still, this close to Nicky with him looming, stiff and unhappy, my heart mushes like a bruised apple. I don't want to hurt this man.

"You're home," I say.

He draws his shoulders back, and he glares at the squat, nondescript building behind me. "You went to the doctor?"

I nod.

"You didn't say you had an appointment." His voice is hard. Distant.

I shake my head. A tic appears at his temple. For a second, it looks like he's going to say something, but he doesn't. He shakes himself, turns, and stalks to the passenger side of his Mercedes. I follow, docile and uneasy.

He opens the door. I slip in and buckle myself while he crosses around to his side. He gets in, and for a second, he just sits there, staring out the windshield at the green tangle of ferns and hackberry in the overgrown lot next door.

I set my purse at my feet as a vague worry pokes at the back of my mind. Something's not right, something besides the fact that Nicky's angry. I run the last few minutes back in my mind. Leaving the dim clinic, the brightness of midday slapping me in the face. Seeing Nicky when I didn't expect him. Stopping short. The quick conversation with Marissa. Marissa driving away.

Nicky opening the car door like he does for me, every time. Except he didn't touch the small of my back to guide me in.

He couldn't.

Because he opened the door with his left hand, not his right. Which he never does.

In the seat beside me, Nicky seems to rouse himself, takes a sharp breath, and puts the key in the ignition. The motion is stiff. Forced. His face is carefully blank.

He's hurt. His arm. Thoughtlessly, I reach out and grab him. He sucks in a hiss.

"What happened?" Dread freezes my chest. It's my greatest fear. Nicky leaves and doesn't come back. I tell him every time that he doesn't have to go. We have enough money. If we live frugally, we can get by for years. We can get jobs under the table. He doesn't listen.

And I don't fight him.

Because we don't fight.

"What happened to your arm?" I raise my voice. He clenches his teeth and makes to turn the key. I clutch his hand, tight, squeezing. "No. Stop. Tell me."

"It's nothing."

He's wearing his jacket. It's eighty-five degrees and eighty percent humidity. I drop his hand and reach for the jacket with half an idea to pull it off so I can see. "What's wrong with your arm?"

I can't do more than tug the lapel aside before Nicky reaches over to grab my wrist.

"I'm fine," he says. "You can see I'm fine."

"I can't see anything."

"It's only a flesh wound."

"A flesh wound?" The words are horrible, and he says it like it's nothing. Like he isn't everything to me. I stop trying to take off his jacket. He lets my wrist go. My hand falls to my lap.

For a second, I stare out of the windshield, too, at the mind-blowing greens of this place we've made our home, the leaves as huge as elephant's ears, the reds and yellows, still so hard to wrap my brain around after growing up with the comparatively muted colors of western Pennsylvania.

That's what happened to my life when we left. I was numb, and now everything's too bright, too big, and I know it's better this way, but sometimes happiness feels like salt in a wound. Sometimes love feels like sheer terror.

I try to take a deep, calming breath, but instead, I burst into tears. Chest-racking sobs. I don't know what Nicky does. I can't see anything.

"Zita," he says, not angry now.

"Never again," I shout, jarringly loud in the airconditioned interior. "No more jobs. No more." I dash tears away, but it's like bailing water out of a sinking ship. "You don't leave me ever again. Do you understand?"

I can feel him staring at me, aghast and on the verge of panic, because I know this man like the back of my hand, and in this moment, I know without a doubt that if I'd told him in no uncertain terms 'no more jobs' last month or last year, he would have done it.

But I hadn't put my foot down because I can't—because women don't tell men what to do. And I might be stronger now for myself, but what about for him?

I sob harder. Nicky's hand hovers in the space between us, unsteady, because his arm is hurt. A *flesh wound*. Less gently than I intend, I push his hand back down.

I grab the hem of my cotton shirt, bury my face in it, and cry my heart out. Years' worth of scalding hot tears, every single one I've ever eaten, I let out in an idling car in an empty parking lot of Consultorios Médicos Gorgona while Nicky sits like a silent sentry by my side.

After a long, long time, I finally run out, blinking like I'm coming awake. Nicky is watching me, grim, his right arm tucked now to his middle like a broken wing.

I sniffle, smooth my damp and wrinkled shirt the best I can, and haul myself out of the car. Nicky straightens in surprise.

"You obviously can't drive," I tell him as I squint in the sunshine. My raw eyeballs burn.

I cross behind the car and open his door. He's already shaking his head.

"You're upset," he says, making no move to get out of the driver's seat.

"But at least both my arms work." I back up and glare, chin hiking. "I'm not playing, Nicky." He hears the quaver in my voice and his body braces like it anticipates a blow. I make a show of wiping my cheeks, although they're dry now, albeit tacky from the tears. He grimaces, and with an exaggerated show of reluctance, jiggles the gear stick, checking that the car's in neutral and unbuckles his belt.

While he walks himself back around to the passenger side, I settle myself in behind the wheel, pulling the seat forward and adjusting the mirrors. He tries really hard to hide his wince, but I'm tuned into this man's every twitch.

"Don't worry. You can put it back the way it was." I give him a slightly battered smile.

He grunts in disagreement. The poor man had found the perfect, unable-to-be-replicated mirror angles, and now he'll never achieve perfection again, but for me, he'll grit his teeth and buckle up.

I give him another, stronger smile. He relaxes a bit in his seat.

When I throw the car into reverse, he tenses right back up. I roll my window down and open it up when we get to the highway. Nicky's body tenses, but soon enough he gets used to going twenty whole kilometers over the limit and settles back, rolling his own window down. Past Coronado, I surprise him by turning off toward Boca De Tete instead of heading straight for San Carlos.

He raises an eyebrow.

I firm my jaw. He's not the only one who can be mysterious. I pass a little café we love to the guesthouse next door. Little lodges and bungalows are everywhere down here. On weekends, they fill with folks from the city, but during the week, they're almost abandoned.

"Wait here," I tell Nicky and hop from the car. Luckily, I don't have to hunt long for the proprietress. She hears us and emerges from an outbuilding, and it doesn't take but a few minutes to get the key to a room overlooking the pristine and empty pool.

I half-expected Nicky to have gotten out and cased the joint, but I think I've thrown him enough with my out-of-character moves that he's still in the car when I get back. I open the door for him. He gazes up at me with narrowed eyes, shaded by thick black lashes.

He really is the most beautiful man I've ever seen. My heart prickles like when you wake up after you've slept on your arm and the blood begins to flow again. Looking at him hurts like that and feels like the same kind of relief.

I lead the way across the porch. He follows. I unlock the door and swing it wide. He enters first, his gaze darting to the corners. He goes and inspects the bathroom and draws the blinds. Light still filters in from a high transom. Like most places in these tourist towns, the space is bright—there's a mirror in a yellow frame and the wooden chairs around a circular table have been painted blue, red, and green.

I drop my purse on the settee and half-push, half-pull Nicky to the bed. It usually wouldn't take any urging on my part, but he's wary of my mood.

I'm not quite sure what I'm going to do next, either.

I make him sit on the foot of the bed, and as I ease his jacket from his shoulders, he's a second too slow hiding a wince of pain. My hands fall to my side, and he takes over, folding the jacket and laying it neatly beside him, all the while watching me, sober and intent, his dark eyes somehow bright too in the mellow daylight.

I begin to unbutton his white dress shirt. Even though he's wearing a white tank underneath, it's damp from sweat. I peel the undershirt off, too. He helps while favoring his right arm. It's wrapped from the shoulder to the elbow. The bandage is clean and neat, and there's no blood seeping through. Still, the sight makes my eyes well again.

Nicky grabs my wrist with his left hand and draws me between his knees. "Don't cry. It's not as bad as it looks."

"Tell me what happened." There's an edge of demand in my voice that I don't recognize.

His thumb strokes the soft skin over my pulse point, and he gazes up at me with what I think of as his smoldering eyes, stoking a familiar swishy feeling in my lower belly. I extricate my wrist.

"Quit stalling. I want to know exactly what happened."

His smoldering eyes grow guarded in an instant. "I got shot."

"Shot?"

He grunts.

"By who?"

He draws in a long-suffering breath, his gaze shifting to over my left shoulder.

How hard is it to say "some Russian?" My intuition's hollering. A flood of fear rushes into my chest.

My voice drops. "What did you do?"

He exhales again. "You were being weird."

"What?" My brain scrambles to catch up. I was expecting some action movie replay, a job gone wrong, nothing to do with me.

"You've been in the bathroom a lot. And you've been wiping your search history on your phone."

I have. I didn't want him to know what I was considering. "I'm not cheating on you," I say.

"I know that."

Of course, he does. He knows me inside out. Of course, he noticed that I've been distracted.

"You could have talked to me about it." So says the woman who did not talk to him about it to the man who never talks about anything.

He snorts, but it's a soft snort, no hostility, only the shared understanding that we're both full of shit.

I sigh and plop down next to him, my shorts riding up so my bare thigh presses against his summer weight wool pants. "Tell me."

It takes him a minute to speak. "I thought you were unhappy. With me."

A sliver of regret jabs my heart. I had no idea.

We're both terrible at this relationship thing. For a while, at the beginning, I'd lapse into acting like I did with Paul—the pick me who cooked and kept herself pretty and had no desires of her own—and it pissed Nicky the hell off. Whenever he'd had enough, he'd haul me into bed and whale on my pussy until everything was messed up beyond recognition—my hair, our dinner plans, my ability to fake anything.

It was therapeutic if a little too intense for everyday life.

We've gotten better since then. Lisa and Marissa are both never-ending founts of wisdom and advice they've heard from books and TikTok, but mostly, Nicky and I have stumbled into what works. He watches me, and I stay close. I take care of myself, and like a symbiont, he's happy.

But I have been distant. And worried. I broke the pact.

"I'm not unhappy," I tell the wall with the big window looking out onto the pool.

"You've been on the bike every night."

"Not for too long." He's right, though. I've fallen back into a bad pattern—storing up calories to ward against future disaster. I'm aware of the issue. I've been beating myself up plenty for not urge surfing, for not practicing mindfulness, for not utilizing my support system.

"You're in the guest room all the time, just staring. Do you want to move in there?" he asks the wall. We are really aces at communication.

"No." I also don't want to tell him what I'm doing in there. Not yet. "And quit changing the subject. What happened to your arm?"

He blows out a sigh and bends back to stare at the white stippled ceiling. "You remember Vinny Bianco?"

Vinny from back home? I haven't thought about him for years. He's muscle for Lucca Corso, the guy who dragged me out of my bed the night they gave me to Nicky. "What about him?"

His face hardens, and he leans forward, bracing his forearms on his thighs. He can't settle. He's hurting. Worried. I press my leg more firmly against his, press a little closer into his side.

"I went back to Pyle and dragged him down four flights of stairs," he says.

I blink. "What the fuck?"

He darts me a wounded glare. "He hurt you."

"Years ago!" My brain fumbles, information slip-sliding from my grasp. Nicky went back to Pyle. Lucca's territory. We have a truce, negotiated by the Russians, but it won't hold if Nicky goes waltzing back into town, roughing up Renellis. And he was shot! He could've been killed. And for what? "Why? Why would you do that?"

"I told him to be gentle," he tells the polished hardwood floors. "He wasn't."

"So you decide to get revenge now? *Years* later?"

He tosses a shoulder. The one without the flesh wound.

"And Vinny shot you?"

He shakes his head, his jaw tensing as he shoots me a glance. Oh, I'm not gonna like this.

"No, that was Lucca," he says.

My stomach drops like a stone. "What the fuck, Nicky?"

He slides me another aggrieved glance, like I'm the crazy one here. "I didn't plan for it to go down like it did. Vinny lives in my old place in Lucca's building. It was a coincidence."

"A coincidence that Lucca busted you dragging his man down four flights of stairs?"

Nicky doesn't have the audacity to keep up the "who would've predicted" pretense. He sighs and goes back to balefully staring at the floor.

"You could've been killed." My aching eyes begin to burn again.

Nicky bumps my arm with his shoulder. "It was never a possibility. He didn't have a clear shot. He just winged me to be an asshole."

That doesn't make me feel the least bit better. "Explain to me again how this happened."

With another gusty sigh, he says, "I heard Vinny was living in my old place. I still had the key. I took a chance. He hadn't changed the locks."

"Well, that was his first mistake."

Nicky's gaze narrows on the floorboards. He doesn't correct me, but I can read his mind. He doesn't consider that Vinny's first mistake.

"So I grabbed him. Trussed him up. Dragged him down the hall to the stairs."

Unbidden, memories of the night Furio was killed flash across my mind. My acrylics digging into the paint in the upstairs hallway as they were ripped off. Biting my tongue as my ass smacked on each wooden step. My body colliding with the wall in the landing. Vinny's black rubber clogs, inches from my face.

My heart pounds. It feels like another lifetime, and also like a split second ago.

"You dragged him down the stairs?" I ask.

He shrugs. "More like threw him down. But yeah."

"And Lucca just randomly showed up?"

"Yeah. With Tomas. And a pregnant girl."

"Who?"

"I don't know her." Nicky's eyes go vague like he's thinking back. "She stood between Lucca and me at the bottom of the stairwell. He told her to move. She wouldn't. He took the only shot he could, over her shoulder. I ducked."

"Jesus Christ."

Nicky's lips soften for a moment. "Lucca said we're even now."

"He did?"

Nicky shrugs again. "There's something different about him."

"You're both insane."

"Maybe."

"Definitely." We all are. "If you do something that reckless again, I'll shoot you myself."

"Okay," he says.

"No. Seriously. I'll kill you."

"Okay." His lips are curving at the corners. He's not taking me seriously.

"I'll leave you, Nicky. I will. And you'll never find me."

His mouth flattens, and guilt scores my chest. I drop my head to stare at his polished black shoes.

"That's a lie. I won't ever leave you," I tell the floor.

"You're unhappy," he says softly.

"No. I'm not." I reach blindly for his hand. He grabs it immediately, flesh wound be damned. That's my Nicky.

We talk about unconditional love like it's the greatest good, the most beautiful possible thing, but the truth is that this is a shitty, evil world. When you give food to a starving man or water to a man dying of thirst, they puke. The body treats it like poison.

You have to learn how to take that kind of love. You have to learn how to give it back.

"I went to the doctor to get my IUD removed," I tell him. "Today. I did it. It's out."

For a minute, we sit in silence, staring together out the perfectly clear window at the smooth turquoise pool surrounded by empty lounge chairs, the lush palms and foliage beyond, the bright blue sky in the distance, reflecting the gulf.

Nicky holds my hand tightly. I hold his back.

At one point, he coughs, but he doesn't say anything. We just sit there together, terrified, in love.

"You want to make the guest room a nursery?" he finally says. "We can buy a bigger place."

"I like our place. I want to do a frog theme."

"Rana dorada?" he says.

"Yeah. Golden frogs." I peek up at him, my mouth curving upwards.

His smile breaks across his face, and then it disappears in an instant. "But is this gonna mess up you getting better?"

"No. Maybe. Probably. But I'll keep getting better. I'll start over." That's pretty much what living with this is anyway—starting over, day by day, minute by minute.

"We don't have to do it."

I hear the longing in his voice. I recognize its echo deep inside myself.

"Why can't we have what we want?" I ask him like he asked me a long time ago.

"The house, the yard, a dog?" he says while I turn to him, push him back—gently—and straddle his waist, careful of his arm, knowing that even though I'm the one pushing him back, he's the strong one. He's letting me climb on top of him, giving way to me.

"The cottage, the lawn, the peacock that's always standing in the middle of the road." I smile down, wriggling so that his hard cock presses against my now throbbing pussy. "The happy sister-in-law, the crazy wife, the baby."

"The baby," he repeats, his left hand finding my waist, squeezing my hip, his smile so wide it crinkles his eyes.

"The baby," I say as I wrangle down my shorts and panties, fumble with his zipper, and free him, stroke him to the base, angle him and sink down, wet and ready for him. My eyes drift shut, and I inhale. The room smells like clean sheets and the distant scent of frying plantains. And Nicky.

He fills me, stretches me, and I ride him, feeling the flex of his hips against my inner thighs, listening to his breath quicken and shallow.

I love this man.

"I want your baby," I whisper, and he wraps his left arm around me, twists me, lays me flat on my back and lifts my leg by the knee, hitches it high so he can drive deeper, riding me until I catch fire and explode, until I'm limp and dopey underneath his broad chest and taut stomach.

He pulls out, and immediately cups my pussy, shoving cum back inside me with his fingers, while he kisses my forehead, my cheeks, my chin.

"My strong, brave wife," he says. "I love you. I love you."

And I believe the second part with my whole heart. One day, I'll believe the first.

About The Author

Cate C. Wells writes everything from mafia to motorcycle club to small town to paranormal romance. Whatever the subgenre, readers can expect character-driven stories that are raw, real, and emotionally satisfying. She's into messy love, flaws, long roads to redemption, grace, and happily ever after, in books and in life. Along with stories, she's collected a husband and children along the way. She lives in Baltimore when she's not exploring the world with her family. She loves to chat with readers!